TEM)

Francis Henry Durbridge was born in Hull, Yorkshire, in 1912 and was educated at Bradford Grammar School. He was encouraged at an early age to write by his English teacher and went on to read English at Birmingham University. At the age of twenty one he sold a play to the BBC and continued to write following his graduation whilst working as a stockbroker's clerk.

In 1938, he created the character Paul Temple, a crime novelist and detective. Many others followed and they were hugely successful until the last of the series was completed in 1968. In 1969, the Paul Temple series was adapted for television and four of the adventures prior to this, had been adapted for cinema, albeit with less success than radio and TV. Francis Durbridge also wrote for the stage and continued doing so up until 1991, when *Sweet Revenge* was completed. Additionally, he wrote over twenty other well received novels, most of which were on the general subject of crime. The last, *Fatal Encounter*, was published after his death in 1998.

Also in this series

Paul Temple and the Front Page Men
News of Paul Temple
Paul Temple Intervenes
Send for Paul Temple Again!
Paul Temple: East of Algiers
Paul Temple and the Kelby Affair
Paul Temple and the Harkdale Robbery
Paul Temple and the Geneva Mystery
Paul Temple and the Curzon Case
Paul Temple and the Margo Mystery
Paul Temple and the Madison Case
Light-Fingers: A Paul Temple Story (e-only)
A Present from Paul Temple (e-only)

FRANCIS DURBRIDGE

Send for Paul Temple

COLLINS
CRIME
CLUB

COLLINS CRIME CLUB

An imprint of HarperCollins*Publishers*
1 London Bridge Street
London SE1 9GF
www.harpercollins.co.uk

This paperback edition 2015

First published in Great Britain by
LONG 1938

Copyright © Francis Durbridge 1938

Francis Durbridge has asserted his right under the Copyright,
Designs and Patents Act, 1988 to be identified as the author of this work

A catalogue record for this book is
available from the British Library

ISBN 978-0-00-812552-3

Set in Sabon by FMG using Atomik ePublisher from Easypress

CHAPTER I

Conference at Scotland Yard

'Superintendent Harvey and Inspector Dale, sir!'

'All right, Sergeant, you can go. Let me have the map some time before noon.'

Sir Graham Forbes, the Commissioner of the Metropolitan Police, stood up to greet the new arrivals. He was a tall man with iron-grey hair and a sparse figure. Even the black coat and striped trousers, which gave him the appearance of a City stockbroker, could not conceal that his early career had been spent with the Army. He contrasted strangely with the two men who now came into his office at Scotland Yard.

Dale was a man of medium height and build who always seemed unhappy and helpless without his bowler hat, and the umbrella which nobody ever remembered seeing unfurled.

The superintendent was a full head taller. He was a man of mighty frame whose bronzed face might have made the casual stranger mistake him for the more successful type of farmer. But he possessed a fund of wisdom and mellow humour, coupled with an astuteness that he would reveal in some urbane remark, that few farmers possessed.

Superintendent Harvey and Chief Inspector Dale had been placed in charge of the mysterious robberies, the size and scope of which had literally staggered the country. It was now their unpleasant task to give the Commissioner an account of yet another mysterious robbery which had occurred in Birmingham only a few hours before.

'It's the same gang, sir!' Chief Inspector Dale was saying. He spoke quietly, but the calm, clear note of efficiency sounded in his voice. 'There's no question of it. £8,000 worth of diamonds.'

The Commissioner looked worried. Monocle in hand, he strode backwards and forwards across the heavily carpeted room.

'The night watchman is dead, sir!' Superintendent Harvey added.

'Dead?' There was no mistaking the surprise in Sir Graham's' voice.

'Yes.'

'The poor devil was chloroformed,' Dale explained. 'I don't think they meant to kill him. According to the doctor, he was gassed during the War, and his lungs were pretty groggy.'

The news had not put Sir Graham in the best of tempers. 'This is bad, Dale!' he said irritably. 'Bad!' he repeated with emphasis.

'He was a new man,' said Harvey. 'He'd only been with Stirling's a month or so.'

'Did you check up on him?'

'Yes. His name was Rogers. "Lefty" Rogers. He was working at Stirling's under the name of Dixon.'

The hint in the superintendent's words, and the inflexion of his voice was not lost on the Commissioner.

'Had he a record?' he asked.

'He'd a record all right! Everything from petty larceny to blackmail,' Chief Inspector Dale informed him.

The Commissioner grunted.

'Inspector Merritt was already on the job when we arrived, sir,' said Harvey.

'Inspector Merritt? Oh, yes.' The Commissioner paused. 'Who discovered the robbery in the first place?'

'One of the constables on night duty,' answered Inspector Dale. 'A man called Finley. He noticed the side door had been forced open. At least, that's his story!' he added, with a queer note in his voice.

'You don't believe him?'

'No,' Dale replied decisively. 'I think he was in the habit of having a chat with Rogers, or Dixon—whichever you like to call him. In fact, he almost admitted as much. The night watchman used to make coffee, and I rather think P.C. Finley has—er—a liking for coffee.'

The Commissioner appeared to think over the significance of what Dale had told him. 'Do you think he knew Dixon was an ex-convict?' he asked at last.

Dale hesitated a fraction before he answered. 'No. I don't think so.'

'This is the fourth robbery in two months, Dale!' the Commissioner said impatiently, and took a cigarette from the small ivory box on his desk.

'There wasn't a mark on the safe,' Inspector Dale said quietly. 'If it hadn't been for the other robberies, I'd have sworn this was an inside job.'

'What did Merritt have to say?' asked Forbes.

Dale seemed amused. 'He's in a complete daze, poor devil. He'd got some fancy sort of theory about a huge criminal organization. I think Inspector Merritt has a rather theatrical imagination!' he added, with a smile which had some slight measure of contempt behind it.

'You don't think we're up against a criminal organization, then?' the Commissioner asked.

'Good heavens, no! Criminal organizations are all very well between the pages of a novel, sir, but when it comes to real life, well, they just don't exist!'

Sir Graham Forbes grunted. 'Is that your opinion too, Harvey?' he asked, turning to where Harvey was sitting on the other side of his desk.

'To be perfectly honest, Sir Graham, I'm rather inclined to agree with Merritt.' Dale looked at him with obvious surprise, but Harvey continued: 'At first I thought we were up against the usual crowd who were having an uncanny run of good luck,' he said, 'but now I'm rather inclined to think otherwise. You see, in the first place, there are certain aspects of this business which, to my way of thinking, indicate the existence of a really super mind. A man with an unusual flair for criminal organization. I know it sounds fantastic, and all that, sir! I feel rather reluctant to believe it myself, but we must face the facts, and the facts are pretty grim!'

He paused, but Sir Graham nodded, as a sign for him to continue.

'First there was the case of Smithson's of Gloucester. £17,000 worth of stuff. Then there was the Leicester business, £9,000 worth. Then there was the Derby affair, £4,000. And mark you, we had the Derby shop covered. We were, in fact, prepared for the raid. But that didn't stop it from happening. Then, on top of everything else, there's this affair in Birmingham, £8,000 worth of diamonds.

'No, Sir Graham, if we were up against the usual crowd, Benny Lever, "Dopey" Crowman, "Spilly" Stetson, we'd have had 'em under lock and key ages ago. I firmly believe, Sir Graham, that we are up against one of the greatest criminal organizations in Europe!'

Harvey had been carried away by his rising excitement as he recalled the details of the mysterious robberies. Sir Graham had been listening intently, making an occasional note on a pad on his desk. A slight smile of amusement on Dale's face had given place to the utmost seriousness as Harvey continued with his dramatic recital.

'Where was the night watchman when this fellow—er—Finley, discovered him?' the Commissioner asked at last.

'In his usual spot, sir,' Dale answered. 'He had a tiny office at the back of the shop.'

'I suppose you questioned Finley?'

'Good Lord, yes, sir!' replied Harvey emphatically. 'I was with him almost an hour.'

'Did you see the night watchman, Dale, before he died?'

'No, sir, but Harvey did.'

'Well, Harvey?'

'He was pretty groggy when I saw him,' the Superintendent said. 'The doctor wouldn't let me stay above a couple of minutes.'

'Did he say anything?'

'Yes,' said Harvey quietly, 'as a matter of fact, he did.'

Superintendent Harvey spoke strangely, and both the Commissioner and Chief Inspector Dale directed puzzled looks at him.

'Well, what did he say?' the Commissioner demanded.

'It was just as I was on the verge of leaving. . . . He turned over on his side and mumbled a few words. They sounded almost incoherent at the time. As a matter of fact, it wasn't until a minute or so later that I realized what he'd said—'

As he broke off, the Commissioner became more and more impatient.

'Well, what *did* he say, Harvey?'

Quietly the superintendent replied. 'He said: "The Green Finger"!'

'The Green Finger . . .' said Dale.

'Yes.'

'But—but that doesn't make sense.'

'Just a minute, Dale,' said the Commissioner, deep in thought. 'You remember that man we fished out of the river about a month ago. We thought he might have had something to do with that job at Leicester. I think you found his print on part of—'

Dale interrupted him. 'Oh, yes! "Snipey" Jackson. I was with Lawrence at the time we found him. The poor devil was floating down the river like an empty sack.' He paused, then suddenly exclaimed: 'I say . . . don't you remember? Don't you remember what he said just before he died? I'm sure I'm right! Why—'

'He said, "The Green Finger"!' The Commissioner spoke slowly, emphasizing each syllable.

'Yes,' repeated Dale, '"The Green Finger".'

'The—the same as the night watchman,' added Harvey. 'But—what is this Green Finger? What does it mean?'

'That, my dear Superintendent,' replied the Commissioner with dry humour, 'is one of the many things we are here to find out.'

'I don't think there's any doubt that "Snipey" Jackson was tied up with that Leicester job,' said Dale. 'Henderson found two of his fingerprints on one of the show-cases.'

'Yes,' replied Sir Graham. 'I reckon that was the reason why you and Lawrence had the pleasure of fishing him out of the Thames. The people we are up against know how to deal with incompetence; that's one thing I'll say for them!'

'Sir Graham,' asked Dale slowly, 'do you believe the same as Harvey and Inspector Merritt, that we *are* up against a definite criminal organization?'

Sir Graham got up and walked to the fireplace. There he stood with his back to the glowing flames while Dale and Harvey swung round in their chairs until they faced him again. For some time he said nothing. Then at last, he seemed to have made up his mind.

'Yes, I do, Dale!' he said quietly.

'I suppose you've seen the newspapers, Sir Graham?' It was Harvey who asked the question.

A faint flush spread over the Commissioner's cheeks. The subject seemed to irritate him. 'Yes!' he snapped impatiently. 'Yes, I've seen them. "Send for Paul Temple"! "Why doesn't Scotland Yard send for Paul Temple?" They even had placards out about the fellow. The Press have been very irritating over this affair. Very irritating!'

'Paul Temple,' said Dale thoughtfully. 'Isn't he the novelist chap who helped us over the Tenworthy murder?'

'Yes.'

'Well, he caught old Tenworthy!' Dale went on. 'I'll say that for him.' Suddenly he turned towards the superintendent. 'He's a friend of yours, isn't he, Harvey?'

'I know him,' said Harvey.

'Temple is just an ordinary amateur criminologist,' said Sir Graham Forbes, with a vast amount of scorn in his voice. 'He had a great deal of luck over the Tenworthy affair and a great deal of excellent publicity for his novels.'

Superintendent Harvey was inclined to doubt this. 'I don't think Paul Temple exactly courted publicity, Sir Graham,' he said quietly.

'Don't be a fool, Harvey, of course he did! All these amateurs thrive on publicity!'

'Well, you must admit, Sir Graham,' laughed Dale, 'we were a little relieved to see the last of the illusive Mr. Tenworthy!'

'Yes!' exclaimed Sir Graham. 'And just at the moment, I should be considerably relieved to hear the last of Mr. Paul Temple. Ever since this confounded business started, people have been bombarding us with letters— "Send for Paul Temple!"' His tones, impatient and bitter to start with, had gradually worked up into a fury. But he was prevented from going any further. As he finished his sentence, the door opened and Sergeant Leopold, his personal attendant, appeared. The Commissioner looked round, angry at being disturbed.

'What is it, sergeant?' he asked.

'The map, sir,' Sergeant Leopold replied. 'Remember you asked me to—'

'Oh, yes,' the Commissioner interrupted him.

'Put it on the desk, sergeant.'

Sergeant Leopold cleared a space on the fully loaded desk, and left the room. Instead of continuing his heated discussion the Commissioner opened the map and spread it flat over the top of his desk.

'Now, gentlemen,' he said, as the two officers stood up and bent over it. 'This is a map covering the exact area in which, so far, the criminals have confined their activities.' He pointed to the circles, and other marks, which had been neatly inscribed in the Map Room at Scotland Yard. 'You will see the towns which have already been affected. Gloucester, Leicester, Derby, and Birmingham.' He pointed to each of the four places in turn. 'The map, as you see, starts at Nottingham and comes as far south as Gloucester . . . covering, in fact, the entire Midlands.'

The Commissioner stood back from the table. He flourished his hand with all the emphasis he might have used in addressing a large and important gathering.

'Gentlemen, somewhere in that area are the headquarters of the greatest criminal organization in Europe. That organization must be smashed!'

CHAPTER II

Paul Temple

The press of the country had seized on the idea of a mysterious gang holding the Midlands in its grasp, and were making the most of it. Both Spanish and Chinese War news had begun to grow wearisome. Moreover, news editors found it both difficult and tedious to try to follow the latest moves. Only an occasional heavy bombardment, the capture of a big city, or the sinking of a British ship could now be sure of reaching the front pages.

The mere killing of hundreds of men a day had long ceased to be news. There had not even been a really good murder story for months, and editors were falling back on such hardy annuals as Gretna Green and the 'cat' for their very large and strident headlines.

Then suddenly, out of the blue, the 'Midland Mysteries' arrived. The circulations of the evening papers immediately reached heights no national or international crisis could produce. Special investigators made their special investigations and produced lengthy summaries of what they had not been able to find out. Articles appeared by well-known psychologists, judges, the Chairman of the Howard League for Penal Reform, and Mr. George Bernard Shaw.

Every newspaper produced different theories and suggested different methods of apprehending the criminals. One ran a competition for readers' solutions. It was won by Mr. Ronald Garth, a Battersea bricklayer, who was convinced, in no very certain grammar or spelling, that the crimes were a put-up job and part of a new attempt to foster interest in A.R.P. He received a cheque for 10s. 6d.

On one point, however, all the newspapers were agreed. The urgent necessity of sending for Mr. Paul Temple. 'Send for Paul Temple' became almost a national slogan.

His name appeared on almost every poster in the city. His photograph was blazoned from the fronts of buses.

Scotland Yard remained quiet and merely writhed in exquisite agony. They did not enjoy the 'Send for Paul Temple' campaign. Nor did they enjoy reading the letters which reached them by the hundred every day instructing them, in the public's interest, to—Send for Paul Temple!

All this publicity, however, was not without its value, for booksellers very quickly reported high sales for Paul Temple's detective stories, and one of the more lurid of Sunday newspapers, hoping to scoop the rest, commissioned an article by Mr. Temple on the growing rat menace in Britain and paid him the record sum of £1,000 for it. Unhappily for them, on the day it appeared, another equally lurid Sunday newspaper published an article by Mr. Temple on the growing spy menace in Britain, which he had written five years before and for which he received £4 14s. 6d. after his agent, overjoyed at selling the ancient manuscript, had deducted his usual 25 per cent commission.

It had taken Paul Temple six years to rise from the dark obscurity of an unknown author to the limelight of a popular novelist. On coming down from Oxford he applied for a newspaper job and eventually became a reporter on one of the great London dailies. After twelve months of writing everything from gossip paragraphs to sports reports he became interested in criminology, and eventually started to specialise in 'crime' stories.

While still in Fleet Street, he tried his hand at the drama, and in 1929 his play, *Dance, Little Lady*, was produced at the Ambassadors Theatre. It ran for seven performances. In a fit of irritation, caused through the unexpected failure of his play, Paul Temple started his first thriller.

Death In The Theatre! appeared early the following year. It achieved a phenomenal success, and Paul Temple promptly left Fleet Street.

Oddly enough, Temple very quickly acquired a reputation as a criminologist. From time to time he had been asked by popular papers to investigate some sensational crime on their behalf. Thus, although it is not generally known, it was Paul Temple who was really responsible for the arrest of such notorious criminals as Toni Silepi, Guy Grinzman, and Tessa Jute.

On the subject of the present crimes, however, Paul Temple refused to be drawn. To the reporters who called to see him, he was invariably out of town. No telephone number or address could possibly be given. He was thought to be travelling in the Ukraine.

Several energetic reporters, however, went so far as to set up camp stools outside the big block of service flats in Golder's Green where he stayed when in London. The only vacant flat in the building had already been engaged on a year's lease at a rental of £460 (inclusive) by the Queen Newspaper Syndicate of America!

Meanwhile other reporters and photographers patrolled the grounds of Bramley Lodge, Paul Temple's country house not far from Evesham.

Bramley Lodge was an extensive old Elizabethan house which Paul Temple had secured at a very low figure owing to its poor condition. He had managed to have it partially rebuilt without completely ruining the beautiful façade, the old oak beams and other ancient features of the building. In addition, central heating had been installed, tennis courts laid, and a rather delightful rockery planned. Altogether, Paul Temple had contrived to make Bramley Lodge a very comfortable place.

All these alterations had done nothing to spoil it, and Paul Temple was often asked by artist friends (and strangers) as well as photographers, for permission to make some permanent record of the lovely old mansion. Only to Surrealists did he refuse.

The house was set in the middle of a large park with a drive fringed by luxurious old beech trees to the main Warwick Road below. About the exact size of his grounds, Temple felt rather dubious. He had bought a half-inch Ordnance Survey map only a few weeks before and by dint of laborious calculation and lengthy use of compasses and dividers, discovered that he possessed eighty-five acres of very pleasant land. But his confidence in his own mathematical knowledge was not exactly great. ('When I was at Rugby, my marks for mathematics used to be 8 per cent with the most monotonous regularity,' he used to tell his friends.) He had not yet remembered to pass the problem on to more mathematically minded friends and as in addition, all the papers concerning the estate were 'locked away somewhere', he had only very vague ideas about his own property.

On the Monday, two days after the conference at Scotland Yard, Dr. Milton and his niece, Diana Thornley, neighbours of the novelist, had succeeded in penetrating the cordon of newspapermen and were now sitting in the comfortable drawing-room of Bramley Lodge.

They had just enjoyed an excellent dinner prepared under the very personal supervision of Temple himself, for he quite rightly prided himself on his culinary knowledge. In fact, he used to boast that his knowledge of West End restaurants was second to none. Certainly he knew almost every *chef* in London well enough to spend many a half-hour in wistful contemplation of the mysterious processes to which they subjected the raw materials of the meal he was later to enjoy.

The knowledge he thus gained would go to benefit his guests. This evening Dr. Milton and Diana Thornley had certainly appreciated the meal that had been set before them.

Now they were sipping their coffee before a great fire of coal and holly, the men in deep brown leather armchairs, Miss Thornley on a stool by the inglenook. A heavy Turkish carpet softened the room, and the comfortable old furniture seemed to impart an intimate, sociable atmosphere.

The vivacious, dark-haired and dark-eyed girl of twenty-seven who looked as if she had Spanish blood in her, contrasted strangely with the two men. Yet she bore them many similarities in temperament. Impetuous, yet firm-lipped, she was a girl of hard character who looked as if she enjoyed life to the full. That she was not married was a continual source of wonder, and even anxiety, to the country people in the district.

Her uncle showed little family likeness to Diana Thornley. But then, as Dr. Milton explained, she took after her mother, not her father, who was Milton's brother. He had a wiry figure, which looked as if it had seen hardship and could easily face more. He rarely seemed completely at his ease.

He told Temple he had had an extensive practice in Sydney and that he had done some exploration into the great deserts of Western Australia. Now he had come back to the home country to retire. He seemed very little over fifty and was probably younger, very young to retire, reflected Temple. But he seemed to have enough money to spend, and always enough to do to obviate boredom.

Temple himself was a modern embodiment of Sir Philip Sydney. Courtly in manners, a dominant character without ever giving the impression of dominating. He was equally at home in the double-breasted dinner-jacket he was now wearing, the perfect host entertaining his guests, or in coarse, loose tweeds striding along the country lanes.

Nobody was surprised to learn that he preferred rugby football to cricket, although he had played both. Now at the age of forty, he was past the violence of the game but still rarely missed an international match. He had done well in the pack for his college team at Oxford but, strangely enough, he had never got past the selection committee for the varsity side. The fact that he had never secured his blue was a constant source of regret.

He had a habit of leisurely movement and retained traces of what, in his younger days, had been a very pronounced Oxford drawl. On the other hand, you felt that here was a man whose bulk would be no great hindrance to action, and that in a fight it was as well to have him on your side.

Conversation had turned gradually to crime as it often did in that drawing-room. They were discussing the notorious Tenworthy case and Temple's personal contacts as distinguished from his abstract interest in crime.

'A man called Tenworthy murdered his wife by gently pushing her over Leaton Cliffs in Cornwall,' the novelist reminded Dr. Milton. 'That was two years ago, the beginning of my active interest in criminology.'

'You must have taken an interest in the case from the very beginning,' said Diana Thornley. 'Surely you just didn't make a lot of Charlie Chan observations?'

Her uncle looked at her with a kindly and tolerant, yet none the less broad, amusement. 'Don't be silly!' he admonished her. 'Mr. Temple is far too modest. I remember reading about the Tenworthy affair. He made several startling discoveries which the police had entirely overlooked. As a matter of fact, they arrested a young man called Roberts, who had nothing to do with the case, if I remember rightly.'

The details of the case were coming back to the two men now. It had caused a tremendous stir at the time. The newspapers had started a 'Release Roberts!' campaign. Indignation meetings had been held over the country and questions had been asked in the House of Commons. Young Roberts was finally set free and awarded £1,000 as compensation.

'Yes, Len Roberts,' said Paul Temple in a soft voice. 'By Timothy, that boy had a near shave!'

'Well, no wonder all the newspapers are saying, "Send for Paul Temple!"' smiled Diana Thornley, with an excitement that sent a glow of colour into her cheeks.

Her host laughed. 'The newspapers, like your uncle, are inclined to exaggerate my ability, Miss Thornley!' he said. 'I am afraid they see in me what is technically described as "good copy"!'

'I've been reading a great deal about these robberies,' said Dr. Milton. 'They really are remarkable, you know. Four robberies in six months, and all within the same area. I'm

17

not one for grumbling, but I do really think it's about time the police started to show some results.

'Now look at that business in Birmingham only this week. The police haven't even got a single clue!'

'Yes,' said Diana softly. 'The night watchman was murdered too.'

'Murdered?' asked her uncle, with surprise in his voice. 'I didn't know that!'

'Apparently he was chloroformed and didn't recover from it,' explained his host. 'I have a sort of feeling that was an accident.'

'Yes,' said Milton after a moment's thought, his face set in a deep frown, 'perhaps you're right. We shall soon start thinking we've settled down in the wrong country, Diana!' he added, laughing.

They discussed the 'Midland Mysteries' just as in a hundred thousand other homes in the country they were being discussed. Whilst jewellers and diamond merchants tested their safes and burglar alarms, taking the latest precautions of every kind, before nervously rubbing their hands and hoping the insurance companies wouldn't be too argumentative when the disaster inevitably arrived.

'Mr. Temple—' started Diana suddenly.

'Yes?'

'What do you really think about these robberies? Do you think it's the work of an organized sort of gang, or do you think. . .'

'Oh, come, Diana!' interrupted her uncle, with what was probably intended to be an indulgent smile, 'don't start troubling Mr. Temple with a lot of newspaper nonsense!'

Both men began to laugh. To Temple, at least, it was amusing to see this lovely girl displaying so sudden and rather startling an interest in the Midland Mysteries. And Diana was so very serious as well as persistent.

'You know, Mr. Temple,' she said, 'I should really like to know what you think about it all?'

'Well, Miss Thornley, if I were Scotland Yard—' and Paul Temple paused.

'Yes?' she exclaimed eagerly.

'If I were Scotland Yard . . .' he repeated with dramatic emphasis, then with an amused twinkle in his eye he added, 'I should send for Paul Temple!'

They were still laughing when the door opened and Pryce, Paul Temple's manservant, came in. 'Superintendent Harvey of Scotland Yard would like to see you, sir,' he said.

CHAPTER III

Death of a Detective

His words cut off the laughter in that drawing-room with strange abruptness. For a moment no one spoke. The coincidence was too striking. All three sensed drama in the air.

Yet Temple and Harvey were old acquaintances, if not friends. Harvey had often called on the novelist to discuss some complicated case or other over a tankard or two of beer. And often enough, Harvey was brought nearer a solution while Temple was provided with material for yet another of his detective stories.

Their acquaintance dated from Temple's newspaper days when he had once been called on to interview the detective. After that, they had often pooled their knowledge on some case both were investigating and discussed possibilities together. Temple's own peculiar logic, if logic it could be called, often saw the short cut to a solution while Harvey was still lost in side paths.

Whenever Temple was in town, the two would explore Soho together, both its better places of eating and its less reputable clubs, Harvey not caring for the recondite forms of

Continental cooking and infinitely preferring 'a good, bloody steak,' but sacrificing himself to Temple's tastes for the sake of his company. Then they would sit through a show or go into Hoxton or the Elephant and Castle areas to hear the latest gossip among the criminal fraternity.

Nevertheless, this visit was unexpected and almost unprecedented.

'Superintendent Harvey—' said Temple softly. 'All right, Pryce, show him in.'

General introductions were effected, and Harvey very soon found himself a deep armchair into which he sank with a sigh of relief. He lit one of his host's cigars, before explaining that, feeling in urgent need of a break, he was taking a fortnight's holiday. He was staying near Evesham, and had taken the first opportunity of calling on his old friend.

The doctor laughed. 'So glad this isn't a professional visit, Superintendent!'

Milton and Temple lit fresh pipes and talked aimlessly for half an hour or so, until Diana Thomley suddenly suggested it was time to leave.

'No, really, Mr. Temple!' exclaimed Dr. Milton when his host started to protest, 'Diana's right. I never like to be later than ten-thirty if I can possibly help it. And it'll take us at least a quarter of an hour.'

'Very well, doctor,' replied his host. 'But don't let the inspector frighten you away!'

Diana Thornley began to laugh. 'It does look rather like a guilty conscience, doesn't it?' she exclaimed.

As the door of the drawing-room closed, Superintendent Harvey walked slowly over to the sideboard, thoughtfully poured himself out a whisky, touched the lever of a soda water siphon, then returned to his seat.

'I say,' he started, as Temple came back into the comfortably warm drawing-room, 'who did you say that fellow was?'

'Which fellow?' pondered his host. 'Oh, Dr. Milton? He's a retired medico. He bought Ashdown House about six months ago. You probably remember the place – used to belong to Lord Snaresdon.'

The detective frowned. 'Thought I'd seen him before somewhere,' he said uneasily.

'You've probably seen his photograph,' the novelist explained. 'He's only been in this country since last September. He was a specialist in Sydney, I believe, or somewhere like that.'

Rather abruptly Temple changed the topic of conversation. 'Well, what brings Superintendent Harvey to Bramley Lodge?' he asked.

It did not need much of the acumen Temple normally kept so carefully hidden to realize that the real reason was the disturbing series of jewel robberies which Harvey was investigating.

'During the last six months, nearly £50,000 worth of diamonds have been spirited away from under our very noses,' said Harvey quietly. 'And you can take it from me, Temple, this is only the beginning. We're up against something we've never even experienced before in this country. A cleverly planned, well-directed, criminal organization.'

Temple smiled at his earnestness.

'Oh, I know it sounds fantastic,' the detective rejoined. 'I know just what you're thinking, but it's the truth, Temple. You can take it from me – it's the truth!'

'Does Sir Graham know that you've come to see me?' Temple asked.

Harvey was slightly embarrassed by the question. Sir Graham did not like outsiders. Least of all the outsiders

did he like the man the newspapers and their readers were advising him to consult.

'I thought that with you being in the actual district,' Harvey was saying apologetically, 'we might—er—well, sort of—er—'

Temple came to his rescue.

'Sort of have an unofficial chat about that matter, is that it?'

Harvey apologized. After all, a dilettante or connoisseur in criminology could hardly be expected to be officially asked for help by the Chief Commissioner! Nevertheless, Harvey's mind had begun to whirl slightly, and he had decided to benefit by a little of his friend's – unofficial – clear thinking!

True, he possessed some scattered facts and a few suspicions, but there was as yet no path for him to follow. He had ploughed his way through trees and bracken to find one, and had only succeeded in entangling himself the more. There was just a chance that Temple, with that uncanny foresight of his, might spot the way. He began to outline in detail what he knew of the Midland Mysteries, concluding with the recent Birmingham robbery.

'Tell me, Harvey,' asked Temple, 'did you see the night watchman on the Birmingham job, the fellow who died?'

'Yes,' Harvey replied. 'His name was Rogers. He was an ex-con.'

'Did he say anything before—'

'I only saw him for a few seconds,' the detective interrupted; 'the doctor wouldn't let me stay any longer. But whilst I was there, he said very quietly, "The Green Finger." . . . At the time, I thought the poor devil was delirious and talking nonsense. Now, however, I'm not so sure.'

'What makes you say that?'

'Well, about a month ago, Dale fished a fellow out of the Thames. A man by the name of Snipey Jackson. He was wanted in connection with the Leicester job. The poor devil was practically gone when they dragged him into the boat – but Dale is absolutely certain he said exactly the same words as the night watchman.'

'The Green Finger—' repeated Temple quietly; then suddenly he looked up. 'Where are you staying, Harvey?'

Harvey explained that he had booked a room at 'The Little General', a small inn about two miles from Bramley Lodge.

'Don't be silly, old boy!' laughed Temple. 'You must stay here. We'll pop round to the inn for your luggage.'

Pryce was sent to start the car, and ten minutes later the two men were swinging their way down the drive, the brilliant headlamps of Temple's long black coupé cleaving a passage between the great beeches that flanked the drive.

There was no great hurry and Temple did not drive fast. It was fairly cold and he kept the roof of the car closed, although both men had opened their windows and were savouring the keen night air. An exhilarating experience after the warm confinement of the drawing-room. Although the inn was only some two miles away, it was almost ten minutes before they arrived. Neither said very much beyond a non-committal word or so about the rabbits which scurried out, drawn by the car's headlamps, or about the smooth, fast running of Temple's car and the easy way she crested the long slope leading up to 'The Little General'.

Harvey got out of the car alone, explaining that he would only be absent long enough for him to collect his bags and break the news of his sudden departure to the innkeeper. Temple remained in the car, drawing away at his great briar. He heard the door of the inn close, and fancied he heard Harvey talking.

Two or three minutes passed by. Then Temple heard footsteps crunching in the gravel by the roadside. Somebody was approaching the car from the back. Through the driving mirror he could see a man gradually coming nearer. He turned round and recognized the burly figure of Ben Stewart, owner of Battington Farm, and a near neighbour of Temple's. He stopped at the window of the car.

''Ello, Mr. Temple. What be you doing 'ere this time o' night?'

'Hello, Ben!' replied Temple. 'I'm just waiting for a friend of mine. How's the farm?'

The two chatted for a little while about the farm, market prices, and foot-and-mouth disease. Although Temple lived in the country, he knew little more about farming than the average townsman, but he was genuinely interested in it, as he was in almost everything else, and Ben Stewart was one of many who appreciated an attentive audience.

Finally the farmer accepted one of Temple's best cigars. 'Sure make the house smell proper Christmassy, this will!' he chuckled, and vanished into the night.

Temple had switched the car lights off and for a moment or two sat peering ahead into the darkness, vainly endeavouring to follow the farmer's path. He wondered vaguely why Harvey should be so long. It was actually getting a little colder, he thought, and closed the windows of the car.

The only light came from the inn. Two of the windows were lit up. One that was evidently the window of the bar parlour, next to the door, and one upstairs. The crescent of the moon just revealed through the mist the existence of the poplars by the side of the road.

Certainly time Harvey was down with those bags, thought Temple.

A sudden piercing shriek cut into his thoughts. A moment later, the inn door was flung open and the excited figure of little Horace Daley, the innkeeper, appeared. For an instant he stood still, silhouetted against the brilliant light from within. Then, with a second cry of astonishment, he darted forward.

'I say, Mister!' he started, his voice almost unintelligible in the sudden pitch of overwhelming emotion, 'is that fellow a friend of yours, the chap who came into the inn about . . .'

'Yes,' Temple cut him short. 'What's happened?'

'My Gawd, it's awful. It's awful!'

'What's happened?' repeated Temple, a sudden note of apprehension in his voice.

'He's shot himself!'

Temple looked at the innkeeper through the darkness. There was a queer look in his eyes.

'Shot—himself.' he repeated slowly. 'No! No! That can't be true!'

The innkeeper began to wave his arms in a frenzy of excitement.

'I tell you, he's shot 'imself. I was—'

Abruptly Temple cut short his flow of words.

'We'd better go inside,' he said quietly.

CHAPTER IV

Again the Green Finger

Temple closed the door of the bar parlour softly behind him and looked down at the lifeless body of Superintendent Harvey. A trickle of blood flowed from the back of his head. In his left hand he still clasped the revolver. For a few seconds Temple stood there in silence. Then he knelt down to make a more hopeful examination.

It was obviously too late to do anything, however, and after a little while he stood up and began to look around.

The door he had just entered was in the corner of a room about twenty feet long and fifteen or so deep. Just to the right of the door was the window from which had come the light Temple had seen from the car.

Along the far end was the bar counter, with a number of glasses, two siphons, an ashtray, a bowl of potato crisps, and an advertisement for Devonshire cider. Behind the bar counter were stacked a number of beer barrels. There were also shelves for the usual bottles of spirits and a table for the till. The whole comprised a scene typical of a little country estaminet. At the end of the counter, away from the road, was a flap.

Behind it was a door leading to an inner room, apparently the Daleys' living-room. Another door in the wall behind the counter opened on to a little courtyard behind the house.

Ancient high-backed oak benches and tables provided seating accommodation in the little parlour. On the floor between them lay two or three spittoons, clean and well-filled with sand. A thin layer of sawdust coated the floor. There was indeed nothing in the parlour to distinguish 'The Little General' from a thousand other inn parlours in the country, save the quietness and lack of custom of which the Cockney innkeeper continually complained.

Daley watched nervously as Temple took in the various details. Eventually he could restrain himself no longer, and exclaimed: 'Whatever made him do it? He came in 'ere as large as life. Walked across to—'

'Please!' said Temple quietly; then, after a pause: 'Are you on the telephone?'

Daley led the way into the little hall, then upstairs to a coin instrument, seemingly intended for the occupants of the three spare rooms.

Temple lifted the receiver. The urgency in his voice impressed itself on the operator, and he was through to the police almost at once.

'Hello! Sergeant Morrison? This is Paul Temple speaking. Sergeant, you'd better come along to "The Little General". There's been an accident . . . Well, it might be suicide . . . Yes, straight away. Oh, and bring Dr. Thome if you can get him. . . . Oh, I see. Well, in that case, give Dr. Milton a ring and tell him I've been in touch with you. . . . Yes, yes, naturally.'

Temple hung up the receiver and turned away to find the little innkeeper immediately behind him. Temple looked at him with distaste clear on his face. Daley was a bumptious little man, no more than five feet tall, but well-built and clearly tough. A small black toothbrush moustache completed a very ordinary face. His dark-brown, almost black hair was well plastered down with cream. His friends would have called him vivacious if they had known what the word meant. A peculiar twist to his upper lip provided him with a continual leer.

It was clear that there was very little the man would miss. It was equally clear that there was very little of Temple's telephone conversation he had not overheard.

'What did you mean – *might* be suicide? You can see for—'

With superb indifference, Temple ignored the question. Then very firmly, setting out to establish his own authority, he asked the innkeeper what he was doing when Harvey arrived.

'What was I doing?' Daley repeated, obviously gaining an extra moment to collect his thoughts together. 'I was doing a crossword puzzle.'

'Where were you? Behind the bar?'

'Yes!'

Inexorably, Temple continued, determined to express and establish his authority.

'Would you mind telling me exactly what happened?'

Daley looked at him, resistance still showing in his beady eyes. Then after a pause: 'No. No, of course not. This fellow comes in and says 'e's changed his mind about staying 'ere the night. 'E pops upstairs and brings 'is suitcase down. There it is,' he added, pointing to one of the oak benches in the corner of the room.

'Then—'e arsks me if I could change a quid. I says "yes", and goes into the back parlour to get the money. When I gets back I sees 'im just like 'e is now, laying all twisted up like, with the gun in 'is 'and. Strewth, I didn't 'alf turn queer!'

'Was there anyone else here, when he arrived?'

'No, course not. The plice 'as been deserted since 'alf-past eight.'

Temple looked thoughtful for a moment, then went on with his questions.

'Are you the landlord?'

'Yes, that's me. Horace Daley's the name.'

'You're new here, aren't you?'

'Been 'ere about six months. I bought the plice from a chap called Sharpe. Blimey, 'e was sharp all right. This plice is a proper white elephant!'

Temple paced up and down the room slowly and deliberately. Then, still without speaking, he took a penknife from his pocket, cleaned out the burnt tobacco from his pipe and refilled it. Before lighting it, he suddenly turned to Daley.

'Tell me,' he asked, 'could anyone else have come in here whilst you were in the parlour?'

'Yes,' was the reply. 'They could 'ave come from outside or from upstairs.'

But no one had entered from the road, reflected Temple as he put a belated match to his pipe. He had been keeping watch there himself from the car.

'I say,' exclaimed the innkeeper, 'why didn't I hear the shot – that's what I can't understand?'

'The gun was fitted with a silencer,' answered the novelist quietly.

'Coo—'e did 'imself in in style like, didn't 'e?'

For a few minutes Temple stared fixedly at Harvey's body. Then he resumed his steady walk up and down the room.

'Is there anyone staying here at the moment?' he asked at length.

'Yes, an old dame who calls herself Miss Parchment,' was the answer. 'She arrived yesterday afternoon. Says she's on a walking tour of the Vale of Evesham. Don't look much like a hiker to me, though.'

'Have you seen her tonight?'

'Yes, she popped in here about half-past nine.'

'What about the servants?' Temple asked next.

'There's two maids, that's all. The rest sleep out.'

'Oh, I see.'

Daley looked at the corpse with very clear distaste.

'Phew!' he exclaimed. 'He looks terrible, don't 'e? This business 'as made me proper nervy.'

Temple turned towards him. 'I think you'd better fetch Miss Parchment down,' he said at length. 'I'd like to have a word with her.'

'Miss Parchment!' Daley looked surprised. 'What do we want 'er for?'

'The sergeant will insist on seeing her, so there's no reason why she shouldn't be brought down right away.'

'All right,' said Daley after a moment's pause. 'If you say so, Guv'nor.'

'And you'd better tell her what's happened. We don't want her fainting, or anything like that.'

'If you asks me, she'll pass right out!' said Daley, walking towards the hall. Temple watched him close the door, and listened to his footsteps as he started to mount the stairs.

Then very swiftly he passed over to the flap in the counter, raised it, and let himself through. A few strides brought him to the till. He opened it and briefly examined its contents. Then he closed it as footsteps could be heard coming down the stairs, and in a very short while he was back in the middle of the room again, sitting down on one of the old oak benches.

'You've been quick!' he said, as Daley appeared, slightly out of breath.

'Yes!' was the brief answer.

'Where's Miss Parchment?'

'She'll be down in a minute.'

'Have you told her about . . . ?'

'Yes,' interrupted Daley. 'And would you believe it, she was as cool as a cucumber. Talk about some of us men being 'ardboiled! Why, if you . . .' He broke off as a faint rustle came from outside.

Both men turned to look at the door. It opened, and a tall, elderly lady appeared. In spite of her grey hair she carried her sixty years well. There was almost a touch of gaiety in the way she advanced to meet them. She was wearing a nondescript dress of grey tweed, but the flashes from her diamond brooch and earrings immediately drew Temple's attention.

'Miss Parchment?' he asked, as he rose to greet her.

'Yes.' But it was a question rather than a form of assent that came from her lips.

Temple introduced himself. He could exercise almost a spell when he wished, and with a few sentences and a smile, he had put Miss Parchment at her ease and won her sympathy.

The novelist pulled out one of the less uncomfortable-looking of the chairs for her and turned it away from the body. She thanked him with a friendly smile and sat down.

'What time was it when you went to your room, Miss Parchment?' asked Paul Temple, after a time.

'Now let me see,' she replied. 'It would be about—er—ten o'clock. I sat for a short while – reading. I prefer to read in bed as a rule, but the book I'm reading at the moment is so very interesting that—'

'Yes, I'm sure it is.' Temple headed her skilfully off what might too easily have developed into a long digression. Time was short, and Temple had a number of questions to ask before the police arrived.

'I trust you've sent for the police, Mr. Temple?' the old lady asked. 'I do feel—'

'Yes. The sergeant is on his way here now.'

'What a dreadful shock it must have been for you. Personally, I can never understand the mentality of anyone who commits suicide. It always seems to me that—'

Temple looked up at her in quiet surprise. 'What makes you so certain that this is suicide?' he said softly.

'What makes me so certain?' she repeated. 'But surely it must be suicide! Unless, of course, Mr. Daley shot him!'

Mr. Daley had been standing nearby as though mounting guard over the body. He had not taken any part in the conversation, but his head had moved from Paul Temple to Miss Parchment and back again with rapid, sparrow-like movements. Now his eyes seemed to pop out of his head in sudden surprise.

''Ere! None of them insinuations!' he started, and crossed toward Miss Parchment as if nearness would lend emphasis to his words. 'I couldn't kill anyone, see. Not even if I wanted to. Can't stand the sight of blood. Makes me proper queer-like.' Then, as though exhausted by this sudden effort, he stepped back and sat down on a bench about two yards from Temple.

'But there doesn't seem to be much blood, Mr. Daley.'

'There's enough to give me the jitters!' he exclaimed, almost savagely. He walked up to the window and peered out into the darkness. A thought seemed to occur to him and he half-turned.

'And if it comes to that, why wasn't you in bed when I knocks on your door?'

'Because, my dear Mr. Daley,' replied Miss Parchment calmly, 'I was reading.'

'Like to bet it was a murder story!' The innkeeper's voice was heavy with sarcasm.

'You'll lose your bet, Mr. Daley,' she replied sweetly, 'It was a book on old English inns. I'm very interested in old English inns.'

Temple decided to interrupt them. There was still much that he might be able to ascertain before the police arrived. He turned to Miss Parchment to ask how long she had intended staying at the inn.

'I hadn't quite made up my mind,' she replied. 'Most probably till the end of the week.'

The innkeeper promptly took her up again. 'You didn't say that when you signed the register! You said it was only for one night!'

Miss Parchment was not disconcerted. She seemed to find pleasure in treating the irrepressible little Cockney with quiet dignity and endowing him with certain powers of understanding and reasoning.

Almost patronizingly, she replied: 'It was my original intention to stay merely for the one night, but I found this inn so very, very interesting.'

Daley looked at her with astonishment. This was a new phase in a person's character and completely beyond his comprehension.

'Interesting?' he asked. 'What the 'ell's interesting about it?'

It was Miss Parchment's turn to appear astonished.

'Why, so many things, my dear Mr. Daley!' she explained patiently. 'Do you realize the actual inn itself is over five hundred years old? Think of it. Five hundred years!'

But the innkeeper was no antiquarian. 'Well, I've been 'ere the last six months,' he grumbled, 'and that's long enough for me. The blinking place is dead after 'alf-past eight.'

Miss Parchment turned towards Paul Temple who was, oddly enough, thoughtfully considering her statement. 'Five hundred years,' he said. 'By Timothy, that's certainly a long time. But I was under the impression it was built about 1800?'

'Oh, no,' replied Miss Parchment. 'Oh, dear, no! It goes back much farther than that.'

'Then why should it be called "The Little General"?' asked Temple. 'Surely the—'

But Miss Parchment was now thoroughly at home on what appeared to be her favourite topic, and she interrupted the novelist to explain.

'It was renamed "The Little General" about 1805,' she said. 'Before that it had a much more interesting name.'

Daley was looking up at her in wonderment. 'You seem to know a dickens of a lot about this place.'

'It's all in the book I'm reading, Mr. Daley,' said Miss Parchment patiently. 'It's all in the book.'

Horace Daley had for some little while been paying as much attention to the body as he had to Miss Parchment. Horace Daley had a peculiar aversion to dead bodies. And he told them so. He thought it was high time the police came to remove it. Then another idea occurred to him.

'Can't—can't we cover him up or something till the sergeant arrives? 'E looks 'orrible just laid there staring up at the ceiling.'

'Yes, yes, all right,' agreed Temple.

'I'll get a sheet from the linen cupboard,' said Daley. 'Won't be a minute.'

They heard him going upstairs and presently moving about in one of the bedrooms.

For perhaps two minutes they sat in silence.

'Was he a very great friend of yours, Mr. Temple?' asked Miss Parchment suddenly.

'Not exactly what one would call a great friend. He was more a sort of business acquaintance.'

'I see.' Miss Parchment hesitated. 'You know, when I first saw him, I had a vague sort of suspicion that I'd seen him before. Of course, one meets so—'

Temple interrupted her. 'His name's Harvey. Superintendent Harvey, of Scotland Yard.'

Miss Parchment looked up.

'Scotland Yard!' she said softly. 'Oh, dear! Oh, dear!'

There was another long pause. Then Temple said: 'You say this inn wasn't always called "The Little General"?'

'No.'

'Then what was it called?'

Miss Parchment looked at him and there was a peculiar look in her eyes.

'A most intriguing title, Mr. Temple,' she replied at length. 'I'm sure you'll like it.'

Temple waited.

'Well?'

'It was called "The Green Finger",' said Miss Parchment quietly. And she smiled.

CHAPTER V

Room 7

'"The *Green Finger*"!' echoed Paul Temple, intense astonishment showing on his face.

He paused.

'Are you sure of this?' he said suddenly.

'Oh, quite sure,' replied Miss Parchment brightly. 'It's all in the book I'm reading, Mr. Temple. A most interesting book.'

Again Temple started pacing up and down the room, thinking over this new surprise. The coincidence was far too striking. Yet where was the connection? He decided that events must show for themselves exactly where this quaint old inn fitted in with these widespread robberies. He took a cigarette from his case and thoughtfully fitted it into his cigarette holder.

Suddenly the door to the little hall opened and Daley reappeared. Over his arm he carried the sheet for which he had been searching the linen cupboards upstairs.

''Ere's the sheet, Guv'nor!' he started. 'Now we can cover him up a bit.'

He unfolded the sheet carefully, displaying two large holes, several smaller ones, and a number of rust stains, which showed that he had no intention of wasting one of the inn's best sheets. He knelt down beside the body of the superintendent, at the same time keeping up a running commentary on his own feelings.

'If there's anything I 'ates the sight of,' he was saying, 'it's a fellow that's gone an'—' He broke off with sudden alarm in his voice as the sound of footsteps came through the window, and men could be heard talking. ''Ello, what's that?' he exclaimed.

'It sounds to me like the sergeant and Dr. Milton,' replied the novelist.

The voices and the footsteps grew louder, and presently feet could be heard brushing against the mat in the hall, while Temple recognized the suave tones of Dr. Milton, in a litany with the harsher country voice of Sergeant Morrison. Then the door opened and the two men came in, followed by the stolid form of Police Constable Hodges, in every way typical of the village constabulary.

'Good evening, Mr. Temple.' There was a clear, impressive note of authority in the sergeant's voice. 'Evening, Daley!'

He looked round the room and at the recumbent figure of Superintendent Harvey, his legs now covered with the innkeeper's sheet, while his trunk, arms and head projected incongruously, almost as if the dead man were just getting out of some strange bed. The worthy sergeant bristled with pride and self-importance as he made it plain that he was in full command of the situation. It is not an everyday occurrence for one of the big Chiefs of Scotland Yard to meet his death under strange circumstances, and Sergeant Morrison felt that here, at last, was the long awaited personal appearance of opportunity.

'Thank heavens you've come,' the innkeeper said, with a sigh of relief. 'I was just about to—'

A gasp of astonishment broke from Dr. Milton's lips. He had been looking at the tragic scene before him, but only now had he suddenly become aware of the victim's identity.

'It's Superintendent Harvey!' he exclaimed. 'Good gracious, why—'

Sergeant Morrison cut him short. 'If you please, Doctor,' he said, and his voice clearly indicated that there was work to be done.

The doctor accepted the rebuff. 'Oh, yes,' he said. 'I'm sorry, Sergeant.'

He knelt down by the side of the body. With deft fingers he loosened the clothing and started his examination. After a few moments, he looked up.

'Could we have another light on, please,' he asked curtly. 'I can't see very clearly.'

Daley hastened to the switch. The benefits of the electric grid had extended out even as far as "The Little General". Swiftly, yet carefully, the doctor carried out his examination.

Meanwhile, Sergeant Morrison was taking stock of his surroundings. He made notes of the exact positions of the chairs, the benches and tables, and of the general layout of the room. Already the sergeant was beginning to picture a better uniform than the one he was wearing, indeed, he was actually throwing increased authority into his voice and bearing. Fortunately, this did not detract from his efficiency. He was leaving nothing to chance.

'Hodges!' he commanded, indicating with a wave of his hand one of the doors behind the counter. 'Take a look at the back of this place. I think there must be some sort of courtyard.'

'Very good, sergeant,' replied Police Constable Hodges, and disappeared into the outer darkness.

For a while there was silence in the room. Temple was sitting patiently on one of the old forms. Sergeant Morrison remained standing, watching Dr. Milton as though fascinated by him.

'Well, Doctor?' he asked, as the latter started rearranging the clothing on the superintendent's body.

Dr. Milton replaced the instruments in his black leather attaché case and stood up.

'He's been dead about a quarter of an hour, I should say,' was the doctor's verdict. 'He must have died almost instantly.' Certainly it was far too late for the doctor to be of any assistance.

Sergeant Morrison grunted. Then he pulled out his notebook and made a laborious note.

'Now I'd like a few details, if you don't mind,' he said, his writing finished. He turned towards the novelist. 'Was the deceased a friend of yours, Mr. Temple?' he asked.

'Well, not exactly what one would call a friend, Sergeant. But I knew him fairly well.'

Again the sergeant laboriously copied the words into his notebook. Then he turned towards Horace Daley.

'Was he staying the night here?' he asked.

'Well, 'e was an' 'e wasn't, as yer might say, Sergeant.'

'Answer the question!'

Mr. Daley looked alarmingly as if he might splutter forth something even more unintelligible, but the novelist intercepted him.

'Perhaps it would be better if you allowed me to explain, Sergeant,' he said, as he rose from his bench and joined the little group.

'Well?'

'Superintendent Harvey was on holiday,' said Temple quietly. 'He called in to see me about ten-fifteen this evening.

42

Dr. Milton and his niece had been dining with me and were on the point of leaving. Harvey gave me to understand that he was staying the night here at "The Little General". Unfortunately, I persuaded the poor devil to change his mind and stay the night with me. We came down here to get his luggage and—'

'What time would that be?' interrupted the sergeant.

'Oh, about eleven-fifteen, I should say. Certainly no later.'

'Go on,' commanded Sergeant Morrison, preparing to make a note of the details.

'Well,' continued Temple, 'I waited outside for him in my car. After about five minutes or so, Mr. Daley came running out. He was very excited and obviously upset. He told me that Harvey had shot himself.'

The sergeant finished scribbling the sentence down, drew a heavy line across the page, then turned back to the innkeeper.

'Now let's hear your side of the story, Daley,' he asked.

Horace was determined to stand on his dignity. 'Mr. Daley, if you don't mind,' he said, by way of prefix. 'Well, I was standin' behind the bar doin' me crossword puzzle when this fellow comes in and says 'e's changed 'is mind about staying 'ere the night. 'E pops upstairs and brings down 'is suitcase. Then 'e asks me if I could change 'im a quid. I says "yes!" and goes into the back parlour to get the money. When I gets back, I sees 'im just like 'e is now. Coo, it wasn't 'alf a nasty shock, I can tell you!'

Sergeant Morrison knew very little shorthand, but he could write quickly and with fair legibility, and rarely had to ask anybody to repeat something they had said.

He finished writing what Daley had just told him, before asking: 'Had you seen him before?'

'Yes, of course I had,' replied the innkeeper impatiently. 'I was 'ere when 'e first arrived.'

'What time would that be?'

'Oh, I dunno. About five perhaps.'

'Was there anyone in here tonight, when he returned for his luggage?'

Perhaps the question was a little obvious, at any rate it certainly seemed to annoy the little Cockney.

'Yes, dozens o' people,' he retorted, with a wealth of broad sarcasm in his voice. 'About fifteen platinum blondes and a couple o' film stars. We had our gala night, Sergeant. You must join in the fun some time.'

The cheeks of Sergeant Morrison gradually suffused to a delicate hue of pink. From pink they changed as gradually to carmine and then, more rapidly, to a perilously deep purple.

For a moment a serious explosion seemed imminent. Then the danger passed.

'Don't try an' be funny!' was all he could growl at the innkeeper. 'And answer the questions!' he suddenly snapped out.

'Anyone 'ere at a quarter past eleven,' the little Cockney replied unperturbed. 'Coo! Why, the perishin' place is dead after 'alf-past eight.'

'Is there anyone else staying here at the moment?'

'Yes, Sergeant,' answered Temple. 'This lady, Miss Parchment.'

Miss Parchment had been sitting quietly on the chair Paul Temple had offered her some time before. She had not moved. Nor had she spoken. But with her bright blue eyes she had been following everything very intently. There could have been little that she had missed. Nobody had noticed her in the excitement of the moment, and it was with a start of quite real surprise that Sergeant Morrison became aware of her existence.

'Oh, yes,' he said, taking in the fact that here was possibly a source of much-needed information, and corroboration. 'Well, Madam, can—er—you throw any light on this matter?'

'I'm afraid not, Sergeant,' replied Miss Parchment calmly. 'I was in my room reading when Mr. Daley arrived with the news that this gentleman had shot himself and that a Mr. Temple wished to see me. Naturally, I was dreadfully upset about the matter and so of course—'

This was more than Horace Daley could stand. 'You didn't look very upset to me,' he interrupted.

'I have learnt to control my emotions,' answered Miss Parchment sweetly.

For once, the innkeeper had nothing to say in return. Miss Parchment, when she chose, could silence him very effectively with a few polite words, whereas all Sergeant Morrison's abuse, and for that matter anybody else's, only served to stimulate him the more.

Nothing seemed to ruffle Miss Parchment. Even the present tragedy had affected her less than some queer discovery she might have made about one of the old English inns that interested her so much. She had been sitting there in her chair, regarding the scene with a completely dispassionate interest. Now and then a slight smile flickered across her face. Then it vanished again. She clearly had a delicate, almost evanescent sense of humour. Cruder sallies left her unmoved. As unmoved as did the corpse on the bar parlour floor in front of her. The harsher realities of life, and death, appeared to have no part in her scheme of things. From the police point of view, she made an admirable witness in that she was so calm and collected, an advantage even if she had little of any value to tell him.

'Well, Miss Parchment, how long have you been staying here?'

'I arrived yesterday afternoon, Sergeant,' she replied. 'I'm on a walking tour of the Vale of Evesham. I'm interested in old English inns,' she explained with a smile. 'Very old English inns.'

'Yes—er—yes, just so,' replied the sergeant, not too intelligently. He felt perplexed and, for some strange reason, Miss Parchment embarrassed him.

'Could I have your full name and permanent address?' he asked gruffly, trying to make his voice as formal and official as possible, but with little success.

'Amelia Victoria Parchment,' said Miss Parchment, as the sergeant commenced to write, '47B, Brook Street, London, W.1.' With a word of thanks, that was more a sigh of gratitude that this part was all over, he turned back to Horace Daley. There was still the point to be cleared up of how the murderer, if any, could have made good his escape.

Temple had been sitting in his car immediately outside the inn during the actual tragedy, and he was certain that nobody had left or entered from the front of the inn. And the back was apparently impossible. Was it, after all then, a question of suicide?

'Now, Mr. Daley,' the sergeant said, this time with slightly more respect in his voice, 'could anyone have come in here whilst you were in the back parlour?'

'Yes,' he replied. 'They could 'ave come from either upstairs or from the street.'

'What about from the back,' the sergeant persisted; 'there's an open courtyard, isn't there?'

'Yes, but there's no way o' gettin' into the inn except through the back parlour, an' I was in there all the time.'

Sergeant Morrison grunted heavily. The mystery was too much for him.

At that moment the door behind the bar counter opened, and Police Constable Hodges reappeared. He pushed open the flap, waddled through rather than walked, and finally came to rest in front of his superior officer.

'There's nothing in the courtyard, sir,' he reported, 'except a lot of blessed pigeons.'

Horace Daley suppressed a smile.

The sergeant again started an examination of the room. He peered out of the window and went into Daley's sitting-room next door. He stayed about five minutes, not knowing what he expected to find, but nevertheless diligently searching every corner. Close on his heels followed Horace Daley, while the rest of the party stayed in the parlour, talking quietly of the tragedy that had suddenly enveloped them.

It seemed clear that the murderer, whoever he was, could not have entered by the sitting-room. Next, the sergeant opened the door to the hall and slowly mounted the stairs. There was little the sergeant did not examine. He inspected every room, opened every window, looked into every cupboard, almost as if the murderer might still be hidden on the premises somewhere.

At length he returned downstairs, feeling that it was all far more than he could tackle by himself and that the inspector ought to be consulted before anything further was done. He was, at any rate, sure that the murderer – if murder it was – was no longer on the premises, and for the moment there seemed little else to be done. Fingerprints might be taken as a matter of routine, but the bar parlour was used by many different people every day, including chance motorists who felt attracted by the inn's inviting old exterior, and stopped for some refreshment. They could therefore expect to find only a confused medley of fingerprints which it was unlikely would help them very far. The fingerprints on the revolver itself he felt certain would prove to be exclusively Harvey's.

'I wonder if you'd mind running me back to the station, Mr. Temple?' he asked. 'I feel that I ought to have a word with Inspector Merritt about this.'

The novelist agreed. He walked over to the bench in the corner of the room where he had flung down his overcoat, and prepared to face the outer coldness of the night. Then, taking his leave of the others, he left the room to start up the car and warm the engine for the run down to the police station. Meanwhile, the sergeant was apologizing to Dr. Milton.

'The police "doc." is down with the "flu",' he explained, 'and Mr. Temple suggested that you might—'

The doctor cut short his apologies. 'Only too glad to be of service, Sergeant. Think nothing of it.'

'Thank you, sir,' the sergeant replied courteously. Then he turned to where Miss Parchment was still sitting with quiet self-effacement.

'You can go to your room, Miss Parchment. I doubt whether the inspector will want to see you tonight.'

'Oh, thank you,' she replied. 'Good night, Sergeant. Good night,' she added, turning to the others. She wrapped her lace shawl around her neck, and with a parting smile for everyone, she opened the door and was gone.

Throughout the whole trying period, she had remained completely calm and collected. The sight of the body, and the blood now congealing on the back of the head, had not in the least upset her. Not so Horace Daley. Even now, when he might be expected to have grown accustomed to the sight of the body, he was still feeling singularly repelled.

'I say,' he burst out at last, addressing the sergeant, 'what the 'ell's goin' to happen to this fellow? We just can't leave 'im 'ere all night!'

'I'll attend to that, Daley,' said the sergeant, turning his back on the innkeeper and addressing the constable. 'Hodges, I think you'd better wait at the front – and don't let anyone enter.'

'Very good, sir.' The constable buttoned up his greatcoat, and went outside to take up his station.

The sergeant took one last look round the room to make certain there was nothing he had omitted. He felt he had done all he could, and turned to Dr. Milton.

'We'll be as quick as we can, Doctor,' he said.

'That's all right, Sergeant.'

He let himself out and hurried to the car where Temple sat waiting, the engine of the car purring, ready to leap away. He nodded to Hodges in passing, and even as he shut the door of the car, Temple was lifting his foot from the clutch pedal and pressing down the accelerator. The brilliant headlamps threw into light the wide sweep of road ahead, and the great car disappeared into the night.

Inside the bar parlour, Dr. Milton and Horace Daley were left alone. For perhaps five minutes neither of them spoke. Both sat on the hard benches of the bar parlour, now gazing at the body, now turning away to stare idly into space.

It was Horace Daley who broke the silence.

'They've gone!' he said in a low voice, far too low for Constable Hodges to hear.

The doctor nodded.

'I don't like it,' said Horace suddenly, with a note of alarm in his voice. 'I don't like it.'

There was an expression of contempt on Milton's face. 'Don't be a damned fool,' he said, keeping his voice low. 'Everything's turned out perfectly.'

They relapsed into the same tense silence. Daley got up and walked across to the window. After a pause he turned.

'Have you had any more information about the Leamington job?'

'Yes,' said the doctor. 'It came through this morning.'

'Well?'

'We meet on—Thursday.'

Horace Daley whistled his surprise. 'Thursday,' he said. 'Here – or at your place?'

Dr. Milton smiled.

'We meet here,' he said at length, 'in Room 7!'

CHAPTER VI

The Knave of Diamonds

Paul Temple picked up his last fragment of toast and proceeded to double its size with butter. Then he carefully scraped up the marmalade left on his plate and lowered it gradually on to the precarious foundation. As the butter began to ooze on to his thumb and forefinger, he inserted it in his mouth and began to chew contentedly. Then he swilled it down with strong black coffee.

Paul Temple had finished his breakfast.

It was a little after nine on the Thursday morning after the death of Superintendent Harvey. Much had taken place during those two days, but little towards helping the police in elucidating the mystery. Nevertheless, his death and the subsequent police investigations were making admirable breakfast-time reading for some millions of honest, hardworking Britons. The case helped to stimulate their minds gently back to the realities they would have to face during the coming day.

Pryce, Paul Temple's manservant, was regaling his master by reading out to him the accounts in the morning papers. Papers of various political hue and of various degrees of

sensation were propped up on the table, against the marmalade jar, against the coffee pot, in fact, against every convenient object against which they could be propped. Nevertheless,
Temple found it easier, conducive to good digestion, and
infinitely preferable to have the accounts read aloud to him.

He had a vast desire for the better things of life, and
preferred to give his concentration to his bacon, toast and
marmalade, and to gaze out of the French windows of his
breakfast-room at Bramley Lodge on to the great trees and
lovely undulating country outside. While Pryce was reading,
he did not therefore have to yield him his full, undivided
attention, but could take in the main essentials more or less
subconsciously.

Pryce picked up one of the more sober of the morning
papers, circulating only in the Midlands, and started reading.

'In a locked room at the police station here tonight,
Chief Inspector Dale discussed with Mr. Paul Temple,
the celebrated novelist, the incidents leading up to the
tragic suicide of Superintendent Harvey of Scotland
Yard. It is believed that, shortly before his death,
Superintendent Harvey discussed with Mr. Temple the
mysterious—'

But Temple had had enough. 'Righto, Pryce!'

'Shall I read you what the *Daily Page* says, sir?' asked Pryce.

'No. I think we'll leave that to the imagination.' Temple
poured himself out a little more coffee.

'Did anyone call yesterday while I was at the station with
Inspector Dale?' he asked.

'Several reporters, sir. Oh, and a rather elderly lady by the
name of Miss Parchment.'

Temple looked up in surprise. 'Miss Parchment!' he echoed, almost to himself. 'Now what the devil does she want?'

'The lady didn't leave a message, sir.'

Paul Temple extracted a cigarette from a nearby box, finished off his coffee, and strolled towards the open window. Below him, worn stone steps descended to a carefully planned garden where early flowers were already adding colour to a picturesque setting. The velvet lawn, its grass thick and smooth with the careful cutting, rolling and general tending of centuries, attracted him. Temple looked at a world far removed from the world of robbery and sudden death. But he was not allowed to digress for long. Pryce's voice was recalling him back to reality.

'I'm afraid several of the reporters will be returning this morning, sir. They seemed quite determined to have a word with you.'

'I don't want to see any of them,' said Temple impatiently. The Press men had one by one been giving up their quest. They had found it far too unprofitable lying in wait for Paul Temple. Nor could they even obtain any pointers from his movements. Nevertheless, the bigger, sensational papers and the agencies had kept their men on in the hope that they might suddenly get a lead towards really big news. Most of the men were fairly certain that Harvey's death was no suicide, and that it was closely bound up with the 'Midland Mysteries'.

Suddenly, a memory of something that seemed to belong to a bygone age came to Temple and he changed the topic.

'By Timothy, I must get down to that serial, Pryce. I promised to let "Malpur's" have the first instalment by the end of May.'

But Pryce was not so easily led astray from the reports he had to make to his master. He had a very high idea, and ideal, of his duties as a manservant. Temple, he felt, needed a little guidance from time to time, especially with that section of his affairs over which Pryce held charge. The serial could wait. There were still weeks to go, not merely days. A long session with a dictaphone would very quickly see the end of the first instalment.

'There was one reporter who seemed very insistent, sir,' said Pryce. 'She simply wouldn't take "No!" for an answer.'

Temple smiled. 'Wouldn't she, Pryce?'

'A very pretty girl, too, sir,' added Pryce. 'If—er—I may say so?'

'By all means say so, Pryce. A very pretty girl who wouldn't take "No" for an answer. Sounds interesting.'

Pryce was endeavouring to remember the young lady's name. He had made a particular note of it at the time because he thought it had sounded a rather peculiar name for a member of the opposite sex.

'Ah, I remember, sir,' he said suddenly, 'it was Trent. Miss Steve Trent.'

Temple was not greatly interested but he forced himself to reply.

'Well, if Miss Steve Trent calls round again you can tell her—'

He did not complete the sentence. An electric bell started ringing. It was the bell to the front door.

'It'll be Inspector Dale,' said Temple, as Pryce moved towards the hall.

Temple stretched forth his arms in a mighty, luxurious yawn, tossed the cigarette he was smoking into the hearth, and proceeded to fill his pipe. One or other of his big briars was his constant companion. He went through an ounce and a half of tobacco every day although a doctor had warned

him long before that two ounces a week should be his limit
if he wished to keep his heart sound. The warning, like
most other warnings he had received during his life, had
not frightened him.

His cultured manners and his breeding formed the best
disguise and mask he could desire. There was nothing blunt
about Paul Temple. To the casual acquaintance, he even
seemed soft-hearted. But behind that smooth exterior was a
forceful character and a courage that few even suspected the
existence of. It showed only in his strange calmness which
nothing could upset.

He sat down on the slope which led down to the garden
and savoured the fresh warm air of the new day. His dreams
were cut short by the sound of excited voices in the hall.
He listened and distinguished Pryce's voice raised in loud
expostulations while a woman's voice alternated in more
subdued tones.

'I'm very sorry, madam,' he heard Pryce saying, evidently
trying to preserve his normal dignified bearing while at the
same time forcibly trying to carry out his master's bidding.
'Mr. Temple is out.'

Once again came the lower undertones of a woman's voice,
but Temple could not catch what she said. His curiosity was
aroused, however, and he strode to the door and opened it
to find Pryce barring the way to a pretty girl who did not
look as if she were much more than twenty. Pryce was clearly
not above using force. In fact, as Temple appeared, he was
actually trying to push her out of the hall.

But she had the advantage of youth and agility against
Pryce's age and bulk, and she had managed to make considerable progress through the hall when Temple came to see
what was happening.

'What the devil is all this?' he exclaimed.

Pryce was very illuminating.

'It's the young lady, sir,' he managed to exclaim.

'Which young lady?'

'The—er—the reporter, sir.'

Temple remembered Pryce's description of the girl 'who wouldn't take "no!" for an answer,' and smiled.

'Oh. Oh, I see,' he said quietly.

The girl was smiling too.

'May I come in?' she asked pleasantly.

Temple hesitated. 'Yes, I think perhaps you'd better,' he said at last.

He led the way into the comfortable lounge where he had entertained Dr. Milton and Diana Thornley two days before. Unconsciously, he bowed his strange visitor into a comfortable armchair and produced Turkish and Virginia cigarettes for her to smoke. Miss Trent took one of the latter, lit it and smiled happily at him.

'He's very determined, isn't he,' she said, referring to Pryce.

Temple, normally the most self-possessed of men, was taken aback.

'Yes—er—yes, very.' Then suddenly he remembered that even though his charming visitor was certainly more good-looking than Pryce had led him to expect, she had literally broken into his house.

'I say, look here,' he expostulated, 'you can't come bursting into people's houses like this!'

'I'm sorry,' she started without seeming to display any great depths of misery, 'but—' And her voice tailed away as if she had other and far weightier topics to think about and discuss.

'You are Paul Temple, aren't you?' she asked, almost abruptly.

'Yes,' said Temple quietly.

Miss Trent had a knack of putting herself so completely in the right that Temple began to feel almost as if he were the offender.

'I tried to see you yesterday, but your man said you were out.'

'Well—er—what is it you wanted to see me about?'

Steve Trent looked up at the man she had forced to be her host, and her face gradually became very serious.

'Do you think Superintendent Harvey committed suicide?' she asked.

Temple looked at this pretty girl sitting before him with sudden interest. She was certainly a very earnest reporter.

'My dear Miss Trent, I don't see that it makes a great deal of difference what I think,' he said non-committally.

But Miss Trent was not so easily evaded.

'Please! Please, answer my question. Do you think Superintendent Harvey committed suicide?'

The words came with a rush. There was deep emotion in her voice.

Temple stared at her with surprise in his eyes. 'By Timothy, you are a remarkable young woman! First of all you insult my . . .'

Miss Trent interrupted him.

'You haven't answered my question!' she said firmly.

Temple had encountered many reporters in the course of his career, but this girl was something new in his experience. That she was extremely pretty, Temple had seen as soon as he set foot in the hall during Pryce's severe efforts to restrain her. But then many girl reporters are pretty. And like the beautiful, glamorous women spies of popular fiction, they can often use that beauty with great advantage, both while extracting information from unwilling victims and coping with recalcitrant editors!

But there was something about Steve Trent that distinguished her from other women reporters in Fleet Street. Her eyes shone clear and bright, with no hard sophistication to mar them. Yet they spoke of experience, of difficulties, even dangers encountered. They were dark-blue eyes, one curiously lighter than the other, and they sparkled with the vivacity of her nature.

She was now wearing an elegant costume of dark-green tweed under which the lustrous silk stockings that emphasized the contours of two admirable legs looked slightly incongruous. A rather shapeless deerstalker type of hat crowned her luxuriant blonde hair. In every respect, as Temple and everyone else who met her thought, she was an eminently attractive young woman, in dress, appearance and character. The sort of woman for whom Elizabethan poets would have torn their hair out searching for epithets sufficiently far-fetched.

Temple took it all in, as he sat on the settee opposite her, wondering exactly what to make of this lovely young criminologist. At length he answered her question.

'No!' he said quietly. 'I think Superintendent Harvey was murdered.'

'I knew it! I knew it!' exclaimed Steve Trent, her voice raising to a high pitch in sudden, unwonted excitement. 'I knew they'd get him!'

'Why do you say that?' asked Paul Temple with surprise.

'Gerald Harvey was . . . a . . . friend of mine,' said Steve Trent slowly.

'Oh, I'm sorry,' he apologized. 'My man told me that you were a reporter and . . .'

'Yes, that's true,' she interrupted. 'I'm on the staff of *The Evening Post*, but that's not why I wanted to see you.'

Again Temple looked at her queerly.

'Why did you want to see me?' he asked at length.

Steve Trent appeared to think for a moment.

'Because I need your help,' she answered suddenly, 'because I need your help more than I've ever wanted anything in my life before.'

Temple was obviously impressed by the urgency in her voice.

'Was Harvey a great friend of yours?' he asked.

Steve nodded. 'He was my brother,' she said softly.

'Your brother!' exclaimed Temple, then: 'When I suggested that your brother might have been murdered, you said: "I knew it! I knew it! I knew they'd get him!" What did you mean by "I knew they'd get him?"'

Steve Trent, alias Louise Harvey, paused a moment, then asked him a question in return.

'Why do you think my brother came to see you, Mr. Temple, the night he was murdered?'

'I don't know,' he replied thoughtfully. 'I'm not at all certain that he had any particular reason.'

'He had,' she answered, 'a very good reason.'

'Well?'

'My brother was investigating the mysterious robberies which have been occurring. He had a theory about these robberies which I believe he wanted to discuss with you.'

'A theory?' queried Paul Temple.

Slowly at first, then gradually gaining confidence, Steve Trent proceeded to tell him her story. It was the life history of herself and of Superintendent Gerald Harvey, the police chief. She had come to see Paul Temple, the novelist and criminologist, not as a reporter after a 'story', but to ask his help.

'About eight years ago,' she explained, 'my brother was attached to what was then called the Service B.Y. It was a special branch of the Cape Town Constabulary. At this particular time, a very daring and successful gang of criminals were carrying out a series of raids on various jewellers within a certain area known as the Cape Town–Simonstown area. My brother and another officer, whose name I forget at the moment, were in charge of the case. After months of investigation, they discovered that the leader of the organization was a man who called himself the Knave of Diamonds, but whose real name was Max Lorraine.

'Lorraine apparently was a well-educated man who at one time had occupied an important position at Columbia University. Eventually the organization was smashed – but the Knave had laid his plans carefully and he escaped. Two months later, the officer who had assisted my brother in the investigation was murdered. It was not a pleasant murder. This was followed almost immediately by two attempts on my brother's life.'

She paused. Paul Temple could see the look of horror in her eyes as the recollection of those terrible days came back to her.

'Please go on,' he said to her at last.

Steve Trent looked up at him gratefully, then resumed her story. The circumstances of the murder of her brother's fellow officer could never be explained.

'A farmer came upon his lifeless body in a ditch by the roadside,' she went on. 'He had suddenly noticed a car by the roadside, apparently abandoned, but with its engine still running.

'There were two bullet wounds in the head. One in the back which had evidently felled him, and one in his forehead, which might have been fired as he lay on the ground.

'The attempts on Gerald's life might quite well have been accidents. But somehow I don't think they were. The first time, a large black saloon car, driven at a high speed, swerved and nearly knocked him down. That was just outside Cape Town.

'In the other case, a large wooden crate containing a piano was being lowered from the upper floor of a house. Gerald happened to be passing: the house was only two or three doors from where he was living at the time. Suddenly, a rope slipped and the crate crashed down immediately in front of him.'

Paul Temple muttered his interest. He waited for Steve to go on with what she had to say.

'From the very first moment when Gerald was put in charge of this Midland case,' she continued, 'he had an uneasy feeling at the back of his mind that he was up against Max Lorraine. I saw him a few days before he came up to see you, and he told me then that he was almost certain that Max Lorraine, alias the Knave of Diamonds, was the real influence behind the robberies which he and Inspector Dale were investigating.'

Steve paused. Then added, softly: 'I think he was a little worried – and rather frightened.'

For a long time Temple said nothing. He realized, only too well, the value of the story Steve Trent had poured out to him.

'Had your brother discussed with Sir Graham, or any of his colleagues, his theory regarding this man Lorraine?' he asked.

'No,' Miss Trent replied. 'No, I don't think so.'

'Why not?'

'Because he knew only too well that they would never believe him.'

'Never believe him?' repeated Temple, puzzled.

'The Knave is hardly the sort of person one can talk about – and sound convincing,' she answered. 'He's like a character snatched from the most sensational thriller and inspired with a strange, satanic intellect.' Steve Trent spoke in a slow monotone, as if reciting a well-learned lesson. She paused and looked up at Temple curiously.

'You think that sounds silly, don't you?' she asked with a half-smile.

'Well, er—' Temple felt a little embarrassed to have his feelings so accurately analyzed, 'it sounds a little unusual!'

At all cost Steve Trent wanted Paul Temple to believe in her. To have complete faith in her story.

'Mr. Temple!' she spoke with the deepest emotion in her voice. 'Do you believe me? Do you believe my story about this man – Lorraine?'

Temple had been wavering. Now he made up his mind.

'Yes.' He paused. 'Yes, I believe you. But tell me, did your brother ever see him; did they ever meet?'

'No!' she replied. 'No, not once. But he knew his methods – he knew everything about him – and he was afraid.'

Paul Temple at last put his pipe down; it had grown cold some time before. Now he plunged his hands into the pockets of his well-worn tweed jacket and finally brought out with some triumph a cherry-wood pipe. This he proceeded to fill with great deliberation. Filling a pipe was a very serious business with Paul Temple. If careful filling were going to provide him with a better smoke, then carefully filled it should be. He applied the Principle of the Conservation of Energy to himself very literally, and had no intentions of wasting energy that could be better devoted to other purposes. After a few seconds had elapsed he pressed the bell-push by the side of the mantelpiece.

Pryce's face showed the surprise he felt when he came in. Fully convinced of some strange romance suddenly blossoming forth, his respect for the mental powers of the man he almost worshipped, decreased very violently. Although Miss Trent was very nearly thirty, Pryce numbered her with the bright young things, of whom he heartily disapproved.

As soon as Pryce had received his instructions, Temple came back to the subject.

'That night your brother came to my house, he told me that he was firmly convinced that a well-directed criminal organization existed. But he didn't mention anything about this man – Max Lorraine. Why not, I wonder?'

'I don't know,' replied Steve Trent. 'He intended to, I'm sure of that. He wanted your help over this case. He had a very great admiration for you.' Then she produced another surprise.

'It was Gerald who persuaded me to start the "Send for Paul Temple" campaign in *The Evening Post*!'

The victim began to laugh. 'By Timothy, you certainly started something.' Then he again became very serious. 'A little while ago, you said you chose the name of "Steve Trent" not only for professional reasons, but partly for another reason too. What did you mean by that?'

'Gerald was terrified that Lorraine might find out that he had a sister,' she replied quietly. 'Even in Cape Town, Gerald made me live with relatives under an assumed name.'

'Was he naturally cautious over everything?'

'No,' she answered. 'But he knew that Max Lorraine would stop at nothing.'

At that moment Pryce came in with a large pot of coffee on a tray together with milk and a plate of biscuits. He put the tray down on a low table between them, and quietly withdrew. Both were glad of the moment's respite.

Temple slowly poured out the coffee.

Steve Trent settled happily in her chair. Already, the slight lines that worry might have brought below her eyes were beginning to disappear. It would be idle to say that she felt at ease. Steve was one of those people who felt at ease anywhere and everywhere. But she did at last feel that she had won Temple's sympathy and support, and the thought was very comforting. She lit a cigarette and with great satisfaction exhaled a cloud of blue-grey smoke.

'Your brother must have known a great deal about this man,' Temple resumed at last.

'Yes, a great deal,' she replied. 'And the day before he died, he passed that information on to me.'

'To you!' exclaimed Temple with surprise. 'That may mean danger. Great danger.' He spoke impressively. 'You realize that?'

'Yes.'

Temple paused to let the full significance of his remark sink in. Then he asked her another question.

'What is it you know about Max Lorraine?'

'I know that he has a small scar above the right elbow, that he smokes Russian cigarettes, and is devoted to a girl who answers to the name of Ludmilla,' said Steve slowly.

Temple rose to his feet and started pacing up and down the room as though digesting this information. It was not until after some minutes had elapsed that he again spoke.

'Miss Trent, you said you wanted my help. You said you wanted my help more than you've ever wanted anything in your life before. What did you mean by that?'

'I meant that from now on I want it to be Paul Temple versus Max Lorraine!'

For a full two minutes Temple again remained silent. Still, he did not seem sure that he wanted to follow his inclinations and take a hand in this struggle. Then he began to laugh, rather quietly at first.

Steve Trent looked up at him as if wondering what new phase of himself he was going to show. 'Why are you laughing?' she asked.

'I was just thinking of something Pryce said before you arrived here.'

'Well?'

'He said, you simply wouldn't take "no" for an answer!'

CHAPTER VII

The Shaping of a Mystery

That same afternoon, 'The Little General', only two or three miles from Paul Temple's house, was the scene of a strange gathering. There were many men at Scotland Yard who would have given a year's salary merely to have heard the conversation that took place in that mysterious Room 7.

Now that the body of Superintendent Harvey had been removed the inn had become famous, quite literally, over-night. Motorists, cyclists, and hikers arrived in a never-ceasing stream to see the place where the well-known police chief had met his unexpected fate. Detectives kept a close watch on all visitors, not that they entertained the hope of making an arrest, but they applied the old adage that a murderer always revisits the scene of his crime, and they did not intend to fail merely because they had neglected such elementary principles.

Chief Inspector Dale had made several visits to the inn. While in no way striving after the spectacular, he was spending as much time as he could on the 'Midland Mysteries', and he had delegated as much of his ordinary routine work at Scotland Yard as possible on to his subordinates. He had called on Paul Temple and had had long conversations with all who might know anything that had any bearing on Harvey's death.

So far, however, the police had found no clue that might lead them towards a solution of the robberies and the death of Superintendent Harvey.

A few hours after Steve Trent and Paul Temple had been discussing the mysterious and elusive Max Lorraine, Dr. Milton was sitting, together with two other men, in Room 7 at 'The Little General'. Horace Daley, the innkeeper, hovered vaguely in the background. But the innkeeper was not his normal ebullient self. He now very definitely yielded precedence to Dr. Milton, who was in full charge of the proceedings.

'Is that quite clear, Dixie?' the doctor was saying.

'Yes, it seems quite clear,' answered the man known as "Dixie". 'Diana will be parked at the corner of Regent Street. I've got to get from the jeweller's to the car – pass the stuff over – and then mingle with the crowd in front of the dress shop.'

'Yes, that's right,' Milton agreed. 'And stay there,' he ordered; 'don't make any attempt to sneak away until the crowd moves!'

'Don't worry, I won't!' said Dixie.

'Have you looked the place over?' inquired the doctor.

'Yes. I had a look round this morning.' Dixie paused. 'Not very difficult. I should be out in a little under seven minutes.'

'Good.' Dr. Milton turned to the man known as "Skid". Both Skid and Dixie were young men, not more than twenty-five, or twenty-six. Both were wearing cheap, ready-made lounge suits. Skid was a sharp-featured man who spoke quickly and never wasted his words. Dixie, on the other hand, to whom Dr. Milton had already been talking, was almost moonfaced. He appeared of a pleasanter disposition than Skid, and even showed traces of a real sense of humour. He was tall enough to be a guardsman, and was a good head taller than Skid.

Dr. Milton now took a map out of his pocket and opened it on one of the little tables. 'Now, Skid, I want you to have a look at this map,' he said. 'You see Regent Street? That's where Diana will park the car. Now take a look at the Parade. You can see the jeweller's and the dress shop the moment you come round the bend. The Chief wants you to come round that corner at seven-forty precisely. You should reach the dress shop about seven-forty-one. Then let it rip! Got that?'

'Yeah,' replied Skid, implying that all this sort of thing was to Skid as easy as sleeping; 'I got it all right.'

'And we want a good job made of this,' continued Dr. Milton. 'No half-measures. Straight through the dress-shop window, you understand, Skid?'

Skid nodded. 'Sure!'

'We want noise, and plenty of it!'

'Don't worry,' answered Skid, somewhat impatiently. 'I'll wake up the whole blasted town.'

'Good,' said the doctor, finally satisfied that his instructions had made the necessary impression.

Horace Daley moved towards the group and took out the home-made cigarette which hung down from the corner of his mouth.

'Well, thank Gawd it's you on the lorry, an' not me!' he said.

'You'll be all right, Skid, provided you keep your head,' said the doctor again. 'All you've got to do is make it look genuine.'

'It'll look genuine all right!' Skid assured him.

'Well, I hope so!'

Dixie had been regarding the scene with clear impatience over his face. In their own sphere they were competent workmen and he felt that Dr. Milton ought to be more certain of them. But he still had a question to ask.

'Do I wait for the smash before I—'

Dr. Milton interrupted him. 'No, at 7.40 get to work. You won't have much time, but it shouldn't take any longer than the Gloucester job.'

'Don't worry about me, Doc,' said Dixie. 'I'll be out of there in no time. Have you got a list of the stuff?'

'I'm expecting Diana with it.' Dr. Milton paused significantly. 'She went to see the Chief this morning.'

For a few moments no one spoke.

'I say, Doc!' It was Skid who broke the silence. 'Who is this fellow who calls himself the Knave? He's been running us around now for three months, and we haven't even so much as had a glimpse of him. Don't you think ...?'

Dixie did not let him finish his sentence. 'Well, it doesn't worry me who the fellow is!' he exclaimed. 'He can be Sir Graham Forbes himself, as far as I'm concerned. All I know is, he can certainly organize. A cool forty thousand in three months. Boy, that's what I call money!'

'I'm not grumbling!' replied Skid. 'I'm just sort of curious, that's all.'

'Same 'ere!' ejaculated Horace. 'Who the 'ell is the Knave, Doc?'

Dr. Milton began to laugh. 'You'll find out my friends. All in good time! All in good time!'

Dixie came back to the matter in hand. 'I say, Doc, where do you come into this Leamington business? Does Diana ...?'

'As soon as you pass the stuff to Diana, she drives to Warwick. I take it over at Warwick, and get the stuff back here. Horace does the rest. It'll be in Amsterdam by Saturday.'

'Any idea what cut we're going to get out of this?'

'I'm not sure, Skid,' the doctor replied. 'Frobisher's got a pretty heavy stock. There's a ring worth £6,000.'

'Six thousand!' repeated Skid, almost savouring the words with his tongue.

Dixie whistled. 'The Knave can certainly pick 'em!'

Suddenly they heard a loud knock. Even the nonchalant Skid jumped.

'There's somebody at the panel!' he whispered, with alarm.

Dr. Milton hastened to reassure him. 'It's only Diana.'

'Blimey!' was Horace's comment. 'You ain't 'alf jumpy!'

In the far wall, away from the hall door, a panel moved, disclosing an open space. Then a figure appeared, and the four men recognized Diana Thornley. The opening in the wall was about a foot above the floor and some four feet high. Normally, it was completely invisible, effectively camouflaged by the old oak panelling.

Diana Thornley stepped out of the opening, and came towards the waiting men.

'Sorry I'm late, Doc!' she apologized. She turned to see Horace Daley closing the panel behind her.

'No, don't shut the panel!'

'Why not?' asked the doctor.

Quietly, almost with reverence in her voice, Diana answered him. 'The Chief's coming!'

'Here?' exclaimed Dr. Milton.

'Yes.'

'Oh!' There was a pause. 'Still I think we'd better shut it,' he said, and signed to Horace Daley to do so.

'He's coming here? The Knave?' asked Dixie, with surprise.

'Yes,' answered Diana. 'He's got the Birmingham money. It came through this morning.'

'Blimey, that's quick work!' came from Skid. For the first time the air of bored indifference had fallen from him. He smiled very broadly.

'Have you given them the Leamington details?' Diana was speaking to Milton, yet there was a note of authority in her voice.

'Yes.'

'How do you feel about it, Skid? Think you can manage the smash all right?'

A smile spread across Skid's face, and he rubbed his hands.

'As easy as falling off a log!'

'Good,' said Diana, obviously pleased, 'but we want as much row as possible, remember that!'

'Sure.'

'And don't forget to dash back to the shop, Dixie,' she continued. 'There's bound to be a crowd.'

'O.K.,' was the reply. 'Have you got a list of the stuff?'

Diana opened her handbag. From its capacious depths, she extracted three folded quarto sheets of paper. It was a list of the articles about which they had inquired, complete with their values. She passed it across to Dixie. He looked down the list, page after page.

'Any good, Dixie?' inquired Horace somewhat anxiously.

'Any good,' repeated Dixie with a wealth of intonation in his voice. 'Any good—'

At that moment, another knock came from the mysterious panel. It was Horace this time who looked round in alarm. 'What's that?' he asked nervously.

'It's the Chief,' Diana informed him. 'Open the panel, Doc.'

Dr. Milton walked quickly over to the wall and fingered the oak panelling. Presently the panel began to move.

Dr. Milton stepped forward.

In an impressive voice, he made his announcement.

'Gentlemen, meet the Knave!'

Absolute astonishment greeted his words. For a few seconds, no one spoke.

'The Knave, but—' said Horace Daley at last.

Then they all began to speak at once.

'I thought you said the Chief was a—' Skid was not allowed to complete his sentence. Dixie's amazement made him almost shriek his surprise.

'But—but this isn't the Knave!' he shouted. 'Why . . . Why—'

Dr. Milton looked round with satisfaction and amusement.

'Surprised, gentlemen?' he asked. 'Surprised?'

Again he looked round, this time into each of their astonished faces. Then he began to laugh, slowly, deeply.

CHAPTER VIII

A Message from Scotland Yard!

During the previous summer Paul Temple had spent several months in Holland and he had noticed, with amusement, that on several of the houses miniature windows were fitted into the front doors. Most of the windows were also equipped with stout grills for protection. Now, however, when callers were frequent and newspaper reporters had become an intolerable nuisance, he was beginning to appreciate the advantages of such a device. He summoned carpenters from the nearby village, and much to their astonishment, they found themselves fitting such safety windows in all the doors at Bramley Lodge.

It was no insignificant precaution. Paul Temple fully realized that the Lorraine gang would stop at nothing. They were quite capable of despatching a member to Bramley Lodge and putting a simultaneous end to his investigations and existence.

But now, however, it was quite impossible to enter Bramley Lodge by force. Not that Temple admitted to any fear in this respect. But he had to keep out reporters and had installed these little windows purely for this reason. That they also protected him against the gang, however, was certainly an additional advantage, not to be readily underestimated.

On the Saturday at the end of a very eventful week Steve Trent had to undergo inspection through the grill for the first time. At about ten that morning she had left her office behind Fleet Street and stepped into her fast sports car. It was a low, black under-slung model with an engine whose six small, but very powerful cylinders, gave her as much speed as any driver could cope with. Moreover, Miss Trent was still young and unspoiled enough to get a renewed thrill out of speeding.

It provided her with a means of escape from the hard and often sordid details of her daily work. Letting her hair stream out, and with the windscreen flat down in front of her, she would press the accelerator hard down with an exhilarated feeling of freedom. She had reached the office soon after half-past eight on this particular Saturday morning in order to complete a weekly woman's article, and then fled from the building before an unfeeling news editor could prevent her from keeping her appointment with Paul Temple.

Late the night before had come a telegram from the novelist asking her if she could possibly come and have lunch with him the next day. 'Interesting news to discuss,' was the intriguing reason he had given. Steve Trent wondered what the urgency was that had persuaded Temple to send for her in such an unusual fashion. Nevertheless, as she resolutely set her alarm clock for seven o'clock the next morning, she felt tremendously elated.

And she felt even more elated at the near prospect of the meeting as she swung her car out of Tudor Street towards Blackfriars Bridge and the hundred odd miles to Bramley Lodge. A traffic block at the Blackfriars Bridge junction which

disregarded the regular 'Go!' signal of the traffic lights held her up for nearly ten minutes.

But somehow, on this particular morning, Steve did not seem to care.

At last she was able to release the brakes and, earnestly praying that no vigilant police patrol car would be drawn to her by the lusty roar from the car's exhaust, she started down the Thames Embankment. Looking periodically into her tiny driving mirror, for the reflection of any suspicious-looking car in the rear, she shot along the wide clear road at just over fifty.

Two and a half hours later, she had parked the car in the drive of Bramley Lodge and was undergoing Pryce's careful inspection through the little grill. This time, there was none of the enmity Pryce had been forced to display on the first occasion she had called.

In fact she had already won a unique place in the old man's affections.

Steve Trent had a happy knack of making people like her, at times even against what they firmly believed to be their better judgment. Like Temple she assessed people, not by the rank they held, but at their real value as human beings, and in Pryce Steve found the completely efficient manservant, old-fashioned in his ideas, perhaps, but nevertheless faithful, solid and reliable, who could carry out for the novelist all the many duties of a bachelor establishment.

On the few brief occasions he had seen her, she had completely enslaved Pryce. So much so that, when Temple asked him the day before to prepare lunch for them both and to 'do your stuff because Miss Trent will be coming,' he set out to provide a meal fit for a proverbial princess. And Steve Trent enjoyed it to the full when it was set before her.

Nearly as much as she enjoyed being in this lovely old room. Its oak panelling gave it a character which Temple had managed to preserve with the help of, or perhaps in spite of, some real Chippendale furniture an aunt had left him. 'Always be kind to wealthy aunts,' had been his never-failing maxim after that occasion. Through the windows the fruit trees could be seen in full blossom.

In the summer it was a very proud host who placed bowls of apples and pears, peaches and less common fruits before his appreciative guests.

The sight of the luxuriant white blossom outside the dining-room windows kept Steve Trent chattering like an excited child. Already her girlhood memories of the even more luxuriant blooms of South Africa were growing dim, and in London she had far too little opportunity of tasting the joys of the countryside.

By common consent, neither of them said a word about Steve's brother and the crimes that had led their paths together. But Max Lorraine, the mystery man, and his gang of jewel thieves were not very far from the thoughts of either of them. Both regarded this lunch together as something in the nature of a respite. And both host and guest kept up a steady chatter of current events. They talked of Mr. Coward's versatility, the capriciousness of editors, the publicity value of Mr. Hore-Belisha, the lack of good shows in town, and kindred topics. Each seemed to feel it was essential to go on talking, if only to keep at bay the dark shadow of the powerful gang behind the 'Midland Mysteries'. They could discuss all that over their coffee later in the afternoon.

And all too soon the coffee stage was reached. Paul Temple made his usual apologies at this time of the year for 'not being able to give you fruit out of my garden: you will have to wait a bit for that!' but he produced quite excellent substitutes from foreign climes. The dessert seemed to have the effect of making them silent. After a while they got up and Temple led the way into the lounge.

It was a rather chilly day, and a great fire was burning in the ingle. A number of logs were piled up by the side, drying in the heat of the flames and imparting a pleasant but keen aromatic smell to the room. He pulled up a comfortable armchair for his guest at one corner of the inglenook and produced boxes of Virginia and Turkish cigarettes for her. These Turkish cigarettes were made for Temple by a Greek who kept a little cafe in Shaftesbury Avenue, and Paul Temple, in his self-imposed role of being the perfect host, was very proud of them. They were of excellent tobacco, and the cigarette itself was attached to a gold-tipped tube of equal length which formed the mouthpiece.

He himself took a Virginia and inserted it carefully into his ivory cigarette holder.

'Would you care for a liqueur, Steve?' he asked, as he started pouring out the coffee.

Steve Trent hesitated. 'No, I don't think so, thanks.' But then, how was Steve to know that one never refused a liqueur at Bramley Lodge? Temple's cherry brandy had an almost notorious reputation.

'Nonsense!' exclaimed Temple. 'By Timothy, this coffee needs it. Pryce,' he called, 'a cherry brandy for Miss Trent.'

Pryce had been tactfully hovering in the background waiting for this very command. He, at all events, had no delusions about the cherry brandy at Bramley Lodge.

'Certainly, sir,' he replied, and proceeded to pour out precious drops of the rosy liquid. Then he set the bottle down conveniently and temptingly on the sideboard, and silently withdrew.

'Well, it was very decent of you to come down from town at a moment's notice like this,' Temple started at last. 'I hope it wasn't too inconvenient?'

'No, of course not, but—' and she paused, 'but why did you send for me so suddenly?'

'Well, Steve, because . . . oh, by the way, I've decided to drop the Miss Trent,' he added a little inconsequently. 'It reminded me of a rather elderly lady I met at a garden party. She thought I was part author of *Gone With the Wind*.'

A ripple of happy laughter floated across the air.

'I sent for you, Steve, because I've been thinking of what you told me the other day.'

'You mean, about my brother and—Max Lorraine?'

'Yes.' Paul Temple hesitated. 'If your brother was right, and this man Lorraine, alias the Knave of Diamonds, really is the big noise behind these jewel robberies, then I think you ought to tell Sir Graham all you know about him.'

'He'd never believe me!' she exclaimed. 'This man Lorraine is—'

'I'm not so sure that he wouldn't, Steve,' Paul Temple interrupted. 'The Commissioner isn't quite such a fool as people think. He's got his head screwed on all right. Even though he won't send for Paul Temple!' he smiled, as an afterthought.

'But they don't even believe my brother was murdered!' Steve Trent put in excitedly. 'If they think he committed suicide, then they're—'

Paul Temple was able to stem even Steve Trent's rapid flow of words.

'I can prove to them that he did not commit suicide,' he said quietly. 'If they need any proof!'

'You can!'

'Yes. According to Horace Daley, the landlord of "The Little General", when your brother came downstairs, he asked him to change a pound note, and Daley then went into the back parlour to get the money.'

Steve Trent looked at Paul Temple expectantly.

'Well,' he continued, 'why should he go into the back parlour? There was thirty-seven and sixpence in the till behind the bar counter. It doesn't make sense.'

'How do you know this?'

'Because I examined the till when Daley went upstairs to fetch Miss Parchment down. In fact, that's why I sent him.'

Steve Trent showed she realized the importance of his discovery. Nevertheless, she had no intention of being so blinded by it that she could not see any of the other facts.

'Of course, there may be a perfectly simple explanation,' she said. 'Perhaps the landlord didn't want to—'

'Oh, yes. There may be quite a simple explanation. But there's just one other little point. Your brother was holding the revolver in his left hand.'

Steve Trent looked puzzled. 'But Gerald *was* left-handed,' she said.

'Yes, of course,' replied Temple, quietly. 'That's just the point.'

'What do you mean?' asked Steve.

'I mean, my dear Miss Trent, that your brother was murdered by someone with a little too much imagination and not sufficient intelligence.'

A journalistic training had sharpened Steve Trent's already quick powers of perception. Moreover, she never accepted facts at their face value but preferred to look both behind and beyond them.

'But if it's so very obvious that my brother was murdered, why do the police think he committed suicide?'

'What makes you so certain that the police think he committed suicide?' asked Paul Temple.

'Why, it's been in all the newspapers, and even at the inquest, they . . . they—' she broke off, apparently in deep thought. Suddenly she exclaimed with a queer note of surprise in her voice: 'You think they *know* he was murdered?'

'I'm almost sure of it.'

'Then why on earth did they make out it was suicide?' she asked. 'Surely—'

'I expect they have a reason, Steve. And I shouldn't be surprised if it isn't a very good one.'

Paul Temple slowly stretched his legs, poured more coffee out for each of them, then strolled towards the sideboard and returned with the bottle of cherry brandy between his fingers. He refilled their glasses and offered Steve another of the Turkish cigarettes she had liked so much.

Then he blew through his long cigarette holder, watched the butt end of his cigarette go flying into the fire, and carefully replaced the holder on the mantelpiece. Paul Temple was by no means a cigarette smoker, but he liked an occasional cigarette, especially while drinking tea or coffee.

He now brought forth the briar pipe which had been his constant companion for three years. It was alight and going well before he sat down again.

'Who was the lady that was staying at the inn? Miss . . . er . . .?'

'Miss Parchment?' asked Temple. 'She's a retired school-mistress with a passion for old English inns. Very old English inns. Why do you ask?'

'Oh, no particular reason,' Steve replied. 'I noticed her at the inquest, that's all.' She paused. 'I called in at "The Little General" last time I was down here. I don't trust that man Daley – there's just something about him that makes me suspicious.'

'Yes,' agreed Temple quietly. 'Yes – I can understand that. As a matter of fact, there's something rather peculiar about the inn itself, if you ask me.'

'Why do you say that?'

'Well, according to Miss Parchment, the inn wasn't always called "The Little General"; it used to be known as "The Green Finger"!'

'"The Green Finger" . . . that's a peculiar name.'

'Yes, it's peculiar in more senses than one,' replied Paul Temple. 'After the Birmingham robbery, the night watchman died. He was chloroformed. Before he died, however, he said "The Green Finger".'

'You don't think this inn – "The Little General" – is used as a sort of meeting-place? That would account for—'

Temple interrupted. 'Yes. I did think of that,' he said quietly.

'It might be a good idea to have the place watched.'

'Merritt's watching it,' Temple informed her. 'He'll let me know if anything funny happens.'

Steve puckered her brow. 'Merritt? Who's Merritt?'

Paul Temple looked puzzled in turn. Then he burst out laughing. 'Don't tell me you've never heard of Inspector Charles Mortimer Merritt! Dear, oh dear, he would be flattered!'

Steve appeared to think for a moment or two, then her forehead became its normal attractive self again.

'Oh, I remember. He was helping Gerald and Chief Inspector Dale over the jewel robberies. Is he a friend of yours?'

'By Timothy, yes!' exclaimed Paul Temple. 'Merritt and I get along like a house on fire.' He grinned widely. 'He's a funny little devil, always got some wild sort of theory at the back of his head, but he's really as cute as a box of monkeys. I'm sure you'd like him.'

'Have you known him long?'

'About five or six years,' replied Temple, as he took his briar out of his mouth and carefully scraped the burnt ash out of it. 'He hasn't been in this country all that long. He was out in New Zealand for a little while, I think, or somewhere like that. If he wasn't so damned rude to his superiors,' he added with a smile, 'they'd have had him at the Yard ages ago.'

'Paul!' exclaimed Steve Trent suddenly, and the new note of friendly familiarity made Paul Temple look over to her with an unexpected pleasure, 'do you really think I ought to tell Scotland Yard what Gerald thought about the Knave being responsible for—'

'Yes, I do, Steve. Believe me, I'll do all I possibly can to help you, my dear. I promised you that, but until Scotland Yard finally decide to—'

The telephone bell ringing outside interrupted him in midsentence.

Presently, the ringing stopped and they heard Pryce's voice. 'Yes, sir, this is Bramley Lodge! Yes, sir . . . I'll see if he's in!' After a little while Pryce came into the drawing-room.

'Chief Inspector Dale on the telephone, sir,' he said.

'Dale!' said Paul Temple with some measure of surprise. He left the room and picked up the receiver off the small table in the hall.

'Hello? Yes, Paul Temple speaking. Hello, Dale, how are you? I'm pretty fit, thanks. Pardon? Yes. . . . Yes . . . When does he want to see me? Mm. . . All right. Tell Sir Graham

I'll be there. Thanks for ringing. Goodbye!' He replaced the receiver and came back into the drawing-room looking rather amused. 'That was Dale of Scotland Yard!' he informed Steve. 'He was speaking for the Commissioner.'

'Speaking for the Commissioner,' repeated Steve with obvious surprise in her voice.

Temple nodded.

'They want to see me!' he said quietly.

'To see you. That can only mean . . .'

'It can only mean one of two things,' said Paul Temple slowly, 'they either want to know the reason why your brother visited me the night he was murdered, or they've decided—'

Steve completed the sentence for him.

'To send for Paul Temple!'

Temple looked at her with a smile. 'Yes,' he said. 'To send for Paul Temple.'

CHAPTER IX

Smash-and-Grab!

Royal Leamington Spa, or just simply Leamington, if you find its full title a little too pretentious, is a comparatively innocuous watering-place a couple of miles from Warwick and a hundred miles or so from London. It is very proud of its traditions. So, for that matter, are Blackpool and Brighton, but they are traditions of a somewhat different order. Leamington has never really quite grown up. It still thinks of the day when Queen Victoria paid it a visit and it suddenly became 'Royal'.

When the worthy inhabitants of Leamington opened their newspapers on the morning after Paul Temple had had lunch with Steve Trent they were justifiably startled. Royal Leamington Spa quite definitely did not extend a warm welcome to smash-and-grab raiders!

On the particular Saturday evening to which the reports referred, dusk was already beginning to fall. A beneficent Providence, aided perhaps by the borough council and kindred bodies, had decreed that Leamington's shops must be closed on Thursday afternoons. Consequently, the greater part of Leamington's more permanent residents were now completing their weekend shopping, while a few early holiday makers helped to crowd the streets. Here and there, a far too modern cinema blazoned its attractive lights and strove to attract the younger element of the population to some soul-stirring drama emanating from Hollywood.

By the clock on the tower of the town hall, the time was exactly twenty-five minutes to eight.

At that moment a large maroon-coloured saloon car of American make drew up by the kerbside. At the wheel sat a lovely girl who looked in the early twenties. It was her dark complexion, together with her almost black hair against which scarlet lips seemed to form a danger signal, that attracted the attention of Police Constable Roberts. Oddly enough he was also attracted by a rather unusual wristlet watch the girl was wearing.

Police Constable Roberts had done nothing all the afternoon except keep a paternal eye on the crowds of shoppers. Now and again, he had been forced to instruct some unwilling driver that he must not park his car by the pavement.

Proper parking places had been provided and they had to be used. The normal traffic of the town would never get a chance of passing through Regent Street if every motorist suddenly decided to park his car when, and where, he thought fit.

This beautiful young motorist, however, was rather a different problem. For one thing, reflected the policeman, she was quite obviously a stranger to the Spa and did not seem to appreciate the difficulties where parking was concerned. Her flashing smile, however, was having a far greater effect on him than he cared to admit. Nevertheless, he had his duty to perform.

'I'm sorry, miss,' Police Constable Roberts cleared his throat, 'but you can't park 'ere.'

'Oh, really, officer,' smiled the girl, 'I'm most awfully sorry – I promised to meet a friend here and—'

'Sorry, miss!' replied the still obdurate policeman, 'you'll have to take it round to the Square.'

The motorist began to make the most of her feminine charms ('vamped me proper' the constable told his friends afterwards when discussing the episode). Gradually, very gradually, she could see the policeman beginning to relent.

'But couldn't I stay here for just a little while? I know it's most irregular, but—'

Police Constable Roberts succumbed at last. 'Well, er—' He smiled back at her. 'It won't have to be for long, miss!'

'No, of course not. It's really most awfully kind of you!' she returned, with the most melting gratitude in her voice.

She had vanquished him completely. The police constable even felt it incumbent on him to apologize for his abruptness.

'Oh, that's all right, miss. Sorry to be such a nuisance, but you know what it is – we fellows have to keep on the job.'

'Why, yes, of course!' she agreed, with yet another of her flashing smiles. It encouraged Police Constable Roberts to linger awhile. He really did seem to be getting along rather well with this charming young person, he told himself.

'I was only saying to the sergeant last Monday,' he commented by way of making conversation, 'the whole parking problem could be settled as easy as pie if only the local authorities would have the common-sense to . . . to—'

He broke off in mid-sentence. No longer were his eyes fixed inside the car. He took his foot from off the running board, his arm from the convenient resting-place of the open window. He was staring behind the car, up towards the crest of the hill.

'What's the matter?' asked the girl suddenly.

'Look at that lorry coming down the hill!' replied the constable with obvious alarm in his voice. 'He's going all over the place. Why . . . something must be . . . must be . . . Good God, he's going for the pavement—' Police Constable Roberts staggered back from the car with bewildered astonishment.

The lorry – a great lumbering old vehicle – had crested the hill at a speed that was far from good for it, and was continuing its reckless journey.

Down the hill it came, in a mad, headlong rush. A front and back tyre were already flat. To and fro it slithered, hitting the pavement on either side of the road. It was quite obviously out of control. The driver could be seen tugging at the wheel but without any signal success.

As the lorry passed by on its appalling career, people jumped into the road to watch what would happen to it.

Thirty yards away from the stationary car the lorry gave another violent lurch. A split second later it was on the pavement.

With a deafening crash, the lorry crashed into the front window of a dress shop. The great sheet of plate-glass was smashed to bits. Splinters flew out in all directions. Then came the grinding crash of wood as the lorry came to a solid obstruction. It stopped dead. As it stopped, its electric horn began to sound. It went on and on, its terrific din adding to the utter confusion.

Torn dresses and silk underwear hung over the bonnet of the lorry forming a queer, grotesque garb. The entire upper storey of the house was kept from collapsing only by the roof of the lorry which supported it.

The shop had already closed but the owner, a middle-aged woman, was still busy with an assistant clearing up accounts and writing orders. Both had narrow escapes from being crushed alive as the lorry ploughed its way through the showroom and forced back the counter on which they were working.

The overpowering noise of the horn drowned nearly every other sound. But through it could nevertheless be heard the loud clanging of a bell, as though an ambulance were already trying to secure a passage through the vast crowd that had immediately collected. Actually, an ambulance had been sent for and was now on its way. Not only had four people, three of them women, been seriously hurt by the lorry as it hurtled over the pavement. A number of others had been cut by flying glass from the showroom window. Not ten minutes after the crash the ambulance was on the spot and its attendants busy on their work of mercy.

From all sides people were pushing their way to be present at this extraordinary scene. Through the mob came Police Constable Roberts, elbowing his way with grim determination. 'Make way there!' he shouted. 'Make way there! If you don't mind, sir! Step on one side, madam! Get off the pavement, please! Step on one side, please!'

He had to muster all his energy together to force his way through a crowd of people who were much too intent on snatching a glimpse of the lurid scene. At last he managed to reach the centre of the crowd.

The driver of the lorry was clambering down from his seat, unhurt, as he reached the centre of the throng. 'It was the steering, Constable,' the driver explained. 'As soon as I came round the corner, something seemed—'

'We must stop that horn,' interrupted the policeman. 'Where the devil is—' He paused, as he became aware of the bell still ringing insistently. 'Hello, what's that bell? Sounds to me like—'

'It's the burglar alarm,' said Skid quickly. 'The wires must 'ave been across the window, and—'

The crowd suddenly began to push their way forward again and Police Constable Roberts was literally forced away from the lorry. 'Step on one side, please,' he shouted with obvious indignation. At last he got back to the driver.

'Can't you stop this—'

Both men had to shout their loudest. The ringing of a bell, the continual blast of the lorry's hooter like a factory siren, added to the cries of the mob, all combined to make a bedlam which was beyond the solitary power of the policeman to control.

'Just—Just a minute, Constable,' interrupted the driver nervously. 'I—I feel like a bag of nerves.'

'It's a miracle to me no one was killed,' Police Constable Roberts went on. 'Why—' Again the noisy ringing of the burglar alarm together with the monotonous but strident blast from the lorry's electric hooter stopped him from speaking. 'We must stop that noise,' he shouted above the din. 'Step on one side, please.' He drove his way forward making for the driver's cab of the lorry. Suddenly the constable pulled a loose wire he noticed under the bonnet and the noise miraculously stopped. About the same time, ambulance men had arrived and were pushing their way through the crowd to attend to the prostrate forms on the pavement.

As the town hall clock was striking 7.45, Dixie appeared by the side of the maroon-coloured car. The car was still parked where, a few minutes ago, the constable had vainly endeavoured to persuade its driver to move on, and had been conquered by Diana's sex appeal. Dixie carried a small brown attaché case.

'Have you got the stuff?' asked Diana quickly.

'Have I! My God, what a smash! It sounded just as if it was on top of me. Is Skid all right?'

'I don't know. Drop the bag in the back. Be quick!'

'I think I ought to come with you and—'

'No!' was the sharp reply. 'Get back to the dress shop and mix with the crowd. Be quick, Dixie. Be quick.'

'O.K.,' replied Dixie. 'And take care of that bag.'

He placed the attaché case on the floor in the rear compartment. Then closed the door. A gear lever was snicked into position and Dixie was nearly sent flying as the car shot forward. A second later Diana was out of sight. Dixie turned and plunged into the crowd which was still struggling violently outside the dress shop.

CHAPTER X

Comparing Notes

The Midland jewel robberies served at least one good purpose. Steve Trent and Paul Temple now shared one common aim. Their tastes, their aims, so dissimilar in many ways, now fitted together perfectly. The liveliness and the external flippancy which were part of Steve Trent's make-up were set off by the more sedate nature of Paul Temple. Indeed, a queer form of platonic friendship had arisen between the two. Although it is doubtful whether either of them would have chosen such a hackneyed word as platonic to describe their friendship.

Paul Temple had told Steve to regard Bramley Lodge as her home, to come and stay whenever she wished, indeed to feel that she had an actual share in the place.

On this particular afternoon, after the two had finished lunch together, Temple announced that he would have to spend the next two or three hours dictating his serial, and that he also intended to do a few chapters on a new book if he had any time over.

He had a large room with a balcony overlooking the garden which he regarded as his office and library. This was upstairs on the first floor. Bookcases lined the walls up to the ceiling. On the whole, it was a mixed collection, and although they included many of the books which had helped him on to his degree, they also included many whose names were more or less unknown, save by the solvers of the more erudite of acrostics and crossword puzzles.

All the cases were glass fronted, save one section which comprised his most used reference books. Fiction spread itself over the house. In the lounge were several bookcases filled with thrillers. Paul Temple, indeed, had formed one of the best collections of thrillers and detective stories in the country. His bookseller had a standing order to supply him with thrillers as a matter of course.

Other novels sprawled about in the dining-room, the drawing-room, and elsewhere in the house. Odd cases even found their way into the hall and into the spare bedrooms. But while Paul Temple read as widely as he did furiously, he was in no sense of the word a bookworm. He had taken up literature as a trade rather than an art, and he instinctively kept well abreast of the latest moves and developments.

After Temple adjourned to the library Steve decided to wander about the grounds for half an hour, then to come back and map out two or three new features for *The Evening Post*. She had already accepted Temple's invitation to stay for supper but had made up her mind to leave for town immediately after the meal. She had to be back in Fleet Street early the next day. But first Steve had a 'story' to telephone to her editor.

The 'story' of the climax to their 'Send for Paul Temple' campaign. As Temple left her to start his work upstairs, she began scribbling a few lines on a pad to read out to the telephonist at the office. Already she could see the posters that would throng the streets forty-eight hours later—'Paul

Temple Sent For!' The news would still have to be ambiguous, however, as Temple was not yet sure exactly why Sir Graham Forbes wanted to see him.

That evening, a few minutes after they had finished supper, there was a ring at the bell, followed by Pryce's now habitual inspection through his little grill. He opened the door and came in to announce Inspector Merritt.

Paul Temple jumped up and went out to welcome him. 'Hello, Charles. This is a pleasant surprise.'

'Just thought I'd drop in for a chat,' replied the inspector. 'Happened to be passing.'

'Why, yes, of course,' exclaimed Temple, at the same time introducing the inspector to Steve.

'I hope I haven't interrupted a private—' Temple cut him short.

'No, of course not, Charles,' he replied with a smile of amusement. 'Have you had dinner?'

'Yes, but if there's any of that really excellent brandy of yours, then—'

'Help yourself, old man. It's on the cocktail cabinet.'

Merritt looked round and saw the bottle of fine old brandy where its owner had indicated. He poured a little into the bottom of a big glass which stood in readiness, and warmed it in his hands before savouring it. Inspector Merritt appreciated his host's fine taste for the better things of life. And not least of them, in the inspector's opinion, was the wonderful old matured brandy Temple always managed to acquire.

Meanwhile, Steve had risen from the luxurious depths of the armchair into which she had sunk after dinner, and declared her intention of returning to town. She felt the two men might be more at their ease if she made her departure.

In any case, it was already half-past eight, and she was still faced with the long drive back to London.

'Well, I really think I ought to be getting along, Paul,' she was saying. 'If you're coming up to town on Monday, then—'

'I'll pick you up about three. We'll go along to the Yard together, Steve.'

'You really think I ought to tell Sir Graham all I know about—' Steve Trent spoke quietly and very seriously. Temple hastened to reassure her.

'Yes. Yes, I do.'

Steve hesitated for the last time. Then she made up her mind. 'Very well. Good night, Inspector,' she added brightly.

Paul Temple went out with her to the car which had remained parked in a corner of the drive all day. The engine started up after Steve had touched the starter once or twice. Then suddenly she turned a switch, and flooded the drive with the brilliant flood of light from her headlamps.

Temple noticed her hand resting on the side of the car, and after a little while he took it in his own. 'Look after yourself, Steve,' he said softly.

She smiled, slowly disengaged her hand, pushed the tiny stump of a gear lever into position, and with a roar of the engine was gone. As the car's lights lit tree after tree down the long drive, Temple stood watching her; then as he saw the car turn into the lane which led into the main London-Warwick road, he walked slowly back to the house.

'I say, look here, Paul,' Inspector Merritt started, with some slight embarrassment and no little alarm, 'I hope I haven't butted in on a private little—'

Temple hastened to relieve him. 'No, of course not, Charles. Of course not. How's the brandy?' he asked inconsequently, both to change the conversation and to try to forget the alarm he suddenly felt for Steve Trent's safety.

'Fine!' answered the inspector, in no way discouraged. 'She's a pretty girl, isn't she?'

'Yes, yes, she is rather. Surprised you've never met her before. She's a reporter on *The Evening Post.*'

'Did you say her name was Trent?'

'Yes, Steve Trent,' answered Temple. 'At least, that's the name she works under on the newspaper. Her real name is Harvey. Louise Harvey. She's the sister of Superintendent Harvey, the fellow who was—'

Inspector Merritt looked startled. 'Sister!' he exclaimed with surprise.

'Yes. Why, what's the matter?'

'Oh, nothing, only . . . only I never knew Harvey had a sister.' The inspector paused to assimilate this new fact. 'Why wasn't she at the inquest?'

'She was, but she didn't give evidence,' replied Temple. 'Well, any news?' he asked at length.

'I've had the inn watched,' Inspector Merritt replied. 'Everything seems to be above-board as far as I can make out. I checked up on that "Green Finger" story. The inn did used to be known as "The Green Finger" – but that's certainly going back some years.'

'I still think there's something funny about that inn, Charles,' Paul Temple replied. 'I don't know what it is, but I intend to find out.'

Merritt looked thoughtful. 'Yes, I think there's something there too,' he said slowly.

'By the way,' continued Temple, 'you might be interested to know that the Commissioner wants to see me.'

'He does!' exclaimed Merritt, obviously surprised. 'Well, that's certainly good news.'

'Of course, he may only want to ask me a few questions about this business with Harvey. On the other hand—'

Merritt suddenly interrupted him.

'Oh, just a minute, Paul!' he exclaimed. 'I *have* got a little news which might interest you. One of my men went into "The Little General" yesterday morning, and on coming out, he bumped into a fellow known as Skid Tyler.'

'Skid Tyler,' repeated Temple, puckering his brows.

'Yes. Know anything about him?'

'I don't know,' said Temple thoughtfully. 'Skid Tyler . . . Skid—' Suddenly he jumped up. 'Yes, I've got him!' he exclaimed triumphantly. 'He used to be a driver at Brooklands. He was warned off the track in 1930 and served a term of imprisonment in 1931 for share-pushing . . . or was it '32? I'm not sure which.'

'Well, that's the fellow anyway.'

'I wonder what he's doing at "The Little General",' said Paul Temple thoughtfully.

'Yes – that's what I wondered. I sent a man back to trail him, but the idiot bungled the job, and Skid disappeared.'

Paul Temple put down his pipe at which he had been puffing steadily for the last half-hour, and took his cigarette holder from the mantelpiece. Oddly enough Temple very rarely smoked cigars although he always had a selection in stock for his visitors, and he now passed a box over to Inspector Merritt. They were Brazilian cigars— 'Havana tobacco, but grown in Brazil,' Paul Temple explained to him; 'I think they're much better than plain Havana cigars. Hope you like them.' Merritt took one, peeled off the thin wooden covering which protected it, cut the end off and lit it. Then he settled back into his comfortable armchair.

'Did you check up on Miss Parchment?' Temple asked him at last.

'Yes,' he replied. 'She's all right as far as I can make out. Retired schoolmistress. Lives alone in a small flat near the Tottenham Court Road. Passionately fond of reading and old English inns. Seems a hell of a life to me – but it sounds genuine enough.'

Temple walked up and down the room, occasionally flicking the ash off the end of his cigarette.

'Somehow,' he said at last, 'I feel sure that in some peculiar way, Miss Parchment fits into all this mystery about "The Little General". . . Harvey's murder . . . and the jewel robberies.' He paused. 'I don't know how . . . but I'm sure she does.'

'Well, your hunches aren't often wrong, Paul,' Merritt replied, 'but I fail to see how an innocent old dame with a passion for—'

The telephone ringing outside cut short his sentence. Temple got up and with an apology left the room. Pryce was probably some distance away downstairs in the servants' quarters, and there seemed little need to bring him up while the call was in all probability one he would have to answer.

After a moment or two he came back into the room with the instrument in his hands, a long extension cord trailing behind him. 'It's for you, Charles,' he explained, putting the instrument down on the low table. With a word of thanks the inspector picked up the receiver.

'Hello! Yes, speaking! Oh, hello, Sergeant. Yes . . . yes—' He looked up at Temple significantly.

'Yes . . . Go on . . . When did it happen? . . . Good lord! Yes, yes, of course . . . You'd better pick me up here. Yes, goodbye.'

Throughout the conversation, Inspector Merritt had rapidly been growing more and more restless. Now, as he replaced the receiver, he jumped out of his chair and almost rushed up to Temple who was standing with his back to the fire.

'What's happened?' asked Temple quickly.

'They've done it again.'

'You mean . . .?'

'It's Leamington this time. Frobisher's, of Regent Street. £14,000 worth of stuff.'

Temple whistled. 'By Timothy!' he exclaimed.

'There'll be hell to pay over this,' went on the inspector irritably.

'When did it happen?'

'About an hour ago. Practically in broad daylight. That smash sounds a dam' funny business to me.'

'What smash?'

'A lorry crashed into a dress shop which was next door to the jeweller's,' Merritt explained. 'There was such a devil of a row over the smash that no one took the slightest notice of what was happening next door.'

'Sounds like a cover,' said Temple thoughtfully.

'Yes, that's what I thought.'

For a few minutes, neither of them spoke. Both were too busy assimilating news of this latest development. Inspector Merritt's first spasm of sharp excitement had gone and he sat down again in his armchair, and relit the cigar he had been too busy to continue smoking.

Suddenly Temple turned. His face was set in an expression of grim determination.

'Charles. Tell them to hold that lorry driver.'

'Why?'

'Because, by Timothy,' said Temple, 'I'll bet a fiver it's Skid Tyler.'

CHAPTER XI

Murder at Scotland Yard

'Would you mind taking a seat, sir, and I'll see if Miss Trent is in.'

The sentence had a slightly unpleasant ring in its familiarity. But then, reflected Paul Temple, with a smile, you can't be too careful in a newspaper office. Reporters and the editorial staff often find it quite essential to their personal well-being to be out to certain callers. For exactly the same reason, the telephone operators had standing orders never to divulge to chance inquirers on the telephone the home address of certain members of the staff.

Temple sat down in the hard solitary chair the waiting-room possessed and waited for Steve Trent to come down. He looked at the clock. It was exactly three. Time was an important factor in his life, and he liked to keep his appointments to the minute if it was humanly possible. He had telephoned Sir Graham Forbes at the Yard and told him he hoped to be along with 'a surprise visitor' at about quarter-past three. That would just give him easy time to drive from *The Evening Post* offices along the Embankment to the police headquarters.

He had not long to wait in the little waiting-room. A page boy came downstairs closely followed by Steve Trent, 'looking even more charming than ever,' reflected Temple. She was wearing a business-like costume of black and white check tweed which looked smart, would stand up to office wear, and was far from being masculine. Steve was very fond of tweeds, and if possible even wore them in summer weather. 'Only that appalling mess of a hat she's wearing to spoil the effect,' Paul Temple told himself. But then Paul Temple, like so many men, was just a little old-fashioned where female hats were concerned.

Her flashing smile of welcome showed the pleasure she felt at meeting Paul Temple again. She had another smile for the commissionaire as she went out, a habitual gesture which endeared her to that section of the staff—'not stuck up like some of the others,' the commissionaire commented.

Together they walked over to Paul Temple's car which was waiting outside, and drove to Scotland Yard. Steve Trent had a host of questions to ask. Nevertheless, neither of them spoke during their short drive. Both seemed to give their thoughts to the coming interview.

At the Yard, they were quickly escorted to the Commissioner's office on the first floor. Sir Graham Forbes had a warm, if somewhat embarrassed, greeting for Paul Temple.

'I told you over the telephone that Miss Trent has a story to tell that will greatly interest you, Sir Graham,' Temple began.

As soon as he heard that Steve was Superintendent Harvey's sister, and that she knew a great deal about his work in South Africa, the Commissioner showed an interest he had certainly not felt on being told that a girl reporter from *The Evening Post* was being brought to see him. In fact, unknown to Paul Temple, Sir Graham had turned a delicate shade of puce when he had been told about her over the telephone.

Sir Graham now made sure his guests were comfortable, and ordered tea to be sent in to them. Then he opened a drawer in his capacious desk and produced a small box.

'A cigarette, Miss Trent?' he said, placing the box before her.

Steve noticed the cigarettes were a brown colour and she hesitated before accepting one.

'They're Russian,' explained Sir Graham. 'I'm sure you'll like them.'

After Temple had offered her a light, Steve slowly commenced her story. She was slightly nervous at first, but gradually gained confidence.

'It's an interesting story, Miss Trent,' said Sir Graham Forbes as she came to the end. 'Er—very interesting. You say that from the very beginning your brother was under the impression that the brains behind these robberies was this man—er—Max Lorraine – the man who calls himself "The Knave of Diamonds"?'

'Yes.'

Sir Graham turned to the novelist. 'What do you think of all this, Temple?'

'Well, Sir Graham,' he replied, 'I don't think there's any doubt that we are up against a definite criminal organization whose activities are directed by a man who is, well to say the least of it, out of the ordinary run of criminals.'

'Yes, I agree with you there,' the Commissioner replied. 'But that doesn't necessarily mean that we are up against this man Miss Trent talks about, the Knave of Diamonds.'

'No, but nevertheless I think we are, Sir Graham,' replied the novelist. 'Harvey was no fool. Harvey was convinced in his own mind that we were up against the Knave – and he was murdered!'

'What makes you so certain that Harvey was murdered?'

'It was as obvious as daylight,' Temple replied. 'He was holding the revolver in his left hand, and the poor devil had been shot through the back of his head. It was on the left side of his head, and Harvey was left-handed all right, but I hardly think he was a contortionist into the bargain.'

'Yes, that's true,' agreed the Commissioner. 'Harvey was murdered.' He said it not merely in agreement and acceptance of Temple's argument, but revealing what actually was thought at the Yard. 'We spotted it immediately,' he went on. 'I was surprised the doctor didn't.'

'The police doctor was down with the flu,' Temple informed him. 'A Dr. Milton came along with the sergeant – he's a retired medico who happens to be an acquaintance of mine.' He paused, then added thoughtfully: 'Still, I must admit I thought it was rather funny he never noticed it.'

They paused while the Commissioner poured out more tea for them. Then he turned to Steve.

'Miss Trent, when was the last time you saw your brother?'

'Shortly before he visited Mr. Temple,' she replied.

'Oh, I see. Did he seem cheerful and in normal health?'

'Yes, I think so,' answered Steve. 'We never really saw a great deal of one another, you know, Sir Graham. My work kept me busy quite a lot, and he was always dashing out of town on some case or other.'

'Yes, of course.'

'I saw Merritt last night,' said Temple suddenly, 'and he told me about this business at Leamington. Did you hold the driver of the lorry?'

106

'Yes,' the Commissioner replied. 'You were right about that, by the way. It was Skid Tyler.'

'Have you questioned him?'

'Not yet. Merritt's bringing him here this afternoon. I've got a feeling that Tyler might talk.'

'Yes, he might,' replied Temple, inwardly marvelling at the amount of personal interest the Commissioner was taking in the case. He was certainly not underestimating its importance, and by undertaking work he normally had to leave entirely to the chiefs of the C.I.D., he showed the effect the robberies, as well as the Press agitation, had made on him.

'I don't expect he'll know a great deal,' the Commissioner continued; 'he's most probably one of the small fry. On the other hand, you never can tell.'

Paul Temple thought it was time he changed the subject. So far, the visit had been more or less confined to a discussion of Steve's story. He had not yet been told why Chief Inspector Dale had telephoned to arrange an appointment.

'Sir Graham—' he started.

'Yes?'

'Why did you send for me this afternoon?'

The Commissioner coughed. He proceeded to look embarrassed, as embarrassed as he had been when they were originally ushered into his office.

'Yes, I've—er—I've been waiting for you to ask that question,' he said.

'Well, Sir Graham?'

'Ever since these robberies first started, there has been a definite campaign both in the newspapers, and amongst a certain section of the public, urging us to—er—to—'

'To Send for Paul Temple?' put in Steve.

'Yes, Miss Trent. To—er—send for Paul Temple,' the Commissioner agreed. 'Well, I don't mind telling you, Temple, the whole damned campaign got me rattled. I was convinced in my own mind that there was nothing you could possibly do in this matter. Now, however, I'm not so certain.' He hesitated a moment before continuing.

'You see, Temple, and I'm sure I can speak in confidence before Miss Trent, there are certain aspects of this business which are very confusing and which, instead of getting clearer, tend towards leading us further and further into a confusing mass of what seems to be on the surface melodramatic nonsense. But is it nonsense? That's just the point. Now take all this business about "The Green Finger".'

He paused and slowly lit another cigarette.

'We know that "The Little General" used to be called "The Green Finger". We know that the night watchman murmured "The Green Finger" before he died. But what does it mean? What is "The Green Finger"?

'And then, secondly, there's the matter of the district. That's been puzzling me a lot lately. Why should this organization confine its activities entirely to the Midlands?' Once again the Commissioner paused, as if endeavouring to underline the importance of his words.

'And there's yet another point,' he continued, 'and believe me, a very important one. How, in heaven's name, are they getting the stuff out of the country – and they *must* be getting the stuff out of the country, because if it was still over here, you can take it from me, Temple, we'd have it back in twenty-four hours!'

Temple nodded. He appreciated only too well the significance of Sir Graham's words.

'The Press have been very irritating over this affair,' continued the Commissioner, 'and their attitude has, at all cost, to undergo a change. We need every possible assistance that the Press can offer. In fact, not only the Press, but—' He did not complete the sentence, although it was quite obvious what he meant, instead he turned towards Steve Trent.

'Miss Trent,' he said, with a smile, 'I see you are dying to print all this in your paper, quite exclusively. I think that would make what I believe you would call a nice "scoop". Well, I give you full permission to do so. But I think it would be safer for yourself if you made no reference to your part in this affair.

'Later this afternoon I am holding an informal sort of Press conference at which I shall be going over some of the ground we have covered during our chat.'

The Commissioner poured himself out some more tea, found it was nearly cold, and pressed the bell to order some fresh tea to be made.

'Well, Sir Graham,' Temple now replied, 'I don't profess to be able to work miracles. By profession, I'm a writer – but, well, I must confess I'm very intrigued by certain aspects of this affair.'

'Then we can—'

'You can count on me to give you every assistance in my power, Sir Graham. That I promise you.'

'Thank you, Temple,' replied the Commissioner. 'I was hoping you'd say that.'

As he spoke the door opened, and Chief Inspector Dale walked in. As soon as he saw the visitors, he hesitated.

'Oh, I'm sorry, sir,' he apologized. 'I thought you—'

The Commissioner cut him short. 'Come in, Dale. Come in. You know Paul Temple, I believe?'

'Yes, yes, of course,' he replied.

They shook hands and the Commissioner introduced him to Steve Trent.

'I thought perhaps you'd like to know that Inspector Merritt has arrived, sir,' Dale reported, 'with that man—er—Tyler, Skid Tyler.'

'Oh, yes. When I ring, show them in here,' Sir Graham replied.

'Very good, sir.'

The Commissioner was not quite certain that Skid Tyler should be brought in before Miss Trent, nor whether even Miss Trent would care to hear his story. But she was now closely involved in the whole business, he reflected, and she might as well see this through.

'Would you like to stay while we question this man?' he asked her, after Dale had departed.

Steve was a reporter. And as a reporter, she had had to deal with situations that were far more gruesome than this might be.

'Yes, yes, I would rather!' she replied eagerly.

'Good. I should sit over there in the corner, Miss Trent. You'll be out of the way there.'

Then he walked over to his desk and pressed one of the bell buttons. His personal attendant, Sergeant Leopold, opened the door.

'You rang, sir?'

'Yes. Tell Inspector Dale, Inspector Merritt, and that man—er—Skid Tyler, to come in here.'

'Yes, sir.' The sergeant departed.

Meanwhile the Commissioner rearranged the chairs and waited for the three men to come in.

Presently the door opened again, and Tyler appeared, followed by Merritt and Dale.

110

'Sit down, Tyler,' said the Commissioner. 'No, over there,' he added, pointing to a chair near the fireplace facing his own chair.

'What is it you want?' Tyler started protesting, before the others had even found time to sit down. 'What the 'ell is the idea draggin' me along 'ere – anybody would think I was a blarsted criminal!'

'Be quiet!' said Chief Inspector Dale sharply.

'That's all right, Dale,' said Sir Graham. 'Now listen, Tyler. We're going to ask you a few questions, and if you've got any sense, you'll tell us the truth.' He looked round at the little gathering who were now waiting to hear what Tyler would have to say.

'What were you doing in Evesham at the beginning of this week?'

Skid Tyler did not look even surprised. 'Evesham?' he retorted impudently. 'Never been near the place!'

The Commissioner was not so easily put off. 'My dear fellow, don't for heaven's sake adopt that attitude. Inspector Merritt saw you there, didn't you, Merritt?'

'That's right,' agreed the inspector. 'Outside "The Little General" about three o'clock in the afternoon.'

'What would I be doin' outside a pub at three o'clock in the afternoon,' said Skid sarcastically. 'Now I ask you?'

Temple drew his chair forward. 'Who said "The Little General" was a—public house?' he asked.

'Who said so?' replied Skid, 'why. . . why—' Then suddenly he realized how neatly he had trapped himself. 'What the 'ell is all this about anyway?' he demanded angrily. 'You've got nothing on me. You can't—' He paused, realizing that he was making a very bad matter a great deal worse.

111

'Last week, my dear fellow,' resumed Temple in very calm tones that only served to infuriate Skid and make him splutter with rage and indignation, 'with the aid of a two-ton lorry, you accidentally smashed your way into a very select little dress shop. By a strange coincidence, the shop next door happened to be a jeweller's. By an even stranger coincidence, it happened to be robbed at precisely the same moment that you decided to make a closer inspection of Madame Isabel's really remarkable exhibition of spring underwear.'

'What are you getting at?' Skid shouted.

'I'll tell you what I'm getting at, Skid,' Temple replied. 'But first of all, tell me, are you fond of children?'

'Children!' repeated the bewildered Skid.

'Ah, but then you must be,' continued Temple; 'I was forgetting.'

Skid felt he was being baited. Temple's smooth words were beyond his comprehension. At last, he burst out. 'What the 'ell 'as children got to do with all this?'

'My dear Skid, you surprise me! Don't you realize you're holding the baby? And, by Timothy, *what* a baby!'

'Holding the . . .' Skid did not know what to make of this. An angry policeman he could cope with. But this smooth, calm, deliberate manner of Temple's was something new to him. 'Say, listen,' he started, 'if you're trying to be funny, then—'

'Trying to be funny?' interrupted Temple. 'My dear Skid, I'm an amateur humorist compared with the crowd you've been mixing with.'

'What—do—you mean?'

'What do I mean?' Temple began to laugh. Even the three policemen looked at him with slight bewilderment.

'Oh! Oh! Our old friend Skid drives the lorry! Our old friend Skid smashes into the dress shop! Our old friend Skid gets arrested! Our old friend Skid visits Scotland Yard! Our old . . .'

'Shut up! Shut yer blarsted mouth!'

'My dear Skid,' said Temple quietly, 'don't be a damned fool! Why should you take the "rap"? Why should you—'

'I'm not talking!' Skid was almost hysterical. 'I'm not a squealer! I—I know what's good for me!'

More and more did Skid Tyler feel that he was being driven into a corner by his pitiless foe. More and more he realized that, all unwittingly, he had been giving away precious information, and that he had made it perfectly clear that he was closely involved in the Leamington jewel robbery.

'You'll talk,' said Temple in a determined voice. 'And you'll talk fast. What were you doing at Evesham? What where you doing near "The Little General" inn?'

'I tell you I've never been near the blarsted place!'

'Skid, listen. . . . This isn't a one-sided little affair like share-pushing. This is big stuff. This is Crime with a capital C. And you're in it. In it up to the neck!' Gradually Paul Temple's voice had reached a climax. 'Now talk!' he said softly.

Skid looked up at his merciless antagonist, towering above him. The room was in absolute silence. All felt the tension in the air. Its utter heaviness. At any moment now might come the blinding flash and the deafening roar of thunder.

Skid looked from one face to the other. He saw no pity. Gradually he was yielding. Temple saw it.

So did Forbes, Dale, and Merritt. Still they said nothing. Finally he broke down.

'All right . . . all right—' he moaned. 'I'll talk . . . but first I want . . . a drink. I'm . . . I'm all . . . all shot to pieces.'

It was true. Skid had turned a deathly pale. He was trembling violently from head to foot. With his final decision, it amounted almost to a mental breakdown. Skid was suddenly, utterly, exhausted.

Sir Graham Forbes had got up. 'All right, I'll get you some brandy,' he said. 'I've got some in the cupboard.' He walked over to the cupboard in the corner of the room near where Steve Trent was sitting.

'Excuse me, Miss Trent,' he said. She pushed her chair out of his way. Sir Graham opened the cupboard door and took out a bottle of brandy. As he proceeded to open it, Paul Temple said: 'Skid, what is "The Green Finger"?'

'It's . . . the organization . . . that's been responsible for the jewel robberies.' Skid was now almost incoherent. 'The chief of the gang is known as . . . as the Knave of Diamonds.'

Steve Trent looked up. 'Max Lorraine!' she said softly.

'Have you ever met this person who—'

'Leave me alone! Leave me alone! For God's sake, leave me alone!' Skid's voice had reached a definite hysterical pitch. He leaped up and made for the door, as if in a despairing effort to flee from his persecutors. Firm hands pulled him back into the chair again.

Forbes walked up to him with a glass of brandy in his hand.

'Here – drink this!' he said, giving him the glass.

Skid Tyler seized the glass and gulped its contents down in one draught. The pallor left his cheeks. The strong spirit seemed to bring back life and strength to him. He settled back in his chair.

Paul Temple leaned forward and spoke gently, earnestly.

'Now, Skid, listen,' he said. 'This is important. Have you ever—'

Skid's face was undergoing curious changes, and Temple paused.

'Have you ever—'

Temple stopped. Skid's face had turned a deathly pale and he was sitting back in his chair as though utterly exhausted by long physical and mental effort.

'Skid!' The others crowded round Skid, staring at him in horror. Steve Trent had rushed up. She felt Skid Tyler's forehead with her right hand.

'Skid! SKID!' shouted Temple.

'What's the matter?' asked the Commissioner, with astonishment and horror in his voice.

'Look at him!' answered Temple. 'Skid!' he shouted again. 'Skid! SKID!'

Forbes knelt down by his side. He put his arm round the ex-convict. Dale had taken his wrist and was feeling his pulse. Paul Temple himself had fallen on his knees in front of Skid Tyler's chair. He was holding him by the knees and gazing up into his face.

It was an extraordinary scene.

'What is it?' asked Chief Inspector Dale. 'He looks so—' his voice tailed off into nothingness.

Suddenly Inspector Merritt spoke. 'Pass me that glass, Sir Graham!'

The Commissioner looked curiously at him.

'The glass, but . . . Good God!' he suddenly ejaculated. 'You don't mean—'

He stopped as Temple rose to his feet. Dale released the man's wrist; then he, too, stood up. The four men stood there in silence, amazement and horror on their faces.

'He's dead!' Paul Temple made the announcement quietly. Again that heavy, lasting silence.

'Dead!' Steve repeated, in what was almost a cry of terror.

'Yes, he's dead all right,' said Dale presently. 'What's in the glass, Merritt?'

Inspector Merritt had been standing a little away from the others, carefully examining the glass from which Skid Tyler had drunk.

'Enough poison to kill a regiment,' he announced sombrely.

'But—but that's impossible,' the Commissioner stuttered. 'Why it—it was a new bottle. I . . . I—'

Suddenly the door opened. Sergeant Leopold appeared.

'A lady to see you, sir, by the name of—'

'I can't see anyone,' interrupted Sir Graham irritably. 'Tell her I'm out. Tell her to—'

'Oh, just a minute, Sergeant,' interposed Paul Temple smoothly. He, alone, seemed to have preserved his normal composure. A caller, and a woman at that, who had succeeded in getting herself announced to the Commissioner, interested him. Especially at this particular moment. 'Who is the lady?' he asked.

'It's a Miss Parchment, sir,' said the sergeant quietly. 'A Miss Amelia Victoria Parchment.'

CHAPTER XII

The Plan

For the moment the dead body of Skid Tyler was forgotten. Temple alone seemed to take this extraordinarily timed visit completely for granted.

As Sir Graham Forbes remained staring at Sergeant Leopold as if he were some new species of monster, Temple took it upon himself to issue instructions.

'Ask her to wait a few minutes.'

'Very good, sir,' the sergeant answered, after a pause that was barely perceptible.

'Where's the bottle, Sir Graham?' asked Chief Inspector Dale suddenly.

The Commissioner walked over to a filing cabinet against the wall by the window where he had placed the bottle. The corkscrew and the cork itself were lying near it.

'It's . . . here—' he managed to say. The Commissioner, normally the most alert and ready of men, now appeared completely baffled.

'I can't understand it,' he went on. 'The bottle's a new one. . . . I bought it myself only two days ago.'

Chief Inspector Dale took the bottle and examined it closely. He turned it from side to side, scrutinized the neck, and finally peered intently at the opening, and cork. At last he looked up.

'The stopper doesn't seem to have been tampered with as far as I can see,' he said. Then again he carried on with his scrutiny. 'Just a minute!' Dale hesitated. 'I'm not so sure.' From the Commissioner's desk he took a powerful magnifying glass.

'Someone must have tampered with it!' exclaimed Inspector Merritt. 'Why—'

'Then the poison must have been meant for you, Sir Graham,' said Paul Temple quietly; 'and not for Tyler.'

The Commissioner blinked at him. 'Yes—it—er—looks very much like it,' he said.

Meanwhile the body of Skid Tyler was still lying sprawled out unnaturally on the armchair. They had all been too busy with the strange mystery of his death even to think of moving the body.

'I think we'd better get him into the other room, sir,' Inspector Merritt said, indicating the body with a wave of his hand. 'Then Doctor Parkes can have a look at him.'

'Yes . . . Yes—er—by all means,' agreed the Commissioner. He was still very flustered. Completely gone was all pretence of the usual calm, collected man of affairs. Many Press reporters would have given a great deal to have seen him in this state.

'Oh, and take this bottle,' he added to Merritt. 'See that Mollinson gets to work on it.'

Andrew Arthur Mollinson was the research man. After a careful examination of the bottle, during which he was apt to use apparatus of every kind varying from powerful microscopes to ultra violet rays, he would in all probability be able to give

118

an accurate picture of the history of the bottle immediately preceding the strange murder.

The Commissioner pressed a bell to summon Sergeant Leopold again. With the latter's help, Dale and Merritt picked up the inert mass which had been Skid Tyler and struggled towards the door.

'You might tell the doctor I'd like a word with him,' said the Commissioner, as they were going out.

Slowly, down the corridor, they carried him. Finally laying his body flat on a couch so that Dr. Parkes could make his examination before rigor mortis set in.

'Terrible business!' Sir Graham remarked to Paul Temple, as soon as the door had closed. 'I can't possibly understand how—' Suddenly he remembered that a 'mere wisp of a girl', as he regarded her, had been present right through this gruesome scene, and he turned to Steve Trent with a great measure of fatherly solicitude in his voice.

'I say, I hope it hasn't shaken you up, Miss Trent?'

'No, I'm all right, Sir Graham,' Steve replied. She had faced similar and even worse ordeals before, and she was comparatively hardened to such sights. 'But I'm afraid I shall have to be going,' she continued. 'I have an appointment at four o'clock and I—'

'Yes, of course,' interrupted the Commissioner. 'Of course.'

Steve Trent knew she had a story any newspaper man would willingly have given a year of his life to possess. There was only one thing to do, and that was to get to the office as fast as the first taxi would take her.

It seemed a pity to leave, but then everything of importance had already happened. In very little over an hour's time, Sir Graham Forbes would be reading her account in *The Evening Post*, 'and she thrilled in anticipation'.

First she talked over the question of the story with the Commissioner and with Temple. Sir Graham gave her full permission to report the events of the afternoon exclusively for *The Evening Post*, but she must use her discretion in its presentation. Her own part, her eyewitness account, she could give. But she must not, at any cost, stress the sensational side of the mystery.

They were vague instructions. But Steve Trent understood only too well the mood the Commissioner was in, and she did not care to alienate his sympathies. He had also promised her further information if she telephoned or called later in the afternoon, and it was very much to her advantage not to antagonize him.

The murder of Skid Tyler had engrossed her thoughts to such an extent that she had almost forgotten she was a reporter. But now, Steve began to tremble with excitement as the immense value of her 'news story' began to sink in to her consciousness.

She bade the Commissioner goodbye and thanked him. But her thoughts were elsewhere. Already she was struggling with her 'intro'—the first few lines of the report that she felt sure would cause a sensation in Fleet Street. She arranged to meet Paul Temple at the office in about an hour's time, after her fierce tearing rush was over. Then she said *au revoir* to him, and was sprinting downstairs to the main door. The 'story' was about to 'break'. As Steve hurriedly looked round for a telephone box, she could literally have shouted with excitement. At the same time, she was running through the whole scene again in her mind, ready to write up her account of it.

She turned round the corner and ran as fast as she could into Westminster Bridge Station. Luckily one of the booths was vacant. In a flash she was inside and dialling her office.

'It's Steve Trent here. Will you find me Mr. Watts as quickly as you can? It's urgent!'

A second's wait, and she was through to the imperturbable news editor.

'I've got a terrific "story"!' she started. 'Skid Tyler's been murdered in Forbes's room at the Yard. Forbes gave him a glass of brandy. It killed him. Poison. He was just going to spill the beans. What? Yes. Died in five minutes . . . Yes . . . in a phone box in Westminster Bridge Station . . . No . . . Yes . . . Temple, Dale and Merritt, nobody else, except Forbes himself. . . . Yes, I'm coming over now. Taking the first cab I can find. Goodbye.'

A split second later, and Steve Trent was back on the pavement waving her arm wildly at an approaching taxi.

'*The Evening Post* office, as fast as you can make it. For God's sake, get a move on!' she added, as she flung herself into the back seat.

The offices of *The Evening Post* were nearly always in a state of wild excitement but Steve's telephone call had acted like an earthquake. The number of calls passing through the telephone switchboard was suddenly trebled. Small boys sprinted up and down the corridors carrying pages of proofs. Machines were being stopped. Pages were being reset. Subeditors were swilling down quantities of hot tea.

In desperation the news editor ordered the edition which had just been printed to have the all-important news stamped on the 'Stop Press' column. Two minutes later he countermanded his order so that his competitors would not learn of the extraordinary happenings before his next edition had the full story.

Later, when it was all over, Steve wondered how the newspaper was ever produced, in this state of utter turmoil.

A typist was already sitting at a typewriter, ready to start typing at her dictation. By now Steve had the whole story mapped out in her mind. Throwing off her hat on to the table, she started.

After three sentences, a frenzied news editor rushed in, shouted 'Marvellous, Steve!' pulled the sheet of paper out of the typewriter, and rushed out again. Barely had they got four more lines on to the next sheet when he was back again. With hand on the top of the sheet, he watched for the full stop. Then out came the page, and Mr. Watts had vanished.

In the meantime, the art department had secured a photograph of Skid Tyler and another of Sir Graham Forbes, and blocks were being made with feverish haste in the race against time. Another reporter had already finished writing a brief resumé of the 'Midland Mysteries'.

Meanwhile, completely unaware of this terrifying haste at the offices of *The Evening Post*, Sir Graham Forbes was discussing with Paul Temple the astonishing events of the last half-hour.

'I wonder whether the poison was meant for Tyler,' he speculated, 'or . . . or for me?'

'Yes,' replied Paul Temple in subdued tones. 'Yes, I wonder.'

'It seemed strange that Tyler should be poisoned,' went on the Commissioner, 'just when he was on the point of talking.'

'Yes. Yes, it seems strange, doesn't it?'

For a few moments, neither of the two men spoke. Both seemed to be speculating on this new viewpoint. Was Skid Tyler's death, after all, an accident, and was the poison destined for the Commissioner himself? Or had he been killed because he was just about to reveal all he knew of what was going on behind the scenes of the 'Midland Mysteries'?

'Oh, by the way, Temple,' the Commissioner suddenly resumed. 'A constable at Leamington remembers talking to a girl in a saloon car shortly before the robbery occurred. For some reason or other, he's got it into his head that she had something to do with it.'

'Did he take the number of the car?' inquired Temple.

'No, I'm afraid he didn't,' replied Sir Graham.

'He's written out a pretty good description of the girl, though.'

He walked over to his desk, opened a drawer and took out some folders. From one of them he extracted a sheet of paper from which he started to read.

'Height about five feet four. Dark. Rather good-looking. Dressed in a smart grey costume with a fox fur. She had a set of golf clubs in the back of the car. Oh, and apparently she wore a small black wristlet watch.'

'A small black wristlet watch?' repeated Temple.

'Yes,' said the Commissioner. 'Does that convey anything?' He had noticed Paul Temple's sudden look of surprise as he came to the words 'black wristlet watch'. He was curious to know the reason.

'I don't know,' said Temple quietly. 'It might.'

'We've tried to trace the girl,' the Commissioner informed him, 'but so far we've failed.'

Paul Temple nodded. He got up from his chair, and paced up and down the room. Then he took out his inevitable pipe and carefully filled it. Not until it was smoking to his satisfaction did he speak again.

'Sir Graham,' he started. 'I've got an idea in my mind and—' He hesitated, as if for words.

'Yes?' prompted the Commissioner.

'There's a jeweller's in Nottingham by the name of "Trenchman",' said Paul Temple suddenly, his mind now apparently made up. 'They go in for a considerable number of antiques, and all that sort of thing. I was at Oxford with the junior partner – a fellow called Rice. Alec Rice.

'Now if it became known that Trenchman's had a very valuable stone on their hands, say a blue-white diamond, for argument's sake, it would be a pretty safe bet that our friends would, in the course of time, pay Trenchman's a friendly little visit.'

He paused while Sir Graham Forbes gave thought to his scheme. 'Yes,' agreed the Commissioner, though somewhat dubiously. 'Yes, I dare say they would.'

'Well, I'm of the opinion that the robbery at Leamington, and all the other robberies for that matter, have been very carefully planned and premeditated.'

Sir Graham was still not over-enthusiastic. 'I still don't quite—' he started.

'I'm also of the definite opinion, Sir Graham,' Paul Temple continued, without giving the Commissioner an opportunity to express his doubts, 'that if it became known that Trenchman's had a very valuable stone, the people we are up against would take the trouble to verify its existence before actually planning the robbery.'

Again he paused as if to allow his words to sink in.

Sir Graham Forbes had gradually been growing interested, in spite of himself. Now he looked up with some signs of enthusiasm over the drawn lines of his face.

'Verify its existence?' he repeated.

'Yes,' agreed Temple. 'Now Alec Rice would, I feel sure, help us over this matter. He would supply us with a list of all the inquiries they might receive about this particular stone. Naturally, most of them would be quite legitimate, but there's the possibility, a strong possibility in my opinion, that amongst that list there would be an agent of—'

'Of . . . the Knave of Diamonds!' exclaimed Sir Graham.
'Yes.'

'By Jove!'

All Sir Graham's doubts had obviously vanished. 'By Jove!'
he said again. 'That's an idea, Temple!'

He started walking backwards and forwards along the well-
worn patch of carpet in front of his fireplace. He tossed the
stump of his cigarette into the fire, now dying away through
lack of attention, and lit another of his favourite cigarettes. He
was turning the plan over and over in his mind and his eyes
glinted. Sir Graham Forbes was essentially a man of action.
It was the lack of any method, any campaign, any scheme by
which some information about the Lorraine gang might be
acquired, that had brought about his continual bad temper
of the last few days.

'Now the whole idea would have to be handled very, very
carefully,' Paul Temple continued, embroidering on his plan.
Now that he had got the main outline into form, he was
thinking over the various details to which attention would
have to be paid.

'We're not dealing with fools, remember,' he went on. 'One
or two brief references to the stone might appear in the daily
Press, an article or two in the trade journals, and that's about
all. There must be nothing clumsy or blatant about the way
the existence of the stone is brought to light, or they'd tumble
to the idea immediately.'

'Yes, of course,' assented the Commissioner. It was obvious
by his attitude that the barriers between the two men had
at last been removed.

'I'll get into touch with Rice immediately,' said Paul Temple.

'And now I suppose I'd better see this woman, Miss—
er— Parchment,' said the Commissioner with a mighty sigh.

Paul Temple's plan was now fixed. Sir Graham was leaving the details of its execution to the novelist while he himself kept the guiding reins. Miss Parchment had been waiting his pleasure for some time, and he felt it was time he interviewed her, though the immediate prospect did not fill him with any great satisfaction. Nevertheless, he pressed the bell on his desk.

'Miss Parchment,' said Paul Temple thoughtfully. 'Did she ask to see you, or—'

'No, I sent for her,' put in the Commissioner. 'She was at the inn the night Harvey was murdered.'

'Yes, I know,' said Temple with a smile. 'I questioned her.'

'She's a retired schoolmistress, isn't she?'

'Yes. A retired schoolmistress, with a passion for old English inns.'

At that moment the door opened again, and Sergeant Leopold appeared. Immediately behind him the two men saw the somewhat stately form of Miss Parchment. Her bright eyes seemed to sparkle even brighter as Sergeant Leopold announced her presence.

Sir Graham Forbes rose to greet her. 'I'm sorry to have kept you waiting, Miss Parchment,' he said, 'but I'm rather afraid that—'

But Miss Parchment was not listening quite as intently as she might have been.

She had caught sight of Paul Temple standing a few yards behind the Commissioner, and her face broke into a happy smile of recognition as she started towards him.

'Ah, Mr. Temple!' she exclaimed. 'How nice to see you again. We meet under pleasanter circumstances this time, I hope.' Suddenly she turned her head as if in alarm. 'Or do we?' she added, almost as an afterthought.

'Yes, of course.' Paul Temple reassured her with a smile. 'And how are you, Miss Parchment? Quite well, I hope?'

'Oh, quite well, thank you,' said Miss Parchment happily. Even the Commissioner himself was warming to this strange little woman who reminded him of a fragile piece of old porcelain suddenly placed in a room, the furniture and decorations of which were of the most modern varieties. She appeared perfectly at her ease. With her air of old-world calm and quiet, she was not put off by the go-ahead methods of the younger generation. Perhaps her life as a schoolmistress had kept her young. It had certainly not made her the biased and pompous old woman that so many teachers are apt to become. She was bright, even flippant at times, and seemed to have an air of pouring gentle ridicule on all the most earnest efforts of the younger set. She herself was almost timeless, yet intensely human.

'Very well indeed,' Miss Parchment went on. 'A little sciatica now and again, you know. But nothing to complain of.'

Sir Graham Forbes turned to her. 'Miss Parchment,' he said, 'won't you be seated?'

'Oh, thank you.' Miss Parchment rewarded him with one of her most dazzling smiles, as she took the chair Sir Graham indicated.

Suddenly she seemed to recollect her immediate surroundings. 'Do you know this is the first time I've ever been in Scotland Yard!' she exclaimed. 'It's quite thrilling, isn't it?'

'Yes, er, quite thrilling,' said the Commissioner drily. He took down a box of his favourite cigarettes from the mantelpiece, preparatory to helping himself, and presented them to Miss Parchment.

'Will you have a cigarette?' he asked.

'No, thank you, I—' Miss Parchment broke off on seeing the peculiar colour of the cigarettes. 'Ah!' she exclaimed. 'Russian cigarettes!'

'Yes, I—er—I prefer them.' The Commissioner cleared his throat somewhat heavily. 'Now, Miss Parchment, I—'

Once again Miss Parchment did not seem to heed his words very intently.

'So frightfully clever, the Russians,' she said provokingly, 'don't you think so, Mr. Temple?' she asked, turning towards where the novelist was sitting.

'Yes, I—er—suppose they are,' agreed the latter.

'Tchehov! Ibsen!' went on Miss Parchment. She seemed to have suddenly embarked on a pet theme of hers. Then just as suddenly she stopped. 'Was Ibsen a Russian?' she asked, with rather a strange note of surprise in her voice.

'Miss Parchment!' Sir Graham Forbes was endeavouring to preserve that calm of manner on which he so prided himself. 'Miss Parchment, I should like to ask you a few questions.'

'And why not, Sir Graham?' Miss Parchment spoke with a strange, sudden gaiety. 'And why not?'

CHAPTER XIII

A Present from the Knave!

A few minutes after six o'clock Paul Temple collected a happy and excited young reporter from the offices of *The Evening Post*.

Intense excitement reigned outside the office as they drove away. The vans were beginning to load up. Drivers were cursing. Men and boys were running backwards and forwards. As the fast vans tore away at breakneck speed, other vans took their places. Soon the news would have spread to all parts of London and the Home Counties, as the skilful drivers threaded their way at an amazing speed through the rush-hour traffic.

The editors of the rival papers were already beginning to foam gently at the mouth and mutter harsh words at the failure of their own intelligence service. The morning papers were beginning to get busy on the 'story', wondering at the same time, in some cases, how they could make the most of the sensation without publicizing too much the news-gathering capabilities of a paper belonging to a rival group.

As Paul Temple started up the car, Steve Trent again opened the copy of the paper she had taken with her. There was her 'story', with a streamer headline stretching right across the top of the front page. While the car jolted along, she struggled to read once again the story she had written. 'It's the biggest thrill I've ever had!' she confessed to her companion.

Finally they drew up in a quiet Chelsea cul-de-sac, and Paul Temple was gaily escorted up to Steve's rooms. They were bright, very feminine rooms, yet in the comfort they provided, they were almost masculine. Her sitting-room ('cum dining-room cum lounge cum office cum women's gossip club', as she described it) boasted two very large and very luxurious armchairs, which Paul Temple eyed appreciatively.

A bright plain rust-coloured carpet covered the floor and did most of all to provide an atmosphere which the Germans aptly describe as '*gemuetlich*'. Brown tweed curtains, coloured with a dash of blue, hung over the windows. The furniture in the room was of a sturdy limed pine, 'not too difficult to look at, and jolly cheap,' said Steve in praise.

In contrast with the rich warm colours of her large sitting-room, her bedroom was bright and cool. Nearly everything in it was either cream or blue. Even the carpet was blue, while the walls were distempered in a light stone tint. It was a happy little home that Steve Trent possessed, and Paul Temple's admiration for her and his appreciation of her excellent tastes suddenly jumped up.

But his first remark was one of quiet good humour.

'So this is where you write all those soul-stirring articles for *The Evening Post*!' he said.

Steve Trent, who had been watching him very closely, bubbled over with her infectious laughter. 'Well, I'm glad somebody thinks they're soul-stirring!' she said. Suddenly she became aware that Paul Temple's arms were still burdened with a host of small parcels, the raw material for the *tête-à-tête* evening meal Steve had promised him. There were also some cigarettes, a couple of books, and other little purchases Paul Temple had made.

'Put those parcels on the table, dear!' she told him.

Paul Temple did as he was told, and then subsided into one of the armchairs he had so much admired when he came into the room.

'How long have you been on *The Evening Post*, Steve?' he asked.

'Oh, about eighteen months,' came the reply. 'I started as "Auntie Molly",' she continued with a smile.

'Auntie Molly?' queried Paul Temple, looking slightly puzzled.

'Yes, the—er—the answers to correspondence,' explained Steve. 'You know, the—er—the—' she broke off a little awkwardly.

'Oh, you mean writing articles about—about love, and things like that?'

'Mostly about—things like that!' rippled Steve, and they both began to laugh.

'I say,' said Temple, 'this is a grand little place, isn't it?'

Steve looked pleased. 'I'm glad you like it,' she said.

'By Timothy, yes!' said Temple. Slowly he rose out of the depths of his chair and looked round the room again. His eyes finally rested on her radiogram, an extremely large instrument which occupied a corner of the room. It was clearly no ordinary mass production instrument. Its case was of the limed pine of which the rest of her furniture was made.

'Rather unusual radiogram you've got, Steve!' he said.

'Yes. Gerald bought it for me in Paris the year he—'

A knock at the door interrupted what Steve was saying.

The door opened, and a homely, cheery-looking woman who made up in bulk what she lacked in height, appeared, carrying a tray.

'Ah, tea!' exclaimed Steve. 'I'll help you, Mrs. Neddy.'

Mrs. Neddy was the benevolent Irish woman of uncertain age, though Steve gathered it was at least fifty, who 'did' for her. She would come early in the morning to get Steve's breakfast ready and spend the greater part of the day there instead of the three hours for which she was paid. She had transformed the little flat into a real home for the girl who had no time to perform for herself all the many services she required.

'That's all right, dearie!' Mrs. Neddy said. 'I can manage.'

'Good afternoon!' said Temple.

'Good afternoon to ye, sir!' she answered with her delicious West-of-Ireland brogue.

She set the tea-tray on the sideboard and began to clear the accumulation of debris from the fireside table. Then she set the tray down on it and was about to go out when Steve stopped her.

'Is that parcel for me, Mrs. Neddy?' she asked.

Mrs. Neddy had entered the room carrying a parcel under her arm, and all the while she was clearing the things so that the two could drink their tea in comfort, she still carried the parcel.

'Parcel?' she now asked with some surprise, having completely forgotten its existence. Then suddenly she remembered. 'Why, yes, of course!' she exclaimed. 'It's a good job you mentioned it now! I should 'ave probably gone to bed with it under my arm!'

Steve began to laugh. 'I gather the memory isn't improving!' she said.

'Improving!' echoed the Irish woman. 'Oh, 'tis something shocking, miss. There are times when I wonder who the devil I am!'

The two began to laugh at the kindly but absent-minded Mrs. Neddy. But whatever her faults, and they included the most complete disregard and contempt for any kind of efficiency, she did her work well. She kept the flat absolutely spotless, and the most fastidious of epicures could not have found fault with the excellence of her cooking. It might have lacked the variety of a Soho restaurant, but it was good, tasty, and nourishing.

Steve Trent took the parcel from her and began to inspect it. There was no stamp and no indication of its sender. It was about an inch in thickness and a foot and a half across. 'A plate or a dish of some sort,' reflected Steve.

'Where did the parcel come from, Mrs. Neddy?' asked Steve, rather puzzled.

'It was delivered about an hour ago, by a boy. A cheeky-faced monkey he was an' all.'

'Was there any message?'

'No,' replied Mrs. Neddy. 'No message, dearie.' She had been staring at the tea-tray on the table in what might have been wistful contemplation. 'Lordy!' she exclaimed suddenly, 'I've forgotten the buttered scones! You'll have to be excusing me!'

Gathering her voluminous skirts about her, Mrs. Neddy swept majestically out of the room, bent on retrieving yet another error. Mrs. Neddy was always making errors, but errors of a kind that endeared her to Steve. Besides, she had a way of saving her face that at once completely removed any possible ill-feeling or grievance.

'Mrs. Neddy seems quite a character!' said Paul Temple, as she closed the door.

'She's a dear!' agreed Steve fervently. Then her face became a little more serious. 'I wonder what this is?'

'It looks like a disc of some sort, doesn't it?'

'Yes,' said Steve quietly. She walked over to the sideboard, opened a drawer and took out a pair of scissors. Then she cut the string which fastened the parcel.

'We'll soon find out,' she said, as she pulled back some sheets of corrugated paper and at last extracted a flat cardboard box. Inside was a gramophone record.

Steve looked at Paul Temple, a frown of curiosity over her face. 'I wonder who sent it?' she speculated.

'Isn't there some writing on the—' Temple stopped in midsentence. The girl in front of him had turned a deathly pallor. 'Steve!' he exclaimed. 'Steve, what's the matter?'

She passed him the black disc. 'Look what it says on the record!' she said tensely.

Paul Temple examined the label. 'To Louise Harvey,' he read. 'From the Knave of Diamonds.'

He caught her eye. For a moment neither of them spoke.

'Max Lorraine!' whispered Steve at last.

'Yes!' he agreed.

Steve Trent took the record out of his hands, and walked slowly over to the radiogram.

'Steve!' he said sharply. 'What are you going to do?'

She hesitated an instant. 'I'm going to play the record,' she said decisively.

She opened the radiogram, switched it on, and placed the record carefully on the turntable. 'The set takes a little while to warm up,' she added.

'Yes.'

'Paul!' This time there were traces of anxiety in her voice. 'What do you think is on the record?'

'I don't know. Probably a message from the—' He hesitated. 'Steve!' he said suddenly. 'You're shaking!'

'No,' she replied, though without any great conviction. 'No, I'm . . . all right.'

'Here – I'll set it going. You sit down, dear!'

He took Steve gently by the arm and led her to one of the comfortable armchairs. She sat down in it with an infinite look of gratitude in her eyes.

Paul Temple walked slowly back to the radiogram. For some seconds he looked down at the gramophone record. From where she was sitting, Steve Trent watched him with curiosity.

'What is it, Paul?' she asked at length. 'Why don't you put the record on?'

'Just a minute,' said Temple. 'Just a minute!' He hesitated. 'Aren't we being a little obvious, my dear?'

'A little obvious?'

'Steve . . . Supposing you sent someone you knew a record – a gramophone record. It had no official label, and looked very mysterious. What do you think would be the first thing they'd do with it?'

'Why, play it, of course! That's what everyone would do under the circumstances.'

'Yes, of course it is,' agreed Temple. 'That's what everyone would do under the circumstances,' he added slowly.

Steve looked even more puzzled.

'Paul. . . I don't understand.'

'The person who sent you this record knew that you'd be puzzled by it,' Paul Temple explained, 'and he knew, without a shadow of doubt, that the first thing you'd want to do would be to satisfy your curiosity by playing it.'

'Well?' she inquired.

Paul Temple began to grow a little excited. His reason had told him something he did not even care to think about.

'Steve, don't you see?' he asked urgently. 'That's the whole point! The Knave wants you to play this record – and immediately you do so, his purpose in sending it to you is fulfilled!'

'But—but what is his purpose?' asked Steve. Not yet had she begun to suspect what was in Paul Temple's mind. 'Why should he send me a gramophone record? If it contains a message, then—'

'Any message it contains could have been sent to you in writing,' interposed Temple quietly.

'Yes, I—I suppose it could.' But she was still very puzzled. 'Then what's on the record?'

'Nothing,' said Temple softly. 'Nothing of importance. I'm sure of that.'

'Then why should he send it?' asked the bewildered Steve. 'You said yourself his purpose was to get me to play it! If nothing is on the record, then—'

'Yes, why should he send it?' asked Temple in turn. He, too, was puzzled. 'By Timothy!' he exclaimed after a moment or two. 'By Timothy, Steve!' He hesitated. 'The gramophone!'

'The gramophone . . .?'

'That's what he wants!' said Paul Temple in excited tones. 'That's what he wants He wants you to use the gramophone. Tell me,' he said sharply, 'has it always been in this position?'

'Yes, always, only—' Steve hesitated.

'Well?'

Steve Trent had now caught Paul Temple's excitement. 'It looks as if it might have been moved slightly,' she said. 'It's further against the wall as a rule. Oh, and look at the gauze on the speaker, why—'

'It's been altered, hasn't it?'

'Yes!'

Paul Temple walked back to the radio set and looked at it very carefully. He inspected the switches and the other controls; finally he bent down to examine the grill on the speaker itself.

Suddenly he jumped up and his face was set and determined.

'What is it, Paul?'

'Stand on one side!' commanded Paul Temple quietly; then after a little while: 'Steve, when you want to put a record on, you stand in front of the loud speaker like this, don't you?' And he stood in front of the radiogram, his arm stretched over it so that his hand was just above the tone arm.

'Yes,' she agreed.

'And you lift the arm up and bring it across to the record?' he continued.

'That's right!'

'I'm going to do exactly the same, only I'm going to stand on one side instead – you'll see why in a minute.'

He stood to one side of the radiogram, making sure at the same time that Steve was well back on the other side of the instrument. Then, very gingerly, he picked up the tone arm. He swung it over, as if to start the motor, just before setting the needle down on the groove of the record.

During that fraction of a second the room was filled with a loud, deafening report. A wisp of acrid smoke began to issue from the loud speaker grill.

'Paul—' ejaculated Steve, with a little cry, in sudden alarm.

Temple took her by the arm.

'There's a small revolver hidden by the speaker,' he explained. 'It's been wired up with the tone arm. Immediately the arm was moved, the revolver was fired.' He paused. His

137

next words were ominous. 'Now you know why he sent you the gramophone record. Obliging little fellow, isn't he?'

Steve Trent shuddered visibly as she thought of the narrow escape she had experienced.

'Thank goodness you were here when it arrived. Why, I—'

Paul Temple interrupted her.

'How many people know that your real name is Harvey . . . Louise Harvey?' he said.

'Yourself,' she replied, 'Lord Broadhedge, the proprietor of *The Evening Post*, and Sir Graham Forbes.' She thought a moment. 'That's all.'

Paul Temple nodded. 'And Merritt, Inspector Merritt,' he added. 'I told him myself.'

'Inspector Merritt?'

'Yes.'

For a long while neither of them spoke. Each was preoccupied with this new problem that confronted them.

'What are you thinking of?' asked Steve Trent at last.

Paul Temple hesitated. 'I was just wondering how long Sir Graham had smoked Russian cigarettes!' he said.

CHAPTER XIV

Behind the Scenes

The door opened and Diana Thornley appeared.

'Diana!' There was amazement in Dr. Milton's voice.

'Has he been through here on the 'phone?' asked Diana Thornley irritably, peeling off her gloves and throwing them on to the small oak bench.

The doctor looked up at her in surprise. 'You mean the Chief?'

'Yes,' she replied impatiently. 'Yes, of course.'

Dr. Milton seemed puzzled. 'No, of course he hasn't. I thought you went down to town to see him.'

'I went to town, all right! I waited over three blasted hours in that tube station, and there wasn't a sign of him.'

Surprise gave way to anxiety in Dr. Milton's face. 'I wonder why he didn't turn up?' he asked her.

'I don't know,' she replied thoughtfully.

The two were sitting in the drawing-room of Dr. Milton's house. It was three hours after the death of Skid Tyler at Scotland Yard.

For perhaps half an hour Dr. Milton had been alone in the room, pacing backwards and forwards, smoking innumerable cigarettes, continually looking at the clock.

When Diana Thornley came in, his eyes brightened for a moment, thinking that she might have news. Now both were sitting in front of the fireplace, equally dejected.

'You haven't heard anything further about Skid?' asked Dr. Milton suddenly.

'No,' she replied. 'They're still holding him, as far as I know.'

'I hope to God Skid doesn't talk,' he added anxiously. 'That's all I'm worried about.'

Just then the door opened, and a tall man moved slowly into sight. Snow Williams was a rather sinister individual in the late forties. He was wearing a drab, grey overcoat, and underneath it an equally drab grey suit with badly worn shoes. He was very thin, and the deathly pallor of his gaunt cheeks added to the unpleasantness of his appearance.

Even the hardened Diana Thornley felt uncomfortable in his presence.

Slowly, he came forward until he stood with his back to the fireplace. Then he took off his overcoat, hung it carefully over a chair, and lit one of Dr. Milton's cigarettes. Only then did he speak.

'Any news?' he asked. His lips barely parted for the words to issue forth. It was a smooth, deep voice, that had, oddly enough, once known a public school, and even a university.

'No,' answered Diana abruptly.

'Didn't you see the Knave?' he continued.

'No,' she replied again, this time even more impatiently.

Snow Williams seemed to share Dr. Milton's nervousness. 'Something's in the wind!' he said anxiously. 'Something's in the wind, if you ask me!'

'Well, nobody's asking you!' said Diana, with obvious irritation in her voice.

Snow was in no way annoyed by her tone of voice.

'It's a devil of a time since the robbery, and we haven't heard a word about Skid,' he continued unperturbed. 'I tell you, he'll talk! He'll talk!'

Dr. Milton looked as if he could scarcely restrain himself. 'Shut up, Snow!' he burst out angrily. Then after a little while he asked: 'Have you seen Horace?'

'Yes,' was the reply.

'What about the stuff?'

'That's all right,' answered Snow. He chuckled in his throat. It was an eerie sound. 'That's all right!' he repeated.

'Then there's nothing to worry about!' exclaimed Dr. Milton. He pointed to a sideboard where stood decanters, siphons, bottles and glasses. 'Mix me a drink, and you'd better mix yourself one too.'

Snow Williams walked over to the sideboard and opened a bottle of whisky. Just as he was pouring it out, a telephone bell began to ring.

'That's the Chief!' said Dr. Milton. 'It's the special line.'

'Yes,' agreed Diana. 'I'll take it.'

She walked over to a cupboard in a corner of the room, pressed a hidden button, and watched a panel slide back to reveal a telephone. She lifted the receiver and started speaking.

'Hello . . . Hello . . . Yes . . . Why didn't you meet me? What? Yes . . . Yes, I'm listening. . .'

'What is it?' put in the doctor anxiously.

Diana signed to him to be still. 'Yes . . . When? . . . Temple? Yes . . . Yes . . . I say, be careful! Milton is here now . . . Yes . . . Yes, all right. Goodbye!'

She replaced the receiver, pressed the button to close the panel, and rejoined the two men.

'Well?' asked Dr. Milton urgently.

'How's Skid?' came from Snow Williams.

Diana Thornley looked hard at them both. 'Skid's dead!' she announced.

'Dead!' echoed the doctor.

'Yes!' Diana Thornley paused. 'He was going to—talk.'

'He . . . he didn't?' inquired Dr. Milton anxiously.

'No. The Knave got him in time.'

The doctor sighed with relief and took the drink Snow was offering him. 'Why didn't he meet you?'

'He didn't say,' Diana Thornley replied. She paused, deep in thought. 'You'd better get in touch with Horace, Snow!' she instructed. 'Tell him we meet again on Friday.'

'Friday?'

'There's a jeweller's at Nottingham called Trenchman,' she explained. 'They've got a new stone. The Chief wants me to have a look at it. I'm going over there tomorrow. If it's as good as the reports say it is, then . . . we'll discuss the matter on Friday with Dixie.'

'Good!' agreed Dr. Milton.

'Oh, and there's just one other point,' said Diana. 'Our friend Mr. Paul Temple has got to be taken care of. Do you think you can manage it, Doc?'

Milton began to laugh. 'What do you think?' He looked at the lovely dark girl before him, now imperious as she was ruthless. He chuckled again. 'What do you think?'

CHAPTER XV

The Wristlet Watch

The plan Paul Temple had suggested to the Commissioner of Police had won wide favour. Here, at last, was a definite move that might lead to something tangible. Up to the present the police had been working completely in the dark, for both of the criminals who could be identified with the crimes, Lefty Jackson and Skid Tyler, had met a sudden and unexpected end. Scotland Yard only knew of men who had worked for the gang; they knew nothing of any of its present members, save that its leader might be a nebulous figure known as Max Lorraine or the Knave of Diamonds.

Now Paul Temple was carrying the war into the enemy camp. He had himself formed one or two shrewd suspicions, but needed confirmation for them. The police themselves welcomed the plan in that it might at last give them something positive to work on.

On the Thursday after Skid Tyler's sudden and mysterious end at Scotland Yard, Steve Trent had driven her little sports car up to Bramley Lodge. An old acquaintance was coming to see Paul Temple, and Steve was anxious to meet him. Temple and Steve were now sitting over their coffee in the lounge, awaiting his arrival. As usual, they had much to talk about, and as usual where journalists are concerned, most of it was concerned with the stranger happenings of the moment in which they were personally involved. In this case, however, although they tried to forget the 'Midland Mysteries', conversation seemed to drift back to the subject quite naturally.

At last Pryce came in to announce the arrival of Alec Rice.

As he entered, Paul Temple jumped out of his seat to welcome him. The two had not met for some years, and the warmth of their greeting showed how glad they were to see each other again. The jeweller was a man who looked at least fifteen years junior to Temple, whereas he could only have been four or five years younger at the most. He was a huge man of breezy manners who swept everything before him. He was now wearing a pair of old and very voluminous grey flannel trousers with an even more ancient Harris tweed jacket. Nevertheless, Alec Rice was not entirely an old public school boy who could talk of little but sport, and had to adopt the exaggerated accent of pseudo-culture. He was essentially a businessman who had thrown off his robes of office to get into these comfortable old clothes for an informal call. Consequently, on being introduced to Steve, he felt it more discreet to withdraw as rapidly as circumstances permitted. Not that Steve made him feel gawkish or boorish at all, but he felt he was both intruding and that his garb was not quite what it might have been. Steve was wearing a long dinner dress of black silk, while Paul Temple, who was by no means a slave to fashion but liked to do 'the right thing', was wearing a tuxedo.

'I'm in rather a hurry, Paul,' he started, 'but I—er—' His voice tailed away in some embarrassment. 'I—er, happened to be passing, and—er—'

Paul Temple came to his rescue.

'That's all right, Alec. You can speak in front of Miss Trent.'

'Oh, good. Well, your little publicity stunt about the "Trenchman" diamond seems to be working all right. We've certainly had plenty of inquiries.'

'Oh?' questioned Temple.

'Most of them, of course, are quite legitimate,' Alec Rice explained. 'People in the trade. Firms we've dealt with for years. But this morning, about eleven o'clock, I think it was, a girl came into the shop. She asked to see some statuettes we had in the window; she examined one or two, and eventually bought one. Just before she was leaving, however, she asked to see your stone. She said she'd read something about it in one of the newspapers.'

He paused. Paul Temple had been listening intently, while Steve had hardly dared move in case she missed a word.

'Go on!' said Temple.

'Well, there's nothing more to tell, really. She admired the diamond we showed her and, and that was the finish of it.'

Paul Temple nodded. It was a sure sign that he was very deeply interested. 'What did she look like?' he asked.

'Dark!' said Alec Rice briefly. 'Sort of—' Again he seemed a trifle embarrassed. Temple suspected at least a few seconds light flirtation between the two. 'Sort of voluptuous!' he explained.

A very feminine ripple of laughter came from Steve. Alec Rice tried to prevent the slight blush he felt stealing over his face.

'Good looking?' questioned Temple.

'Yes,' was the answer. 'Yes, I suppose she was.'

'Well, something must have impressed you about her, or—'

Alec Rice attempted to redeem himself in Steve Trent's eyes.

'As a matter of fact, old boy, I got the impression that all this business about the statuettes was a sort of blind. I think the real reason for her visit was to have a jolly good "decko" at the diamond.'

'Was she tall?' asked Paul Temple.

The jeweller was a little dubious. 'Yes, I—er—I suppose she was,' he said hesitantly.

Paul Temple laughed. 'You don't seem to have been very observant!'

'Good Lord, old boy – you can hardly—' His voice tailed off as he struggled to recollect some detail or other about the girl's appearance. 'I say, just a minute!' he suddenly started. 'I tell you what I did notice. She had a rather snappy wristlet watch. Looked to me as if it was made of onyx or something. It was—'

Temple finished the sentence for him.

'It was black, with a diamond clasp, and a small platinum safety chain,' he said quietly.

Alec Rice opened his mouth with surprise.

'Yes, yes!' he exclaimed as Paul Temple finished. 'I say,' he continued excitedly, 'I say, do you know the girl?'

'I think perhaps I do, Alec!' replied the novelist softly. 'I think perhaps I do.'

Temple rose and took from the mantelpiece a new pipe he had bought a few days before. It was a habitual gesture when he was thinking over some problem. For a few minutes there was silence in the room. At last the jeweller got up.

'Oh, well,' he said, 'I must be toddling!'

Paul Temple was taken by surprise. 'Look here,' he said, 'won't you stop and have a drink or something?'

146

'Sorry, old boy – in a frightful hurry!' Alec Rice was always in a hurry about something or other, with a seemingly endless stream of appointments.

When Temple came back to the drawing-room, after showing his friend out, he found a very puzzled Steve waiting for him.

'Did you know the girl he was talking about?' she started.

'Yes!' answered her host. 'Her name is Diana Thornley. She and her uncle, Dr. Milton, dined with me a fortnight ago.'

'And you noticed the wristlet watch?'

'Yes, I noticed it,' he answered thoughtfully. 'And so did Alec. And so did the constable at Leamington.' He suddenly looked up. 'Do you know, Steve, I think it might be quite a good idea if we paid Dr. Milton a visit!'

Paul Temple liked to take his life in a leisurely fashion. It went with his slight tendency to drawl. He, of all men, always seemed to have an infinite amount of time. Perhaps because the busiest of men are always able to fit even more into their schedule. But Paul Temple was also essentially a man of action. He could take the initiative better than anyone else, and rapid movement and thinking came as naturally to him as they did to Steve. For Steve, too, liked action. She lived in a world of action, for nothing requires more rapid thinking, more rapid work than an evening newspaper. And much as she admired what she regarded as Paul Temple's perpetual pose, she herself could never adopt it.

They thought over the suggestion of the visit to Dr. Milton. To think was to decide.

'No time like the present!' said Steve with expectancy and excitement in her voice.

Paul Temple said nothing. By way of answer, he left the room. Two minutes later he was back, clad in his huge grey camel-hair coat; in his hand, his large fur-lined gloves and battered felt hat.

He looked at Steve a little quizzically.

'Coming?' he asked.

'Right now!' she answered happily. She jumped up and went to put on her coat. She might have been going to a cheery summer picnic.

She had not noticed the highly significant bulge in Paul Temple's overcoat pocket.

CHAPTER XVI

Going Down!

'I should ring again!' said Steve.

She was standing outside Dr. Milton's house with Paul Temple. A few yards away, in the drive, stood the car in which they had arrived from Bramley Lodge a few minutes before.

Once again Paul Temple pressed the bell-push. In the distance they could hear the peal of the electric bell echoing through the house. The noise stopped and everything was as still as before. The atmosphere seemed strained and eerie, as though immediately before a thunderstorm. Steve gripped her companion's arm. Through his thick overcoat he could feel the strength with which she held him.

'There doesn't seem to be anyone in, as far as I can—' He broke off. 'Just a minute!'

Resounding through the hall, they could hear footsteps approaching. Next they heard bolts being drawn and presently the door opened. Before them stood Snow Williams.

'Good evening, sir,' he said quietly.

'I should like to see Dr. Milton,' said Temple. 'My name is—'

'Dr. Milton is out!' the other interrupted. 'He went into Evesham about an hour ago.'

'Oh. Oh, I see,' Temple replied. 'Er, then perhaps Miss Thornley would—'

'Miss Thornley is with the doctor, sir.' Snow Williams spoke in his dispassionate voice, and instinctively Paul Temple felt there was no truth in what he was saying.

'Oh. Er, that's rather unfortunate, isn't it?' he said after a moment's pause.

'Was the doctor expecting you, sir?'

'No,' replied Temple. 'No, I don't think he was. Still, if he's only popped into Evesham, it might be quite a good idea if we waited.'

Snow Williams did not appear to welcome the proposal.

'I hardly think the doctor will be back for quite a little while, sir.'

'Oh, er, don't you?' asked Temple. 'Still, I think we'll wait,' he said pleasantly.

Snow Williams hesitated.

'Very good, sir,' he said at last. 'This way, if you please.'

He closed the door and led the way through a large and stately hall. Their footsteps echoed over the parquet floor. One or two oil paintings hung on the walls. On an old-fashioned carved mahogany stand hung a collection of coats and hats.

The 'butler' opened a door and showed them into a large, comfortable room which appeared to be in frequent use. Newspapers and periodicals littered the tables and chairs. Among them Paul Temple noticed a copy of the *Police Review* and suppressed a smile. On the mantelpiece stood a number of small gilt statuettes. The doctor seemed fond of sculpture. In a corner of the room stood a statue, half life size, of Aphrodite. In the hall, Paul Temple had

seen another large marble statue of Apollo. Dr. Milton was apparently very classical in his tastes, if a little obvious, Paul Temple reflected.

'This is the lounge, sir,' Snow Williams informed them. 'I'll let you know immediately the doctor returns.'

'Splendid!'

'What name shall I—'

'Temple. Paul Temple.'

A look of surprise came into the man's eyes.

'Temple?' he repeated. He paused, then seemed to recollect himself. 'Oh, thank you, sir.'

Then he left the room and closed the door.

Steve Trent did not know whether to laugh or shudder at this strange specimen of humanity.

'Well, I don't think Boris Karloff would keep him awake!' she remarked to Paul Temple.

The novelist began to laugh. 'Behind that rough exterior there probably lurks a heart of gold!'

'Lurks is about right, if you ask me!' laughed Steve.

Neither of them seemed to have any inclination just to sit down and await the arrival of Dr. Milton. Together they started examining the room. All the furniture and decorations were obviously of the best. A beautiful old silk Turkish rug lay in front of the fire. Indeed, the room could scarcely have been more luxuriously equipped.

'I say,' remarked Paul Temple at last, 'it's a pretty impressive sort of place, this, isn't it?'

'Yes,' she agreed. Then she turned to the mantelpiece and pointed to the little figures on it. 'Our friend, the doctor, certainly believes in statues!'

'Nothing particularly modest about 'em, either!' remarked Paul Temple.

Steve rippled with laughter as she contemplated the nudity to which he referred. Meanwhile Temple walked over to give them a closer examination, and Steve began to laugh anew.

'Hello! Hello!' he exclaimed, looking down from the mantelpiece to the grate below.

'What is it?' Steve asked, now serious again.

'Dear, oh dear! It looks as if our friend Mr. Karloff was spinning a little story when he said the doctor and Diana left an hour ago.'

'Why?'

'There's a cigarette-end in the fireplace and it obviously hasn't been there very long, judging from appearances.'

Steve did not take the discovery quite so seriously as her companion. 'Perhaps the butler was having a quiet little smoke!' she remarked. 'That would account for him keeping us waiting.'

'It wouldn't account for the lip rouge on the cigarette, dearie!' said Paul Temple, ironically. 'Unless we've greatly misjudged our friend.'

Steve Trent joined him in front of the fireplace and proceeded to examine the beautiful little statuettes. They were perfect specimens of workmanship. Indeed, two of them looked as if they were of solid gold and worth an immense sum of money. Suddenly Steve came to a stop before one of the statues.

'I say, Paul—' she started.

'Yes?'

'This is a funny sort of thing, isn't it?'

'What is it?' asked Paul Temple quietly.

'I don't know,' Steve answered. 'Looks like a figure of something or other . . .'

Being gifted with an exceptionally large measure of curiosity, Steve proceeded to finger the strange little statue. Its upper half seemed separate from the remainder.

'The top part is quite loose!' she exclaimed as she made the discovery. 'Look, it—' She suddenly hesitated.

Steve had turned the statue round, idly wondering whether it could be unscrewed. As she did so, a section of the oak panelling in the wall, several feet square, began slowly and softly to slide back.

'Paul, look!' she shouted across at him. 'Look!' she repeated.

Paul Temple came to her side and together they stared at this extraordinary discovery. Behind the panel all was intense darkness. Steve, full of excitement, returned to have another look at the little statue.

'No, don't touch the statue, Steve!' Temple admonished her. He felt in his pockets, and extracted a flat pocket electric torch. 'We must have a look at this!' he said softly.

He switched the torch on and flashed the light through the aperture. It was not big enough for both of them to look through, together, and Steve found it hard to restrain her impatience.

'Can you see anything?' she asked at last.

Paul Temple withdrew his arms and head and looked into her anxious eyes.

'Yes,' he said. 'It's just a small room – nothing exciting about it. It's not even furnished.'

'Oh,' said Steve, feeling a trifle disappointed.

'Let's have a look inside!' he said, however. He managed to push back the panel a few inches and started climbing inside. The opening was now just big enough for a man to work his way through. The bottom of the opening was some two feet from the floor. Slowly and carefully, Paul Temple began to clamber through, watching for anything that might happen. Soon he was inside. Then he stretched out his arm to help Steve into the little room.

'Come on, Steve!' he encouraged her. 'Can you get in all right?'

'Yes!' she replied, as she placed one foot on the other side of the panel, unconsciously revealing as she did so a length of perfectly shaped leg. Then she bent down and was soon inside the mysterious little room.

'Not very impressive, is it?' commented Paul Temple.

'It doesn't seem to be used at all as far as I can see,' she replied. Nevertheless, there was very little dust on the floor. Both stood looking round, equally mystified.

'Isn't there a light?' asked Steve.

'Yes, but I'm blowed if I can see the switch,' was the answer. Set in the middle of the ceiling was an opal glass bowl which betokened an electric light. Yet neither of them had noticed any sign of a switch which would work it.

'Close the panel, Steve,' Paul Temple hazarded. 'I have an idea that might work it.'

She pulled the panel. Immediately the little chamber was flooded with light from the bowl above. They could now see their immediate surroundings better, but found there was still nothing extraordinary about them.

'I thought it would,' he said. 'I could see the small notch in the corner of—'

He broke off as a strange noise came to their ears.

'What's that?' he asked.

They listened intently. It was the sound of machinery. It might have been the whir of a dynamo or some electric motor. It seemed to come from somewhere close at hand.

'It sounds like—' Steve Trent started; then she broke off. She had been feeling the panel, trying to push it back.

'Paul!' she exclaimed in sudden alarm. 'Paul! The panel won't open!'

'Won't open!' he repeated, gently pushing her aside. 'Here, let me try.' He struggled hard, but it refused to yield.

'By Timothy!' he said. 'We're locked in!'

They looked round in helpless amazement at their tiny prison.

They pushed at the sides of the chamber, but without avail. Their desperate search for some hidden button or switch that might put an end to their imprisonment met with immediate failure.

'Listen!' exclaimed Temple suddenly.

The hum of the machinery had gradually been growing louder. Now it seemed to fill the little room. An instant later, the floor started to tremble.

'Paul!' exclaimed Steve with immense trepidation, 'Paul! We're moving!'

'Moving?'

'It's the room – can't you feel it? Can't you feel it?'

The hum of the machinery had swollen till now it reverberated in their ears. The entire room was shaking.

Paul Temple paused. Then in sudden astonishment, he realized what was happening. 'By Timothy, Steve – we're in a lift!'

'A lift!' she repeated.

'Keep still!' he instructed.

The two stood watching each other, powerless to do anything.

Slowly, they realized that they were descending, that they were being carried into the depths of the earth. Steve stared at Temple with an expression of bewildered astonishment.

'Paul!' she shrieked. 'We're going down! We're—going— down! We're—going—down!!!!'

CHAPTER XVII

The Secret of the Lift

The hum of machinery continued. For what seemed an eternity Paul Temple and Steve Trent were imprisoned in the slowly descending lift. Neither spoke. Both could only wonder what would be the climax of this strange turn of events. There was scarcely room to move.

There was nothing to be seen. The panel was the only opening, and this was now closed. There was not even a grill of any kind through which they could peer as they descended.

Down and down it went. Seconds lengthened into minutes. Only the continued vibration told them they were still moving.

'We're stopping, Steve . . .' said Temple. Suddenly, almost simultaneously, the lift gave a sharp jerk and the vibration ceased.

'Open the panel, Steve!'

Steve was in a better position to slide it back than Temple.

'I wonder where we are!' she speculated, a little nervously, as she stretched out her arm to open it.

'Probably the bargain basement!' replied Paul Temple, with grim flippancy. 'Here, I'll try that!' he exclaimed, as he saw that Steve's efforts to open the panel were proving fruitless. With a twist of his arm, he had the panel open.

Both looked out through the opening. Dimly they could make out that they were in some kind of vault or passage. They could see two sides, six or eight feet apart. In the rear was nothing but hollow darkness.

Everything was deathly still. The air seemed clammy, even though it was cold. They appeared to be deep under the earth in some kind of queer subterranean corridor.

Paul Temple had now pulled out his electric torch, thanking his lucky stars for having taken it with him, and suddenly pressed the switch.

'Looks like a passage of some sort!' he said.

'Yes,' agreed Steve in a whisper. They made out the stone slabs that lined the sides and the floor. They were slimy and covered with some growth that looked like moss. Stalactites, up to nearly a foot long, hung down from the roof. The passage itself seemed just high enough for a tall man to walk upright. The surface of the walls and ground were wet. A few yards from the lift was a cavity in which were two strong wooden cases with heavy padlocks fastening them, and bound with iron.

'Can you get out all right?' Paul Temple asked.

'I think so,' Steve replied as she started to clamber through the opening. 'They don't give you much room, do they?'

Taking care not to rip her dinner dress, she finally managed to pull herself through. The bulkier Temple speedily followed her. Together they stood in front of the lift peering into the distance which the light from the little electric torch could not reach.

Temple put his arm round Steve's waist to reassure her, and slowly and carefully, watching out for any openings in the ground beneath them, they commenced to move forward. He handed Steve the torch. His right hand he put into his pocket. There, he had his precious automatic, and his fingers closed round it with an immense feeling of satisfaction. He pulled it out and showed it to Steve so that she, too, could share in the feeling of security it gave. With his thumb, he pressed down the safety catch, and as they walked along, held it in front of him, ready for any emergency.

'I wonder where this place leads to?' he remarked.

'I've got a pretty awful sense of direction,' replied Steve, 'but we seem to be going towards the village, as far as I can make out.'

'We'll walk to the end!' he said, after they had gone on a few yards.

The light from the torch began to flicker. The battery was fading. Temple cursed himself mentally for not making sure that it would last. He determined also, if he ever came out of this extraordinary situation alive, to buy a lamp with a hand-operated dynamo.

'Can you see all right?' he asked Steve after a while.

'Not too badly,' she replied.

'This passage is pretty old,' remarked Temple. 'It must have been here for years.'

Silently they trudged on. They were now getting more accustomed to the darkness and to the slippery surface of the stone flags over which they were walking. Now they were beginning to step out in a sharp walk. This was necessary, if only to keep warm in the damp, cold air of the passage.

'Seems fairly long, doesn't it?' said Temple after a few minutes.

Suddenly Steve came to a stop. She pulled herself free from him and pointed into the distance.

'Paul!' she burst out. 'Paul, there's a light!'

The novelist's eyesight was not quite so keen as Steve's, but he strained his eyes to catch a glimpse of the light in the distance.

'Where?' he asked. 'Oh, yes!' he said suddenly.

'It's an oil lamp!' said Steve. 'Someone must have been here quite recently.'

'Someone's been here quite recently, all right!' Temple remarked grimly. 'Don't worry about that. I wonder where the devil this passage leads to?' he added thoughtfully.

Steve began to smile. A fantastic thought had occurred to her. 'Most probably to "The Little General",' she laughed. 'Everything seems to lead towards—'

'By Timothy, Steve!' interrupted Paul Temple, a tremendous elation in his voice. 'By Timothy, you're right!'

'Why, Paul, you don't—'

Paul Temple did not let Steve finish her sentence. He explained the conclusion to which he had jumped from her chance remark.

'"The Little General" lies about a hundred yards from Ashdown House,' he said. 'We must have come fifty yards already—'

'Then you really think this passage leads towards the inn?' Steve interrupted, with obvious excitement in her voice.

'We'll soon find out,' he replied grimly. 'We'll soon find out, Steve.'

Slowly they plodded on. Paul Temple had switched his torch off, but the faint beams from the oil lamp seemed to be reflected backwards and forwards from the shiny walls. There was just enough light for them to make their way. Moreover, they did not care to advertise their approach by using the torch.

Occasionally, one or other of them kicked hard at a stone that projected from the other flags. Otherwise their progress remained uninterrupted. There were no hidden pitfalls, no obstructions against which they might stumble. Only here and there an old barrel, its iron hoops thick with rust.

At last they came to a halt.

'There's some sort of wooden staircase over there!' exclaimed Steve in guarded tones.

'Yes. We're underneath the inn, all right,' Temple whispered. 'I don't think there's any doubt about that.'

They made their way towards the stairs that Steve had indicated.

'Can you hear voices?' asked Paul Temple suddenly.

Steve listened intently. 'Yes,' she said at last. 'Yes, I think I can.'

They could both hear men talking, but it was all too far away to distinguish what was being said.

'If we climb to the top of the staircase, we might hear better,' suggested Temple.

'Yes,' said Steve, obviously keyed up with excitement.

She set her foot on the first step and proceeded to make her way up the staircase, followed closely by Temple.

'Be careful, Steve!' he admonished her.

Taking care not to make any noise, they climbed the old wooden stairs. The voices were growing more distinct now, but at all cost their presence must not be discovered.

Suddenly, a board creaked very loudly. The noise rang through the silent gloom almost like a pistol shot. Both stopped dead. Temple gently pushed Steve to the edge of the stairs.

'Don't walk in the middle,' he whispered.

Keeping close to the rail on the outside, Steve slowly and cautiously picked her way up, with Paul Temple immediately behind her. At last they came to a door from which the voices were now clearly audible.

'Paul, listen!' said Steve, turning round. 'Listen—'

Both stood motionless behind the door. They recognized the accents of Dr. Milton and Horace Daley, the innkeeper. Both appeared angry. Both were raising their voices.

'What's happened to Skid?' demanded Horace suddenly.

There was a pause. Then they heard Dr. Milton's answer.

'He's dead!'

'Dead!' the innkeeper shrieked. 'I thought you said the smash was—'

'It wasn't the smash, Horace,' came from the doctor in subdued tones.

There was a slight pause before Horace spoke again. 'Then what was it?' he said suddenly.

'He—had—to be taken care of.'

'Taken—care—of,' repeated the innkeeper. There was a pause. 'You don't mean the Knave—'

'Yes.'

Steve turned to look at her companion through the gloom, but she could not make out the expression on Temple's face.

'Why should he?' she now heard Horace demand angrily. 'Why should Skid be murdered?'

'He had to go,' the doctor answered. 'He was on the point of talking.'

'How do we know he was on the point of talking?'

'That's what I says,' came from a third voice they could not identify.

'It was the same with Snipey Jackson and Lefty. They did their job well and then . . .'

Dr. Milton cut the innkeeper short.

'Jackson was a fool!' they heard him exclaim. 'And an incompetent fool into the bargain. He didn't even wear gloves on the Leicester job.'

'And what about Lefty?'

'That was my fault,' the doctor replied more calmly. 'I was sorry about that. I only meant to give the poor devil a whiff of chloroform and he passed out on me.'

There was silence for a few moments. Then they heard Horace Daley speak again.

'Yes, well, it sounds all right. But I'm just getting a bit windy. The Knave is just a little too smart for my liking.'

'A little too smart, eh, Horace? How very interesting!'

It was a woman's voice. With a start of surprise, Temple recognized it. He bent over towards Steve and whispered: 'Diana Thornley!'

'If the Knave wasn't smart, we shouldn't be here, my friend,' the doctor continued; 'you can take that from me.'

'What do you mean?' they heard Horace Daley ask, with hesitancy and nervousness in his voice.

Dr. Milton explained. 'The Knave received information about a valuable diamond owned by a Nottingham firm called "Trenchman's". Diana went round there this morning and had a look at it.'

Paul Temple found a cold little hand being inserted into his. It was far too dark for either of them to see more than a dim outline of the other, but he knew by the way her hand trembled that Steve was excited.

'We were supposed to make all the arrangements about the job tonight,' the doctor was saying. 'But this morning, after Diana got back, the Chief rang up and—'

He paused. 'Well?' demanded Horace.

'The Trenchman diamond was a trap – a charming little noose, my friend, for us all to put our pretty little necks in!'

'Strewth!' exclaimed the innkeeper. 'What about Diana?' he asked quickly. 'How do we know she wasn't spotted?'

'We don't know. Diana's got to lie low for a while.'

Once again they heard the mysterious third voice join in the discussion.

'It's a damn good job the Chief found out about Trenchman's, or we should 'ave been in a pretty pickle.'

'Whose idea was it to have a "plant" like that?' demanded Horace Daley. 'I bet a fiver it—'

Dr. Milton interrupted him again. 'It was Mr. Paul Temple's idea, unless I'm very much mistaken. And, unless I'm very much mistaken, Mr. Temple is going to be aptly rewarded for his originality.'

'Then heaven help the poor devil if you get your hands on him, Doc,' they heard the innkeeper burst out. 'D'you remember that Greek fellow . . . and the small drops of acid? I'll never forget his face. Why, he was—'

Dr. Milton began to laugh. It was a hard, cruel laugh, and Steve shuddered violently as she heard him. Temple put his arm about her protectively. The laughter stopped as suddenly as it had started.

'Now listen,' said Milton sharply. 'The Chief's got another idea up his sleeve, and as far as I can make out, it's going to be a pretty big proposition. He wants you all here, in Room 7, on Saturday, at nine sharp.'

'Is—is he coming?' inquired Horace.

'Yes,' the doctor answered. 'Yes, he's coming.' He paused. 'Dixie,' he said, obviously addressing the owner of the unknown voice, 'I want you to meet Snow at the house. I'll see he gets his instructions.' Dr. Milton's voice seemed to grow fainter, as if he were moving across the room.

'Paul!' exclaimed Steve, in an urgent whisper. 'We'd better return to the house.'

Temple nodded. At any moment, now, the door in front of them might open. There was not a moment to lose.

With the knowledge that there were no obstructions or unforeseen obstacles of any kind on the stairs, they were able to go down more quickly than they had ascended. Nevertheless, they took care to avoid undue noise.

'Do you think we'll be able to work the lift?' inquired Steve, as they came to the end of the third and last flight of stairs.

'We'll have to,' was the reply. 'Mind that bottom step!'

'You can see quite clearly when you get used to the light,' said Steve, when they stood in the passage again.

'Yes.' Paul Temple paused. 'Now come on, Steve,' he urged. 'We must hurry.'

They had to cover little more than a hundred yards, and both felt that they would be safer when they were back in the house again. It was dangerous to sprint along the slippery passage, but nevertheless, Temple broke into a sharp trot, with Steve close behind him. The faint, flickering light of his torch, added to the rays from the oil lamp in the passage, helped them to cover the distance fairly quickly. It was not long before they were back at the lift.

'Here we are!' exclaimed Steve breathlessly, but at the same time, relieved.

Then they noticed the panel was closed. In sudden fear, Temple began to struggle with it. It yielded to his efforts.

'Ah!' he exclaimed. 'That's got it. ... Hurry, Steve!'

He bundled her unceremoniously through the opening and quickly climbed in himself. It was the work of another instant to close the panel again.

They had solved the secret of the lift. The panel was at the same time entrance and operating switch. Once again they heard the hum of the electric motor, and after a second or two, they felt the lift slowly moving.

'It's working!' exclaimed Steve a little nervously. 'We're going up!'

Paul Temple nodded. 'I hope Boris Karloff hasn't missed us,' he said grimly.

At last, the slow upward movement ceased and, of its own accord, the panel opened.

Paul Temple looked cautiously out into the drawing-room.

'Is—the room empty?' inquired Steve softly.

'Yes.'

The room was just as they had left it. In all probability their absence had not even been noticed. Paul Temple stepped through the opening and turned round to assist Steve.

'Careful!' he warned. He paused and looked round. 'Now how do we close this panel from the . . . Oh, the statue, Steve!'

'I'll do it.' Steve walked quickly over to the little statue she had discovered, gave it a twist, and to her satisfaction saw the panel close.

'Good!' exclaimed Paul Temple.

'Now what . . .?' she asked. 'Are we going to wait here, or—'

'No. I think we've seen enough of Ashdown House for the time being. I'll get hold of this butler fellow and tell him we're not waiting.' He looked round. 'Is that a bell push?' he asked, pointing to the wall by the fireside, where Steve was standing.

'Yes. I'll ring.'

She pressed it. Then they sat down in two of the armchairs the room boasted and tried desperately hard to look both very bored and very innocent. At last they heard footsteps in the hall outside.

'He's coming!' said Temple softly.

The door opened, and Snow Williams appeared.

'You rang, sir?'

'Yes,' said Temple with such a perfect air of indifference that Steve had difficulty in keeping her face straight. 'We've, er, decided not to wait for Dr. Milton. Perhaps you'd be kind enough to give him my kind regards?'

'Certainly, sir.' Snow led the way to the door without any apparent suspicions. 'Good night, sir! Good night, Miss!'

Steve and Temple drank in the fresh air greedily. Both felt glad to be outside again. As they walked slowly over to the car neither of them spoke. Both seemed to have far too much to think about. Paul Temple folded a rug over Steve's knees, made sure she was comfortable, then pressed the self-starter. After two or three turns, the engine was firing, and he slipped the gear lever into position. A few moments later, they were shooting down the drive towards the main road which would take them back to Bramley Lodge.

After a mile or so, Paul Temple suddenly came to a stand-still beside the road and switched off his headlamps. Steve looked round at him in surprise.

'Why have you stopped?' she asked.

'Because I want to have a chat with you, young lady!' he replied.

'Oh, Mr. Temple!' said Steve flippantly and with a laugh.

'Steve,' he said very soberly, 'I'm worried.'

'Worried?' she echoed, now serious again; 'Why?'

'I'm worried because you're mixed up in this affair. These people are dangerous. They'll stop at nothing. You've got to watch yourself, Steve. You've got to watch yourself.'

'Don't worry . . . I will!' she said reassuringly. 'You're very sweet!' she added gently.

'Ever since that incident in your flat . . . with the record . . . I've been very anxious for you.' There was urgency in Temple's voice. 'Can't you go away for a little while, Steve. Perhaps—'

'No,' she replied decisively. 'No, and even if I could – I shouldn't. This is my affair, Paul – my affair more than anyone else's – the Knave of Diamonds killed my brother, remember—'

Her knuckles were clenched and Temple noticed the row of white spots where the bones were forced against the skin. Her lips were pressed firmly together. Paul Temple realized that his passenger could be a very determined little person when she chose.

'But Steve—'

'But that isn't everything,' she continued firmly. 'The whole affair is much deeper than that, Paul. . . much deeper.' For a few moments, she sat in silence, her face set in a deep frown. 'From the very beginning of the Cape Town–Simonstown robberies eight years ago,' she continued thoughtfully, 'I knew, and hated, the name of Max Lorraine. I knew that sooner or later . . . I should have to face him. Please believe me, Paul, when I say—'

Again Temple interrupted her. 'Steve, listen!' he said suddenly. 'We agreed that it would be Paul Temple versus Max Lorraine. You heard them talking in that room at the inn: and you know the type of people we're up against.' He paused expressively. 'Steve, for my sake – you've got to keep out of this!'

'But Paul—'

He refused to let her say what she wanted. 'I shall make a point of seeing Sir Graham first thing tomorrow morning,' he said, 'the inn must be raided on Thursday, at all cost!' Suddenly, he changed the subject. 'Steve, there's something I've been wanting to ask you.'

'Well?' There was something in the tone of his voice that had aroused her curiosity.

'You remember, you told me, that when your brother was investigating the Cape Town–Simonstown robberies he worked with another officer, a man who was later murdered by Max Lorraine?'

'Yes,' she answered. 'Yes, that's right.'

'Tell me – what did they call that man?'

Steve tried to recall the name of the man to mind. 'Bellman!' she exclaimed at length, 'Sydney Bellman.' Then after a pause she said: 'Why do you ask?'

'I was just wondering,' said Paul Temple quietly, 'I was just wondering.'

CHAPTER XVIII

The Commissioner's Orders

It was with some sense of satisfaction that Paul Temple mounted the steps which would take him into the hall at Scotland Yard. On the occasion of his visit there with Steve Trent a few days ago, the first he had paid since his newspaper days, he had felt remarkably like a guilty schoolboy being hauled before his headmaster for cheating.

But now he had something definite to report to the Commissioner. Indeed, Temple had hoped that his story would make Sir Graham feel glad that he had invited the novelist to co-operate. Even the stolid policeman at the entrance seemed more friendly and greeted him with a cheery, 'Good morning, Mr. Temple!' as he pushed his way through the glass doors.

It was clear that Paul Temple was expected. He had driven down from Bramley Lodge early that morning, and as he had started long before the roads had become cluttered with their more normal traffic, he had made excellent progress.

After a light breakfast, he had stepped into the car just before eight o'clock. There were no large towns to pass through and the needle of the speedometer frequently wavered between sixty and seventy. The car's brakes were good and Temple was a competent driver. At a quarter to nine he was skirting Oxford, along the by-pass, and by ten o'clock he had reached the Western Avenue and was passing Ealing. Here he stopped to telephone Scotland Yard and make an appointment with the Commissioner.

He was due to meet Sir Graham at twelve and this gave him time to visit his club and glance through the morning papers before driving over to Whitehall.

The policeman on duty had escorted him to the table where Paul Temple had duly filled up the inquiry slip, without which not even the most exalted visitor seems permitted to leave the portals of Scotland Yard. He had then telephoned the Commissioner to make sure he was disengaged, after which he led the way up the broad flight of stairs to the Commissioner's office on the first floor.

Sir Graham had a warm welcome for him. The urgent telephone call of a few hours before had certainly surprised him, and he was now more than anxious to hear what had brought Paul Temple to town so early.

Temple commenced his story. He gave a full account of his adventure in the passage at Ashdown House on the previous evening, and of Alec Rice's visit.

Sir Graham Forbes did not conceal his interest as he listened to the story of the lift, and the thrilling exploits which Steve Trent and Paul Temple had shared.

'By gosh,' he said at last, 'it was a lucky chance that Miss Trent touched the statue!' He paused. 'You say this passage runs from the doctor's house into the actual inn itself?'

'Yes, Sir Graham!'

The Commissioner grunted. 'Do you think this passage is a recent innovation or—'

'No. It's been there for donkey's years: it must have been. I daresay it was used by smugglers originally as a sort of storing house. Why, some of these old English inns have—' Paul Temple broke off.

'What is it?' asked the Commissioner.

'I wonder if Miss Parchment knew that there was a definite connection between the doctor's house and "The Little General"?' said the novelist quietly.

'Miss Parchment?' Sir Graham Forbes looked puzzled. Then suddenly he remembered. 'Oh, the retired schoolmistress! Good heavens, why should she know anything about it?' he asked with a laugh.

'I, er, just wondered, that's all.' Temple occasionally liked to surround himself with an air of mystery. Certainly, he never went out of his way to enlighten people as to his thoughts.

'You know,' continued the Commissioner, dismissing Miss Parchment from his mind, 'the thing that beats me, Temple, is how this fellow, the, er, Knave of Diamonds, discovered that the "Trenchman" affair was a trap!'

'Well,' Temple replied quietly, 'the answer to that is quite simple, Sir Graham.'

The Commissioner looked up in surprise. 'Quite simple?' he repeated.

'The Knave is here,' said Temple slowly. 'He knows all our plans, and everything about us.'

Sir Graham Forbes jumped up from his chair and stood looking down at his visitor.

'Good God, Temple!' he exclaimed with amazement, 'are you suggesting—'

Paul Temple interrupted him. 'I'm suggesting nothing, Sir Graham, that the facts themselves do not indicate!' he said firmly. 'Skid Tyler was murdered, remember, here, in this very office, because he was on the point of divulging the identity of the Knave of Diamonds.'

Sir Graham Forbes was silent. He walked up and down the room for a few moments, then stopped near his desk and lit another of his cigarettes.

'Yes,' he said at last. 'Yes, you're right, Temple.' He paused again. 'Then who is the Knave?'

'I don't know,' was the answer. 'But I may have a pretty good idea within twenty-four hours!' There was a quiet certainty in Temple's voice.

'Within twenty-four hours?' echoed the Commissioner, puzzled by Temple's words.

'There's a meeting to be held at "The Little General" tomorrow night at nine. And the Knave will be there!'

'Then—'

'I want about half a dozen of your men to surround the place,' said Temple quickly. 'If anyone attempts to leave, have them picked up. But no one must be stopped from entering the inn, you understand?'

The Commissioner nodded in agreement. 'And the doctor's house?' he asked.

'Exactly the same precautions must be taken. At about 9.15, the men watching the house will close in on it – force an entrance – and come down the underground passage to the inn. Is that clear?'

Sir Graham Forbes did not take offence at Temple's author-itative instructions. Both were obviously carried away by the excitement of the moment.

'Meanwhile,' the novelist continued, 'at 9.15, the men watching the inn follow exactly the same procedure: close in on "The Little General" and force an entrance.'

At that moment a knock sounded on the door and Chief Inspector Dale appeared.

'Oh, I'm sorry, sir!' He stopped. 'I thought—'

'That's all right, Dale!' the Commissioner hastened to reassure him. 'Tell Davis of the Flying Squad I want a word with him!'

'Very good, sir!'

'I should have your men planted at about eight, Sir Graham,' Paul Temple continued as the door closed, 'and then—'

'Don't worry, Temple. I'll see to that all right!'

The Commissioner walked over to the fireplace and flicked the ash off his cigarette. 'It might be a good idea if I came down myself!' he suggested. 'The two of us could join the men at "The Little General", and then—'

The novelist nodded. 'Excellent idea, Sir Graham!'

'By gosh!' exclaimed the Commissioner, finding difficulty in restraining himself. 'We've got him! We've got him this time!'

Paul Temple smiled. 'I wonder, Sir Graham,' he said. 'I wonder . . .?'

CHAPTER XIX

Steve Vanishes!

It was shortly after eight o'clock the following evening. Sir Graham Forbes, Chief Inspector Dale, and Paul Temple were standing in the drawing-room at Bramley Lodge. All three were smoking, the novelist his customary pipe, the two police chiefs cigarettes. Both kept flicking their ash nervously into the grate and into the ashtrays that lay scattered over the room.

There was an air of expectancy, the feeling that something decisive and unexpected was going to happen. The last remaining details of their plan were under discussion.

'Are the men armed, Sir Graham?' Paul Temple asked.

'Some of them are, I believe, aren't they, Dale?' he asked, turning to the inspector who had arranged the practical details of the plan.

'The men watching the house have service revolvers, sir,' Dale explained. 'I thought under the circumstances that—'

'Yes, of course.'

'You understand about the statue, don't you, Inspector?' Paul Temple suddenly asked him.

'Yes, I think so, sir!' he replied. 'It's on the left you say, as soon as you enter the lounge?'

'Yes, that's right. The head of the statue is on a sort of base: as soon as you turn it, you'll see the panel in the wall. I told you about the light, didn't I?'

Dale nodded.

'Good,' said Temple. 'As far as I could gather, the lift works automatically. Immediately you close the panel you'll hear the machinery.'

'I see.'

'I think someone ought to be left behind in the house,' Sir Graham interrupted. 'I should leave Smith, Hodgson, and Mowbray, Dale. We'll pick them up later.'

'Very good, sir.'

For a few minutes, no one spoke. Each seemed occupied in turning over in his own mind the events that were shortly to occur at the inn.

'By the way,' remarked the Commissioner suddenly, 'you have the search warrant?'

'Oh, yes, sir!'

'Good!' Sir Graham turned to his host. 'Well, I think that's about all, isn't it, Temple?'

The novelist nodded.

'We shall be waiting for you at "The Little General", Dale,' he said. 'Good luck!'

'Thank you, sir!'

'And be careful in that passage,' the Commissioner added. 'I expect the devils know the place backwards.'

As the Inspector walked out of the drawing-room both men watched him, and speculated as to what would happen before they met again.

'Dale seems a nice fellow,' Temple remarked at last.

'Yes,' Sir Graham replied. 'A bit reserved, but very efficient. He's only been at the Yard about twelve months.'

The Commissioner walked over to one of the inviting armchairs and sat down. Temple remained perched on the arm of one of the smaller chairs.

'What time is it, exactly?' asked the Commissioner, at last.

'I make it 8.40.'

'How long should it take us to get down to the inn?'

'Oh, about fifteen minutes.'

'Well, there's no hurry.'

'Dale said he had six men at the house,' commented Temple, after a slight pause. 'How many are watching the inn?'

The Commissioner frowned. 'Now, let me see,' he said. 'There's Foster, Robinson.. . . Oh, about eight or nine, I should say.'

'Good. Is Merritt there?'

'No.'

'Then I think the best plan would be for you and I to enter the inn first,' said Temple thoughtfully, 'then if possible we can also . . .'

He stopped to look round at the door, which had suddenly opened.

'What is it, Pryce?'

'There's a lady called to see you, sir. A Mrs. Neddy. I told her you were engaged, but—'

'Mrs. Neddy?' Temple was obviously puzzled. 'Good Lord!' he exclaimed suddenly, as memory came back to him, 'that's Steve's landlady; surely she—'

At that moment, the very large, very flamboyant figure of Mrs. Neddy appeared in the doorway. She was puffing and blowing with sheer exhaustion, and her eyes were shining with an excitement that partly communicated itself to the two men. She was trying to find breath with which to speak, but the sentences she attempted were all equally unintelligible. At last, after standing still for a moment, Mrs. Neddy was able to speak.

'You'll have to be excusing me bursting in on you like this, Mr. Temple,' she started, her Irish brogue stronger than ever in her agitation, 'but—' Mrs. Neddy did not contain enough breath to complete the sentence. 'Oh, dear! Oh, dear!' she spluttered. 'I'm that exhausted!'

Paul Temple knew better than anyone that he had to use all the patience in the world with the good Irish woman. Anxious as he was to know what had brought her to Bramley Lodge at such an extraordinary hour, he nevertheless remained, outwardly at any rate, perfectly calm.

'Sit down, Mrs. Neddy,' he said gently, as he drew a chair up for her, and even helped her into it. 'That's all right, Pryce,' he added to his manservant, who had been looking at the strange scene with a crestfallen air, ready to apologize as best he could for what he imagined was so unwelcome an intrusion.

'I'm sorry to be—' Mrs. Neddy started, as the door closed, and her bosom heaved again as she struggled for enough breath to complete the sentence. 'I'm sorry to be troubling you, sir. But . . . but—'

Again she came to a full stop. Her recent exertion was clearly more than her constitution was able to stand. Her face was still so flushed that Paul Temple felt very serious alarms for the safety of her heart.

'Now, that's all right, Mrs. Neddy,' said Paul Temple, sitting on a chair beside her, and trying his best both to smooth over his own impatience, and relieve Mrs. Neddy. 'Just take your time,' he added.

'Thank you, sir,' said Mrs. Neddy. Then she breathed out a mighty sigh. 'Ah! What a relief!' she murmured.

For a few moments she sat still, growing gradually calmer, her high colour slowly disappearing.

'Now,' Paul Temple started, when he at last felt it was time for Mrs. Neddy to deliver her message, 'do you feel any better?'

'Yes,' sighed Mrs. Neddy. 'Yes, much better, thank you, sir.'

'Good!' he replied. 'Well,' he asked, in a gentle, persuasive voice, 'what is it you want to see me about?'

'It's—it's about Miss Trent, sir,' Mrs. Neddy stuttered, some of her excitement returning as she remembered the purpose of her visit.

'Miss Trent?' Paul Temple paused. 'What about Miss Trent?'

'She's . . . she's disappeared, sir!'

'Disappeared!' repeated Sir Graham, startled in spite of himself.

'What makes you say that, Mrs. Neddy?' asked Paul Temple, still very gently, still concealing from her the increasing perturbation he felt within.

'Well, it's like this, sir,' she began to explain. 'This morning at about half-past nine, the telephone rang in Miss Trent's flat. I was in the kitchen downstairs at the time, and I could 'ear it as clear as a bell, as you might say, sir.

'After a little while, Miss Trent came downstairs. She seemed in rather a hurry, and slightly excited. I asked her if she was going out, and whether she'd be back for lunch or not. Miss Trent said that her editor had sent for her, and that she would probably be back in about an hour and a half.'

181

Mrs. Neddy was very obviously enjoying herself. Now that she had recovered her speech, and it could again be uttered without undue effort, she could watch Paul Temple and Sir Graham Forbes hanging on every word. It was not every day that Mrs. Neddy could secure such an audience, and she was determined to make the most of it.

Paul Temple almost shouted at her in his sheer, tearing impatience. 'Go on, Mrs. Neddy!'

'Well, sir, there's nothing much to tell, really, except that— she never came back. And then, about a quarter to twelve, the telephone went again. I could hear it all over the blessed house. . . . So after a while I went upstairs and answered it, and . . . and—'

'Yes, Mrs. Neddy!' urged Paul Temple, now more anxious than ever.

'It was the newspaper office, sir. They said they wanted to speak to Miss Trent. I told them she had left the house immediately after they first called her. But . . . but . . . but—' Once again Mrs. Neddy began to be carried away by her emotions. She was now very nearly weeping at the thought of what might have happened to her beloved Steve Trent. 'Well, the man at the other end said he was the editor, and that . . . and that . . . they never had called her!'

'My God!' exclaimed Temple under his breath.

'I—I didn't know what to do, sir,' Mrs. Neddy went on. 'I was in a quandary, as you might say. Then suddenly I remembered all those articles Miss Trent used to write about – "Send for Paul Temple", and I thought that if I could—'

'You acted very wisely, Mrs. Neddy,' said Temple quietly, and Mrs. Neddy beamed with joy at this flattery.

'Temple,' exclaimed Sir Graham suddenly, 'you don't think that the Knave . . .?'

Paul Temple's face was grave. 'Yes,' he replied desperately, 'and, by Timothy, we've no time to lose, Sir Graham. No time to lose!'

CHAPTER XX

At the Inn

Paul Temple rang the bell for Pryce and rushed out into the hall to collect their overcoats.

As they came out of the house the uniformed Flying Squad officer sitting in the driver's seat pressed the starter, and the two men had barely taken their seats before the tyres of the car were sending a shower of gravel backwards towards the porch.

'The inn, as fast as you can get there!' barked the Commissioner, leaning forward to the driver.

'Very good, sir.'

In the back the two men began to talk in low tones. It was a strange and highly irregular conversation.

But then, as Sir Graham Forbes explained to the novelist, 'This whole business is so devilish unprecedented.

'You know,' he pointed out to Paul Temple, 'we have to appoint somebody as Harvey's successor. Dale hasn't been with us long enough for the job, and there is nobody else who is properly *au fait* with these, er, extraordinary jewel robberies.'

Sir Graham paused. He was finding it hard to say exactly what he had in mind. Temple thought he knew what was coming, but not even Temple had guessed all that was in the Commissioner's mind.

'Chief Inspector Purley will be taking over Harvey's duties when this business is over. He has done some very good work at the Yard, and we are making him a Super. But that won't help us over the present business.'

Again the Commissioner paused. 'I wonder,' he went on at last, 'I wonder if you would care to take an, er, an unofficial sort of appointment?'

Once again there was a slight pause before he continued. 'Naturally, I can't give you any official rank or standing, but personally I don't see any reason why you yourself should not carry on with what Harvey started.'

Sir Graham Forbes had been staring straight ahead, watching the car's passage through the country road on the way to 'The Little General'.

'How do you feel about it, Temple?' he asked, at length.

For a moment or two Paul Temple did not reply, then at last he said, 'It's very good of you, Sir Graham.'

'I shall tell Dale, of course,' Sir Graham continued, 'and any orders you have to make you can give directly through me, or if you prefer it, through Dale or Merritt. That puts the whole arrangement on a practical footing.'

'Well, it's very good of you to show this confidence in me,' Temple replied. 'I shall certainly do what I can. I think myself the arrangement should work fairly well.'

The two men fell silent. Temple sat considering his new position. A superintendent without rank or standing, a police chief without police experience, office, or salary, a detective who had to give his orders through an intermediary.

186

Nevertheless, Sir Graham Forbes had given him the highest possible token of his appreciation.

They were still thinking over this new arrangement when the brakes shrieked, and the car skidded on the loose gravel to a stop outside the inn. Immediately both men leaped out and hurried up to a figure that loomed out of the darkness.

'Anything to report, Turner?' asked the Commissioner briskly.

'No, sir.'

'Has anyone entered the inn?' Temple asked.

'Not a soul, sir; I can't understand it.'

Paul Temple took the Commissioner by the arm.

'Come along, Sir Graham,' he said quickly.

'You know the signal, Turner,' added the Commissioner. 'Just in case we need you.'

'Yes, sir.'

The Commissioner and the novelist strode towards the inn. Temple opened the door to the hall and led the way inside to the bar parlour.

'The place seems deserted,' remarked the Commissioner, as he looked around.

'Yes,' agreed Temple, after hesitating a moment. 'I wonder if there's anyone in the back parlour?'

'We'll soon find out!' the Commissioner replied. He walked over to the flap in the counter, raised it, and walked through. He then opened the door leading to the back room, and looked inside.

'It looks to me as if we're on a wild goose chase,' said Temple, as the Commissioner came back.

Sir Graham made no comment.

'Where does this door lead to?' he asked suddenly, indicating the other door behind the counter.

'Oh, that leads outside, I think, into a sort of courtyard,' Paul Temple explained. 'You won't find anything out there except pigeons.'

'Well, where the devil is the room you were telling me about?' asked the Commissioner. 'Room 7?'

'Yes,' Temple replied slowly. 'That's what I want to know, Sir Graham.'

'It can't very well be upstairs, because of the passage leading from the house,' remarked the Commissioner.

'No.. . . It must be behind this panelling.'

Temple walked across the room to the wall and started thumping on it with his fist.

'It sounds solid enough,' remarked Sir Graham.

'Yes, but there's quite a gap between this parlour and the staircase. I reckon that's where the room is.'

'Yes, but how are we going to get into it? There must be a—'

'Just a minute,' Temple suddenly interrupted.

'What is it?' asked the Commissioner, after a short pause.

'I thought I heard . . .' Paul Temple started. 'Listen!' he exclaimed.

They could hear sounds from somewhere behind the wall. There were creaks, as if from footboards, then the clear noise of footsteps.

'There's someone behind the panelling!' exclaimed Sir Graham.

'Yes.'

Again they listened. Suddenly a knock was heard against the panelling. It was as if some ghostly hand were repeating the endeavours Temple had just been making.

'That's Dale!' exclaimed the Commissioner.

'Then, by Timothy, he's been quick!' Temple added.

The Commissioner nodded to him. Suddenly he shouted,
'Is that you, Dale?'

Clearly, from somewhere behind the wall, they could hear
the inspector.

'Yes! Where are you?'

'Knock on the wall, Dale!' shouted Temple, by way of
answer.

They listened, and once again they heard the thump on
the wall.

'He's over here, I think,' said the Commissioner.

Together they walked over to the spot which Sir Graham
indicated.

'There must be some way to—' Temple broke off, bewildered by what he saw in front of him.

'Look!' exclaimed Sir Graham Forbes. 'Look! The panel's
moving!'

It was true. Part of the actual panelling in the wall was slowly
swinging backwards. Neither of them could have suspected
its possibility, even from their close inspection of the wall.

'He must have found the switch,' remarked Temple, as
Chief Inspector Dale appeared through the opening.

'Hello, Sir Graham!' smiled Dale. 'There's a room in here,
sir; it seems . . .'

'Yes,' interrupted Temple, 'that's what we're looking for.'

The inspector drew back into the room, followed by
Temple and the Commissioner. The top of the panelling
was not more than five feet high, and they had to bow their
heads as they stepped into the room.

'I was certainly lucky to find the switch for the panel,'
Dale remarked.

'So . . . this . . . is Room 7!' said Paul Temple, when they
were safely inside.

'Where's the entrance from the house?' asked the Commissioner.

'Through that cupboard, sir,' said Inspector Dale, pointing to a large cupboard built into a corner of the room. 'There's another panel. It leads down to the passage.'

'Well, these people certainly picked a good hideout,' remarked Temple. 'Did you find anyone in the house, Dale?' he asked.

'No, sir. But on the small table in the hall I found this.'

He took a wallet from his pocket, and extracted a piece of pasteboard. It was a playing card. The knave of diamonds.

'There's something on the back, sir,' added Dale, as Paul Temple looked at the card.

'My God!' he exclaimed, as he turned it over to read the message inscribed.

'What does it say?' the Commissioner asked.

'It says, "Enter Paul Temple . . . Exit Louise . . . Harvey".'

'Exit . . . Louise Harvey,' the Commissioner slowly repeated. 'Temple!' he exclaimed sharply, 'we've got to find that girl!'

'Sir Graham!' said Dale suddenly.

'What is it?'

'There's someone in the back parlour!' said Dale excitedly. 'Look, you can see his—'

Both Temple and Forbes had turned round and walked across to the door to see who it was. Suddenly Temple recognized the new arrival on the scene.

'Why, it's Merritt!' he exclaimed. 'Come in, Charles!'

'Good Lord, Paul!' exclaimed Merritt, staring with surprise at the open panel. 'What the devil do you . . .?' Then he caught sight of the Commissioner, and broke off. 'Sir Graham!' he ejaculated. 'Good evening, sir.'

'Evening, Merritt. What are you doing here?'

'I came down to see Mr. Temple, sir,' he explained. 'His man told me he was at "The Little General" and—' He stopped, then added slowly, 'Well, it's lucky you're here, too, sir.'

'Why, what is it, Merritt?' the Commissioner asked.

'I'm afraid I've got bad news, sir!'

'Bad news?'

'It's Radcliffe and Chambers, of Malvern, sir. They rang through this evening, and . . .'

'Radcliffe and Chambers?' Temple interrupted. 'You mean the jewellery people?'

'Yes.'

'Merritt!' exclaimed the Commissioner, with sudden alarm, 'You don't mean . . .?'

'Yes, Sir Graham,' Inspector Merritt replied. '£12,000 worth,' he added succinctly.

'Twelve thousand—' Sir Graham whistled with astonishment. 'Good Lord, Merritt, why—'

'When did this happen?' asked Paul Temple quickly.

'About six o'clock,' Merritt replied. 'Apparently a man went into the shop and . . .' He suddenly broke off and felt in the breast pocket of his coat. He pulled out an envelope of buff-coloured paper, and passed it across to the novelist. 'Oh, by the way, Paul,' he explained, 'Pryce asked me to give you this cable. It arrived about five minutes after you left.'

'Good,' replied Paul Temple briskly. 'I've been expecting this. Excuse me,' he added.

He tore open the telegram and straightened out the thin sheet of paper. At last he looked up.

'Interesting news, Sir Graham,' he explained. 'It's from a friend of mine in South Africa. He's attached to the Cape Town Intelligence Department.'

'Well, what does he say?' the Commissioner asked.

'He says, "Sydney Bellman was unmarried, but he had a sister."'

'Who the devil is Sydney Bellman?' asked Sir Graham, with some impatience.

'He was the man who assisted Harvey when he was in South Africa. They worked together over the Simonstown Case.'

'Oh, yes,' replied the Commissioner. 'I remember. Didn't Miss Trent say he was murdered?'

'He was murdered by – the Knave of Diamonds!'

'What does your friend mean by, "But he had a sister"?' inquired Sir Graham.

'I wonder . . .' replied Temple slowly, 'I wonder . . .'

Suddenly a loud knock was heard on the panel. It was repeated almost instantly.

'That's from the cupboard,' said Dale. 'One of the men must have come through from the house.'

'Open the panel, Dale,' commanded the Commissioner.

The inspector walked over to the cupboard, opened the door, and slowly pulled back the panel. Behind it he saw the tall figure of Sergeant Mowbray.

'What is it?' asked Dale impatiently. 'I told you to stay at the house.'

'Sorry, sir,' Mowbray started, jumping on one side and revealing the presence of yet another visitor, 'but this lady arrived at the house and insisted on seeing Mr. Temple. I thought perhaps . . .'

On hearing his name mentioned, Paul Temple had walked up to the cupboard, and he now caught sight of the unexpected visitor.

'Miss Parchment!' he exclaimed, with astonishment.

Miss Amelia Victoria Parchment smiled. 'So we meet again, Mr. Temple!' she said. 'How nice.'

CHAPTER XXI

The First Penguin

'Miss Parchment!' exclaimed Sir Graham, with a surprise in his voice that verged on sheer horror. 'What the devil are you doing here?'

Miss Parchment was in no way perturbed. 'Well,' she answered brightly, 'suppose I said "waiting for a bus," Sir Graham, would you believe me?'

But the Commissioner was in no mood for jesting.

'Miss Parchment,' he answered, with all the dignity and severity he could muster, 'this is no time for flippancy. I warn you that—'

'Sir Graham, please!' implored Paul Temple. He turned from the Commissioner to his strange visitor. 'Miss Parchment, I know why you are here tonight,' he said quietly. 'I know who you are – and what you are. But there's one question you've got to answer me. . . . Where is Steve Trent?'

'Steve Trent?' repeated Miss Parchment, with blank surprise. 'And who, may I ask, is Steve Trent?'

'Her real name is Harvey . . . Louise Harvey. She's the sister to Superintendent Harvey, the man who . . .'

Francis Durbridge

Miss Parchment's tone of flippancy and badinage fell from her like a cloak. She became a more human person, a woman who could be aroused, a woman subject to emotions. Her pose as the retired schoolmistress disappeared completely as she exclaimed with alarm: 'Good God, you don't mean Harvey . . . had . . . a sister?'

'Yes,' said Temple briefly. 'And she's disappeared.'

It was Inspector Merritt's turn to be surprised. He was not aware of all the developments in the case, and could not understand the purport of this strange conversation with Miss Parchment.

'Disappeared?' he now repeated, with open mouthed surprise.

'Yes, Charles.'

Chief Inspector Dale frowned. 'But when did this happen?' he asked. 'Surely you didn't know anything about it when . . .?'

'Steve's landlady arrived with the news shortly after you left for the doctor's house, Dale.'

'Oh, I see.'

The Commissioner was still feeling irritated with what he considered Miss Parchment's unwarranted intrusion. He considered it clearly a waste of valuable time, and he did not hesitate to demonstrate his impatience. He turned to Sergeant Mowbray.

'I think you'd better return to the house, Mowbray,' he ordered.

'Very good, sir.'

'I'll come along with you,' remarked Dale. 'There's nothing further I can do here, Sir Graham.'

The little party had returned to the parlour of the inn when Miss Parchment arrived, but the secret panel in the

194

wall had remained open. Inspector Dale now led the way into the mysterious Room 7, followed closely by Sergeant Mowbray. As the rest of the party turned to watch their departure, they saw the panel slowly glide back into position as Dale pressed the button behind the wall.

Temple pulled forward one of the inn's not-too-comfortable wooden chairs for Miss Parchment, and she accepted it with a pleasant smile. He himself took another chair while the Commissioner remained standing, still a little irritated by the unexpected turn of events.

'Mr. Temple!' Miss Parchment spoke quietly, but with a note of desperation in her voice, 'I should like to have a word with you privately, if possible.'

'Well . . .?'

But Sir Graham was not slow in taking the hint. He turned to Inspector Merritt, who had been hovering rather awkwardly in the background.

'I, er, want to have a word with Turner,' he said, 'so you can come along with me, Merritt.'

'Very good, sir.'

The two men then walked towards the door, leaving Miss Parchment to her interview with Paul Temple. Just before he went out the Commissioner paused. 'Of course, I shall want to see you later, Miss Parchment,' he said.

Miss Parchment nodded.

'Thank you, Sir Graham,' said Temple.

'We'll meet later, Paul,' Merritt remarked, as he joined the Commissioner.

'Who is that man?' asked Miss Parchment, as the door closed behind them.

'Which man?' Temple asked. 'Oh, Inspector Merritt,' he went on with a smile. 'Why do you ask?'

'I wondered, that's all.'

Paul Temple hesitated a moment. He was curious to know the purpose of this strange visit.

'Well, Miss Parchment?' he asked, at last.

Miss Parchment hesitated, then seemed to make up her mind. In her crisp, well-modulated, and cultured voice she started.

'A little while ago, Mr. Temple, you said, "I know why you are here tonight. I know who you are, and what you are—" She paused. 'Is that true, Mr. Temple?'

'Quite true.'

'Then tell me, and please believe me when I say this is important – do the police know . . . who I am?'

'No,' Paul Temple replied. 'No, they don't, Miss Parchment.'

Miss Parchment sighed. 'Ah—well, that's a relief.'

'Why are you so anxious to keep your identity a secret from Scotland Yard?'

'I think you know the answer to that question, Mr. Temple.'

'Yes,' he replied. 'Yes, I think perhaps I do.'

Suddenly, with what was almost a cry of despair, he said: 'Miss Parchment – you've got to help me find Steve Trent!'

The retired schoolmistress smiled. 'I'll help you, Mr. Temple,' she said. 'But first, tell me. Do you know why I am interested in old English inns?'

'Yes,' Temple replied earnestly. 'Yes, I know. Although I must confess I was rather puzzled at first. During the last few days I have made a great many inquiries about the Cape Town–Simonstown robberies.' He paused, then went on significantly, 'I was very interested to learn that the Knave of Diamonds organized and directed his plans from a group of inns all situated in the same area. It was clever of you to assume that he would use the same procedure in this country.'

196

Paul Temple smiled. 'You should have been a detective, Miss Parchment,' he added, as an afterthought.

Miss Parchment smiled, too, then immediately afterwards her face turned serious again.

'Mr. Temple,' she said, 'I think the Commissioner intends to detain me on suspicion, especially after my unexpected presence here this evening. If you could persuade him to refrain from doing so, then I think the two of us might quite possibly stand a very good chance of finding Miss Trent.'

'Yes,' he answered slowly, 'I think that could be arranged.'

There was a slight pause before either of them spoke again. Miss Parchment seemed to be taking stock of her surroundings. At length she said quietly:

'Have you heard of "The First Penguin", Mr. Temple?'

Temple frowned. In spite of its peculiarity the name sounded vaguely familiar.

'Isn't it a small deserted inn on the river – about two miles the other side of Evesham?' he said.

The retired schoolmistress smiled. 'That's right, Mr. Temple!'

CHAPTER XXII

Ludmilla

'Hello! Oh, it's you, Max! No, no, they haven't . . . No, not even Milton . . . I'm still waiting for them . . . Yes . . . Yes, the girl's here . . . I say, Max, is everything all right? Yes. Yes, of course I'm listening . . . Salzburg? . . . I see . . . Yes, I'll tell him . . . Right! Goodbye.'

Diana Thornley replaced the telephone receiver. The look of anxiety was still pronounced on her face. It seemed to make her beauty even more striking. She was sitting in a room at 'The First Penguin'. It was an old Tudor building, but not too well preserved. A succession of owners had let it decay until there were very few visitors attracted by its tumbledown exterior. In the summer a few casual and perspiring cyclists would stop out of curiosity, but the natives of the district all made their nightly pilgrimage to the 'White Swan', which was about a quarter of a mile away on the same road.

The room was sparsely furnished with tables, chairs, an extremely large sideboard, and a dilapidated settee.

The inn itself was built directly on the water's edge, and even from the inside could be heard the sound of the water lapping against the walls. In front of 'The First Penguin' was a neglected garden that a more enterprising proprietor would have turned into a car park.

Diana Thornley appeared ill at ease, and judging from the number of times she glanced towards the door, was obviously expecting someone.

Finally she flung herself down on the settee, and picked up an early edition of the local paper. Suddenly the door opened, and Diana dropped the paper with a start of astonishment.

'You're late!'

It was Dr. Milton who appeared.

'We had a hell of a game with one of the cars,' he answered.

'Where's Dixie and the others?' she demanded sharply.

'They should be here soon.'

'Did you get the stuff all right?' she continued.

'Yes,' Dr. Milton replied. 'I say,' he added suddenly, 'what happened about that girl, Steve Trent?'

'She's here.'

'Here?' he echoed incredulously.

'Yes.'

'That's a bit silly, isn't it?'

'It was the Chief's orders to bring her back here,' Diana Thornley explained. 'That's all I know.'

'Did you have any trouble with her?'

'At first,' she answered, with a determined smile. 'We were nearly picked up in Bond Street – she screamed like hell!'

Dr. Milton grunted. He looked round the room, and suddenly became aware of the bottles and decanters that, together with a siphon and glasses, invited use from the sideboard.

'By gosh!' he exclaimed, 'I could do with a drink. No, I'll mix it,' he added, as Diana got up and began to walk over to the sideboard. He poured out a liberal helping of whisky, added a little soda water, and carried the drink back to the armchair he had selected.

'Dixie was very good tonight,' he said; 'he worked like a trojan.'

Diana had been looking thoughtfully at the doctor. 'I'm glad you arrived first, Doc,' she said. 'I wanted to talk with you.'

'Yes,' said Dr. Milton quietly. 'I wanted to see you, too. That's why I came on ahead.'

The girl glanced at him with a surprised look on her face. 'Oh,' she exclaimed. 'What did you want to see me about?'

Dr. Milton hesitated a moment before he spoke. 'Can't you guess?' he queried.

'No.'

Again he paused, as though making up his mind.

'Then I'll tell you,' he said, with a quizzical smile. 'Six months ago, my dear Miss Thornley, you and the gentleman who prefers to call himself the Knave of Diamonds, picked me off a somewhat dilapidated tramp steamer where, partly through certain misfortunes for which I can assure you I was not to blame, I was acting as a sort of, er, shall we say, general practitioner? Indeed, not to put too fine a point on it, I was down and out!'

He paused. Diana Thornley appeared a little bewildered by this new attitude. She sat quietly watching him.

'Well?' she prompted, at last.

'Well, Miss Thornley—' he broke off. 'By the way,' he suddenly added, 'I think I'll call you Ludmilla. Miss Thornley is a trifle—'

He was not allowed to complete the sentence.

'No one calls me Ludmilla!' she interrupted, and there was no mistaking the determination in her voice. 'No one, except Max!'

Dr. Milton hesitated before he replied. 'Very well, then,' he said at last, 'it shall be Diana. Well, Diana, whereas six months ago I shouldn't have given a twopenny damn about what happened to me, today I find myself in the rather unique position, for me, at any rate, of looking forward to the future.'

'I still don't understand,' came the reply.

'What I am trying to say is this. I sincerely hope that our mutual friend, the Knave of Diamonds, has no intention of depriving me of that future.'

Diana Thornley appeared a little worried.

'Why should you think that?'

'Oh, no particular reason,' he replied. 'But you see, unlike Dixie and Horace, and, of course, Snow, there are times when I find myself doing quite a spot of thinking. This evening, I regret to say, was one of those occasions.'

'Well?'

'Well, Diana,' the doctor continued, 'oddly enough, my thoughts this evening took a rather, shall we say, creative turn of mind?'

Diana looked puzzled, and not a little worried.

'Creative turn of mind?' she echoed.

'Yes,' he replied calmly. 'I wrote a letter. A long letter. Beautifully phrased and charmingly written.'

His ironical words were not wasted. 'I wish to God you'd talk sense!' the girl burst out angrily.

'Very well, then,' went on Dr. Milton, in a more businesslike voice. 'If, by any chance, I happen to have an unfortunate, er, accident, either now or in the near future, my beautifully

phrased, charmingly written letter will be delivered straight
into the hands of the Home Secretary. You will observe
that I say the Home Secretary, Miss Thornley – and not
Scotland Yard.'

'What's in that letter?' she asked desperately.

Dr. Milton began to laugh. 'Shall we leave that to the
imagination?' he asked.

'You damned fool!' she burst out furiously. 'If that
letter—'

'The letter, I assure you, is quite safe!' said Dr. Milton,
calmly interrupting her. 'It will neither be posted nor opened,
except, of course, in what I, at any rate, would regard as an
unpleasant emergency.'

Diana Thornley's eyes were blazing with fury. 'Max has no
intention of double-crossing you!' she exclaimed, with venom
in her voice. 'You've been far too valuable. We respect both
your intelligence and your courage.' She hesitated a fraction
before going on. 'But the others, well—'

'What about the others?' asked Dr. Milton.

Diana hesitated. Then, very slowly, she answered. 'They've
got to go.'

'Why?'

'You know perfectly well why! We're coming to the end
of our rope. Things are getting a bit too hot. They've got a
warrant out for every one of us, excepting the Chief. Temple
overheard our meeting in Room 7 on Thursday. That's why
Max switched our meeting to this place.'

Dr. Milton whistled with surprise. It was no pleasant
prospect that he had to face, and his brow clouded as he
gradually became aware of the full implications.

'If any of the other three are picked up they'll talk,'
continued Diana Thornley. 'We can't take that chance.'

Dr. Milton pondered over her words for a second or so. 'No,' he replied at last. 'Perhaps you're right.'

'Max wants us to leave for Austria almost immediately,' Diana Thornley went on. 'He'll join us later.'

The doctor sat still for a few moments, sipping his drink. Suddenly he looked up. 'Do the boys know about the Salzburg hideout?' he asked.

'I'm afraid so,' she answered. 'That's what makes them so dangerous.'

Dr. Milton murmured assent. 'What about the girl?'

'Which girl?' asked Diana.

'This girl here,' he replied impatiently. 'Steve Trent.'

'The Chief will take care of her,' she told him. 'Don't worry.'

He pondered over the fate of the luckless reporter. 'Why did he bring her here?' he said. 'What's the point?'

'She's Harvey's sister,' came the casual reply.

'Harvey!' Dr. Milton whistled softly. You mean the 'tec Horace murdered at "The Little General"?'

'Yes.'

'I'm beginning to see daylight,' said Dr. Milton slowly. 'So Superintendent Harvey had a sister. . .. I didn't know that.'

'No,' said Diana. 'And neither did the Knave until Mr. Paul Temple kindly supplied the information.'

'Paul Temple!' exclaimed Dr. Milton. The name brought back to his mind the undertaking he had already made. 'I've still got that little matter to attend to.'

'Don't worry about Temple,' she told him. 'While we've got the girl his hands are tied.'

Dr. Milton grunted. He walked over to the window and peered into the outer darkness. Then he turned back into the room.

'Have you heard from the Chief?' he asked, as he pulled back the curtains.

'Yes. He rang through shortly before you arrived. He wanted to know about the Malvern job.'

'I think we might have difficulty getting some of the stuff out of the country.'

'We can deal with that later. But, first of all, there's this other business. . . .'

'You mean—' Dr. Milton hesitated. 'The gang . . .?'

'Yes.'

For a few minutes there was silence. Dr. Milton bent forward, his head in his hands. He was deep in thought. Diana Thornley watched him closely, a slight hint of satisfaction curling her lips. The plans on which she had determined were beginning to take effect.

Suddenly the doctor turned. He had made up his mind. His hands deep in his trousers' pockets, he towered above Diana Thornley.

'Leave everything to me,' he said to her decisively. He glanced behind him. 'Is—is the trapdoor working?' he asked.

'Yes. And the river's pretty high.' The smug look of satisfaction on her face became even more pronounced as she spoke.

'Good,' he replied. He turned round and walked over to a recess in the wall. He drew back the curtains which hung down from the ceiling, and revealed a large wooden flap built into the wall. It was some four feet high, and about the same width. The bottom of the flap hung over the floor. A glistening film over the rusty hinges on top showed that they had been newly oiled. It was the trapdoor of which Dr. Milton had spoken.

'Give me a hand,' he said to his companion, as he loosened the catches that fastened the trapdoor down to the floor. The pair knelt down and pushed hard at the flap. It refused to move. Dr. Milton leaned against it with all his weight, while Diana Thornley pushed as hard as she could.

This time their efforts were more than sufficient to open it. They held it up, and looked down to the murky water of the river below. The trapdoor was built of solid wood, and its heavy weight was increased by the iron supports which gave it strength. It was no easy matter to hold it up. They listened for a few moments to the sounds of the water lapping against the walls of the inn. Then they gently lowered the flap again.

The trapdoor clearly dated from the days when the inn received its supplies from the river. A rusty iron or steel beam projected from the wall with a worn pulley at the end. It was some elementary form of crane which must once have been used for hauling up goods from vessels in the river below. There were also bolts and brackets by which the heavy flap could be held up while the process of loading and unloading took place.

'Not a very pleasant part of the river, Doctor,' remarked Diana Thornley.

Dr. Milton laughed. It was not a happy laugh. 'No,' he replied. 'But it's going to prove useful.' He became more thoughtful. 'Snow will be the first here. Horace and Dixie are coming together.'

'What are you going to do?'

Dr. Milton looked amused. 'You'll soon see,' he told her. He pushed the trapdoor backwards and forwards. In spite of its weight, it could easily be swung to and fro. Only when it was pushed right up did its weight become apparent. There was enough space to push things through without great difficulty. Dr. Milton indicated as much with a graphic gesture.

'They know about the trapdoor, you know,' Diana Thornley remarked. 'It won't be a surprise.'

'I think it will,' said Dr. Milton smoothly. 'The way I shall handle the situation.' He paused. 'Where's the bottle of whisky?'

Diana handed it to him.

'Good. Now we'll each have a drink handy on the table.'

He poured whisky into their glasses, long since emptied, and placed them on the table. Then he opened one of the doors in the sideboard and took out three more glasses. These he put on a tray on the sideboard near the siphon and the bottles.

The latter included sherry and gin. Dr. Milton looked at them for a moment, then picked them up and put them into the cupboard of the sideboard from which he had just taken out the glasses.

Only the bottle of whisky was left. Then he took up his valise which he had left at hand on a chair and opened it. After inspecting its contents for a few moments, he took out a small dark green bottle bearing a red label. Diana Thornley followed his every movement with curiosity.

'What's that small bottle?' she asked him.

Dr. Milton smiled. 'I'm going to add a little extra "kick" to the whisky, my dear, that's all. I think our friends will find it stimulating.'

He unscrewed the stopper and, through a small funnel which he had also taken out of his case, poured its contents into the whisky.

'What is it?' Diana Thornley persisted.

The slight intangible smile spread across Dr. Milton's face. 'I don't think you'd be any the wiser, my dear, if I told you.' Suddenly he became grave again. 'When Snow arrives, be drinking. At all costs, he mustn't suspect anything.'

'No, ah right, but . . . What's that?'

They both stopped to listen. Outside, they could hear the scrunch of a car's tyre on the gravel of the drive leading up to the inn. Then it stopped. A moment or two later, the engine was switched off and they heard the door of the car open and shut, followed by footsteps. The first of their visitors had arrived.

CHAPTER XXIII

A Surprise for Temple

'It must be Snow!' said Dr. Milton. A quick stride took him to the window. He drew the curtains and tried to see through the thick white mist that had spread from the river. Diana Thornley joined him. But neither of them could distinguish more than a dim figure near the car. Then, suddenly, the mist cleared for a moment and showed them a thin man walking towards the entrance to the inn.

'It's Dixie!' Dr. Milton exclaimed.

'Isn't Horace with him?' Diana Thornley asked, as she tried to make out the figure of the other man they were expecting.

'No. He must be coming with Snow later. That's funny—' Dr. Milton hesitated. He looked rather worried. 'Why, I was absolutely—' Again he stopped, as Dixie entered the inn. 'Here he is!' he exclaimed suddenly. 'You know what to do.'

They walked back to the centre of the room and waited for Dixie to come in.

Both were sitting down and Dr. Milton had picked up a newspaper and was casually turning over its pages when Dixie arrived.

'Hello, Dixie. I thought you were coming with Horace?'

'No,' said Dixie, as he glanced round the room. 'We've had a hell of a game. They must have got the alarm out pretty snappy. A rozzer stopped us on the outskirts of Malvern.'

'What happened?' demanded Milton.

'Well—' Dixie found it apparently too much to continue the sentence.

The doctor glanced at him sharply. 'You didn't . . .?'

Dixie interrupted his alarmed request. 'Yes. Snow let him have it!'

'You blasted fool, Dixie!' shouted Milton in a blind fury. 'Why–'

But even the normally nonchalant Dixie was not inclined to take this calmly. 'It's all very well talking,' he said angrily. 'We were in a jam.'

The doctor glared at him. Presently he spoke, this time more calmly.

'Why did you change cars?'

'Snow was all shot to pieces,' Dixie informed him. 'He couldn't drive properly.' He paused, then suddenly added: 'I say, I feel like a drink.' As he spoke, he glanced at the whisky bottle and the glasses.

But Dr. Milton had not been listening too carefully. The shooting of the policeman more than occupied his thoughts. It took him a moment or two to realize that not only did he intend Dixie to drink some of the whisky, but that Dixie was actually playing into his hands by asking for a drink.

'Oh, yes,' he said. And he pushed the tray over towards Dixie. 'Help yourself.'

Dixie took the bottle and poured himself nearly half a tumblerful of the amber fluid. He felt he needed something to pull himself together again.

'My God!' he exclaimed as he pressed the lever of the siphon and watched the soda water spurt into his glass, 'Snow was in a state; we couldn't do anything with him.'

'Is Horace all right?' asked Dr. Milton.

'Yes,' replied Dixie. He took the glass from the table and was about to drink. Suddenly he stopped. There was another question he had to ask. 'I say,' he asked suddenly, 'have you heard from the Chief?'

The doctor nodded. 'He's ringing again later.'

Dixie paused. His thoughts flew back to the 'job' he had just finished. 'This is the biggest thing I've ever tackled,' he said. 'It was one of those—'

But Dr. Milton was not anxious for any detailed account of the robbery. That could come later. There was more important work to be done. While Dixie was still talking, he lifted his glass and said quietly: 'Cheerio, Dixie!'

Dixie was not slow in accepting the hint. He was desperately anxious for a drink and quickly took up his glass.

'Cheers, Doc,' he answered. Dixie's throat was dry and he was obviously in a nervous condition. He gulped down half the glass. But as he swallowed, he stood motionless. His face became screwed up. Slowly he drew his tongue over his lips. He looked first at Dr. Milton, then at Diana. Both were staring curiously at him.

'I say,' he suddenly burst out, 'what the 'ell is the matter with this . . . with this—' He broke off. He took up his glass and looked closely at what remained of the whisky. 'I say, Doc, my throat . . . It's—'

Diana Thornley and Dr. Milton were standing up, still watching him closely. Neither of them spoke. Dixie had put his glass down on the table again. Suddenly he began to claw at his collar in desperation trying to pull it away from his throat.

211

'Doc!' he suddenly shrieked. 'Doc! What is it?' He was desperately alarmed. His eyes, in a lifeless glaze, were fixed on Milton. Now he was holding his forehead, now pressing his fingers deep into his throat, so deep that white marks were left.

'What is it, Doc?' he repeated. 'Oh, God!' he moaned. Then suddenly he collapsed. He had been standing close to the table. During the last second or two he had taken hold of it for support, but even with the support of the table his legs seemed unable to bear the strain. His knees bent forward and he sagged to the ground. As he did so, his chin struck the edge of the table. He lay on his side, groaning, his hands still feeling his forehead and his neck. But there was little life in them now. They could only make aimless movements.

Dr. Milton and Diana had been watching him as though in a stupor. The doctor was the first to recover. He shook himself, as though to throw off the thought of the murder he was committing, and turned to the girl.

'Help me with the trapdoor!' he said briskly. 'Quickly!'

They drew back the curtains they had closed a little while before and knelt down against the flap in the wall. Gradually they opened it, until they had swung it outwards and fixed it with the old bolts.

'Good!' exclaimed Dr. Milton. 'No, I'll attend to him,' he added, as Diana Thornley stepped towards the moaning form of Dixie. 'Now listen – go downstairs and drive his car round to the back. We don't want the others to see it when they arrive.'

'Yes, all right,' she replied. She walked swiftly to the door and closed it behind her. A moment later Dr. Milton heard the sounds of the self-starter followed by the scrunch of gravel as Diana Thornley drove the car to the back of the inn, where it would be hidden from view. He turned to look at the man on the floor beneath him. After a moment's reflection he knelt down beside him. There was little of value in any of his pockets, so Milton started rolling the body along the floor towards the trapdoor.

A last push and Dixie was on his way to the river. Dr. Milton peered after him. Dimly he could make out the black shape falling down to the water below. Suddenly he heard the terrific splash for which he was waiting.

Dr. Milton drew back into the room, pushed back the bolts and lowered the trapdoor into position again. Then he stood up and pulled back the curtains. As he was doing so, he heard a car drive up outside. The noise of the tyres over the gravel stopped, the engine was switched off and an instant later, he heard the car door. At the same moment, Diana Thornley reappeared.

'Here's Snow and Horace!' she exclaimed breathlessly.

'Yes. I gathered that,' replied Dr. Milton. As he spoke, he hurried back to the centre of the room and proceeded to remove Dixie's glass out of sight, so that their suspicions should not be aroused. 'Did they see you moving the car?' he asked.

'No.'

Both looked round the room to make sure all was in order.

'You know what to do?' said Dr. Milton.

Diana Thornley turned towards the curtain hiding the trapdoor. As she did so, Dr. Milton noticed her shudder. Callous as she might be, this girl was not entirely inhuman, he reflected.

'Is . . . Is Dixie . . .?'

'Yes,' he answered as she paused, unable to complete the sentence. 'Now be careful,' he went on in practical tones.

'We must make certain they both drink about the same time or—'

Diana Thornley brought her finger to her lips. 'Here they are,' she whispered.

The door opened and Horace Daley appeared, together with Snow Williams.

Horace looked rather nervous. 'Hello, Doc,' he said. He glanced round the room and nodded to Diana Thornley. Then both men walked in.

'Hello, Horace,' answered the doctor. 'Where's Dixie?' he asked.

'Dixie,' echoed Horace Daley. The question obviously surprised him. 'Hasn't he arrived?'

'No,' replied Milton quietly. 'Why – did he come on ahead?'

'Yes,' put in Snow, now speaking for the first time.

'That's funny,' commented the doctor.

Diana Thornley had been standing away from the little group. Now she walked over towards them. 'I thought he was coming with you, Horace?' she asked.

'Yes – we 'ad a bit of bother, an' changed over. Well, 'ere's the sparklers!'

He put the little attaché case he had been carrying on to the table. The others watched him closely.

'Is that all the stuff?' asked Dr. Milton.

'Yes. I think so.' He opened the case and revealed to their gaze a quantity of glittering diamonds. These he proceeded to scoop out with his hands and deposit on the table. 'Blimey!' he suddenly exclaimed. 'Look at that diamond!' It was a magnificent stone hanging as a pendant from a thin platinum chain.

Dr. Milton ignored his remark. 'Did you stick to the list the Chief gave you?' he asked abruptly.

'He didn't give *me* the list,' was the answer. 'It was Dixie.' The mention of Dixie's name brought his former thoughts flashing back into his mind. 'I say, it's funny 'e isn't 'ere, ain't it?' he added.

'Perhaps he got nervy after that spot of bother we had,' put in Snow.

Dr. Milton interrupted him. He spoke quietly and without thinking. 'It was a pity you shot that policeman, Snow,' he said. 'He's almost—'

'I couldn't help it!' exclaimed Snow a little nervously. 'He was standing there, so . . . damned sure of 'imself, and then—'

''Ere, just a minute!' exclaimed Horace Daley. He had lifted his head sharply when Dr. Milton spoke. 'Just a minute, Doc! 'Ow did you know Snow bumped a rozzer off?'

Milton immediately realized the mistake he had made. 'How did I know?' he repeated, trying to gain time to think. 'Why—'

But Diana Thornley was equal to the situation. While the doctor had been taken aback, she put in calmly: 'The Chief rang up just before you arrived. He told us.'

Horace Daley blinked at her suspiciously. 'Blimey!' he exclaimed. 'News don't 'alf travel! Why, we 'ardly—'

A sudden, piercing scream cut short what Horace was about to say. Steve Trent was suddenly making herself heard from upstairs.

All four looked at the door. Diana and Milton both tried to appear nonchalant. Snow was the first to speak.

'What's that?' he asked suddenly.

''Oo the 'ell is it?' demanded Horace Daley with equal surprise, and certainly greater emphasis.

'It's all right,' Dr. Milton hastened to reassure them. 'Nothing to be alarmed about. Diana,' he added, turning to her, 'take this handkerchief; tie it tight this time. See that she can't talk.'

'Yes, all right.' Diana Thornley took the large silk hand-kerchief Dr. Milton had taken out of his pocket and quickly left the room.

'Who is it?' asked Horace Daley again. 'Who's upstairs?'

'Steve Trent,' Dr. Milton explained. 'She's a reporter on *The Evening Post.*'

'A reporter? Then what the 'ell is she doin' 'ere? You've picked a ruddy good time to 'ave a reporter 'angin' abaht!'

'There's nothing to get alarmed about, Horace,' said the doctor smoothly. 'It was the Chief's orders to bring her back here – that's all we know.' Suddenly he changed his tone and added more briskly: 'What you boys want is a drink. Help yourself, Snow.'

Snow showed his appreciation of the invitation.

'Oh, thanks, Doc,' he said.

'Go on, Horace,' the doctor urged.

'Thanks,' said Horace Daley. 'I don't mind if I do.'

Snow poured himself out a glass of whisky, and then passed the bottle to Horace Daley who followed his example. He was adding soda when the door opened and Diana reappeared with a smile of satisfaction over her face.

'Well,' she said brightly, 'we shan't hear any more from that young lady for a little while.'

'The boys are having a drink, Diana,' remarked Dr. Milton quietly.

'And they deserve it,' she replied warmly. Diana walked over to the table and picked up the diamond to which Horace Daley had already referred. 'This diamond is a whopper,' she said. 'Why, it must be worth a cool—'

'Blimey!' It was Horace Daley interrupting her, 'I almost forgot,' he said quickly. 'I got another packet outside – Dixie 'anded it to me when we switched cars. Shan't be a second!'

'No, just a minute, Horace,' said Dr. Milton, laying a restraining hand on his arm, 'you can finish your—'

But Horace Daley pulled himself free. 'Back in a jiffy, Doc,' he said, as he disappeared through the door.

'He's a hot-headed devil is 'orace!' remarked Snow.

'Yes,' said Dr. Milton quietly.

'Well, cheerio, Doc,' said Snow raising his glass. There was about an inch and a half of the spirit at the bottom of the glass. He was drinking it neat. He looked at them both and smiled.

'Strewth, I feel queer, Doc!' he exclaimed, putting the glass down on the small table. 'Bit . . . bit close in here, isn't . . . isn't —it?' He was finding it difficult to speak. Already he was struggling for breath. Then, as Dixie had done, his hands came hurriedly to his throat.

'Doc!' he suddenly burst out, 'my throat . . . it's—'

He stood still, his chest slowly rising and falling. Suddenly he flung out his arms and fell with his face to the floor.

Dr. Milton was standing in readiness. Quietly, and as efficiently as if he were a porter dealing with some fairly heavy luggage, he began to roll the body towards the curtain.

'What about Horace?' asked Diana Thornley suddenly.

'We'll look after Horace,' he replied grimly.

'You'd better search him,' she suggested, as he got the body to the curtains and was pushing it through the gap between them.

'We haven't time,' was the brief answer. 'Here,' he continued, 'help me with this trapdoor . . . Ah, that's done it,' he said at last, with relief.

He pushed the body of Snow hard against the trapdoor and then, with Diana Thornley's help, contrived to make enough space for him to fall through. The trapdoor slammed and an instant later they heard the splash as Snow reached the river.

'What are you going to tell Horace?' asked Diana Thornley, as they got up and hastened back to the middle of the room.

'I don't know,' he replied thoughtfully. 'We'll tell him Snow's upstairs with the girl.'

'Mm . . . we'd better fill Snow's glass again or—'

But there was no time. 'Here he is,' remarked Dr. Milton as footsteps could be heard outside.

The door opened, and Horace Daley reappeared.

'Blimey!' he started, 'I don't know what's the matter with me. I must be imagining things. I could 'ave sworn Dixie slipped me a packet when we—' He broke off. ''Ello, where's Snow?' he asked suddenly, after glancing round the room.

'He's upstairs talking to the girl,' said Dr. Milton casually.

'Coo,' replied Horace. ''Oo the 'ell does 'e think 'e is, Clark Gable?'

'He'll be down in a minute,' said Dr. Milton, beginning to laugh. 'Here's your drink, Horace.'

'Oh, thanks,' he replied.

'Cheerio!' said Dr. Milton, drinking from his glass.

'Cheerio, Doc.' But the little Cockney did not drink. Dr. Milton looked at him expectantly.

'Why don't you drink?' he asked at last.

'I'm thinking of that rozzer,' Horace replied. 'I 'ope to Gawd Snow did 'im in proper. 'E 'ad a good decko at us.'

'You're nervy, Horace. What you want is a good, stiff drink.'

'Perhaps you're right, Doc.'

For a few moments nobody spoke. Horace Daley seemed to be listening intently. Now and again he glanced curiously towards the door.

'What's the matter, Horace?' asked Dr. Milton at last.

'I'm listening, that's all,' he replied. 'Can't 'ear voices.'

'Why should you hear voices?'

'Why, Snow, o' course. You said he was upstairs.'

'Well,' said Dr. Milton in pleasant tones, 'perhaps he's not talking just now.'

'Then what the 'ell is 'e doin'?' asked Horace Daley abruptly.

Diana Thornley began to laugh. 'You certainly are jumpy, Horace,' she remarked.

'For a man who's just made the best part of a cool five thousand, you don't seem very bright, Horace,' added Dr. Milton.

Horace Daley jerked his head forward. 'Five thousand?' he queried.

'That's right,' said Dr. Milton hurriedly. 'That's going to be your cut of the Malvern job, isn't it, Diana?' he went on, turning to her.

'That's what the Chief said,' she emphasized.

A broad smile spread slowly across Horace Daley's face as the full significance of this sum dawned on him.

'Five thousand smackers!' he said with delight. He clapped his hands together. 'That's what I call money!'

'It's what we all call money, Horace,' said Milton brightly.

Horace Daley began to laugh with glee. 'Blimey!' he exclaimed. 'Will I paint the town red!'

'Well, here's luck,' said Dr. Milton, drinking again.

'Thank you, Doc.'

'Drink up, Horace,' added Diana in what was intended to be a gay voice, but which somehow sounded a little strained.

Still he did not drink.

'Five . . . thousand!' said the little Cockney slowly. 'Coo, fair takes your breath away, don't it, Doc?'

The doctor began to laugh. 'It certainly seems to have taken your breath away. What the devil's the matter with you, Horace? Are you on the wagon?'

'On the wagon?' he echoed, with a perplexed frown on his face.

'Yes,' put in Diana Thornley. 'You're not drinking, Horace.'

'Oh! On the wagon!' he repeated again, this time with enlightenment on his face. He burst out laughing. 'Can you imagine it, Doc? Me—on the wagon! That's good! That's good!'

'Horace on the wagon,' said Diana at last. 'That's certainly funny—'

'I was only on it once, Doc,' he said. 'But I couldn't see straight.'

'Cheerio!' said Diana when the laughter eventually died down.

'Cheerio, Diana,' replied Dr. Milton, and raised his glass. But still Horace did not drink. They looked at him curiously.

'Drink up, Horace.' It was Milton who spoke.

There was a long pause. The three stood around the table facing each other. Horace Daley looked from one to the other.

'Why aren't you drinking?' said Dr. Milton seriously.

For a moment the innkeeper did not answer. Suddenly he straightened himself and pulled a large automatic from his pocket.

'Because I'm not a damned fool, Doc!' he answered sharply. 'Stand away from that door!' he added suddenly, as Dr. Milton took a step backwards.

'Put that gun down, Horace,' said Milton. 'Don't be a young idiot.'

'Stand away from that door!' shouted Horace Daley desperately, 'or I'll blow your blarsted brains out!' A grin spread slowly across his face. 'Drink up, Horace!' he said, mimicking the doctor's persuasive tones. 'Are you on the wagon, Horace? Cheerio, Horace!' He began to laugh, deeply, throatily. Suddenly he became serious again. "Ere!' he said sharply. 'Take this glass, Doc! Take it!'

Dr. Milton's calm vanished. A look of horror came over him. 'No!' he answered desperately. 'No!'

'What 'ave you done with Dixie and Snow?' There was no mistaking the desperation in Horace's voice.

'I tell you, we haven't seen Dixie!' Milton replied. But his voice shook slightly.

'Don't tell your blarsted lies! His car's at the back!'

'Now listen, Horace,' said Milton, his voice persuasive again, 'if you take my tip—'

'I'm taking nothing from you or anybody else,' interrupted Horace savagely. 'I'm giving the orders, see! Now drink this!' He stretched out his glass, while the gleaming black automatic in his other hand remained pointed at the doctor.

'No!' exclaimed Dr. Milton in alarm. 'No!'

'Drink it!'

'Here, I'll drink it, Horace.' It was Diana Thornley speaking.

'You!' he exclaimed, turning in astonishment.

'There's nothing in the glass except whisky,' said Diana quietly. 'Give me the glass and I'll prove it!'

'All right! All right, Miss Clever! If that's how you feel about it—' Horace stretched the glass across the table towards her.

'Thank you!' she said, taking it from him. 'Well, cheerio, Doc!'

She raised it, but did not drink. Suddenly, taking advantage of Horace's amazement, she dashed the contents of the glass into his face. As he threw up his hands in an instinctive effort to protect himself, Dr. Milton raised his arm, and brought his hand down heavily on Horace's head. The groaning body became silent and lay still.

'Smart girl!' said Dr. Milton.

'What did you hit him with?' she asked.

'This revolver!' The doctor disclosed a black weapon which was as dangerous as it looked. 'I had it in my hand all the time, but I was frightened to shoot.'

Diana Thornley looked down at the prostrate figure.

She noticed that he was still breathing, 'He's not dead!' she remarked.

'No, but we'll soon—' Milton broke off. 'What's that?' he added, looking towards the window.

Outside they heard the sound of an approaching car. They looked puzzled and anxious.

'Well, who the devil can that be?' asked Dr. Milton abruptly. They both ran to the window and peered into the darkness. Dimly they could see the outline of a car. A figure was moving away from it towards the inn. Suddenly Diana Thornley drew in her breath sharply.

'Why—' she stammered, 'why, it's that woman . . . Miss Parchment!'

'Miss Parchment!' echoed Milton. 'Is she alone?' he asked.

'Yes. As far as I can see.'

Dr. Milton turned back from the window. There was work to be done in the room. 'Open that cupboard door!' he said. 'We'll push Horace in there!'

'What about the river? Can't—'

Milton cut her short. 'No. We haven't time. It's all right. It'll be a hell of a time before he comes round.'

In one corner of the room a cupboard had been built into the wall. It was wide enough to take a man lying full length, and Dr. Milton opened its door. Then, with Diana Thornley's help, he contrived to drag Horace Daley across the floor. There was no time to be lost, but at last they had the innkeeper inside.

'I say, Doc!' said the girl, thoughtfully, as they walked away, 'who the devil is this woman?'

'Don't ask me!'

'She seems to be turning up all over the place. First she was at "The Little General". Then she was at the Yard when Skid was bumped off, and now she's—'

'I reckon she's a 'tec,' put in Dr. Milton.

'Then what's she doing here?'

'Probably trying to find Steve Trent.'

'Mm.. . . Well, she's got some nerve; I'll say that for her!'

'And she'll need it!' Dr. Milton paused. 'Listen! She's coming through the bar parlour!'

They could hear Miss Parchment moving about in the next room.

'Stand away from the door!' said Milton quietly.

Diana moved back. The doctor seized the knob and suddenly flung the door open. He stood face to face with his unexpected visitor.

'Good evening, Miss Parchment!' he said with sarcastic politeness. The revolver, with which he had just rendered Horace Daley unconscious, was now pointing straight at Miss Parchment, but she appeared completely unconcerned by it.

'Why, Dr. Milton!' she exclaimed, with what seemed the most genuine pleasure. 'How very nice!'

'Come in here!' he ordered sharply. 'And drop that handbag! Drop it!' he added more sharply, as she took no notice of him.

She hesitated a moment, looking from one to the other. 'Very well,' she said finally. She put it down unconcernedly on a nearby chair.

'I do hope that gun isn't loaded, Doctor!' said Miss Parchment with a calm plaintiveness in her voice. 'Your hand is quite shaky, and . . .'

Dr. Milton interrupted her sharply. 'Miss Parchment!' he started. 'What are you doing here . . . at "The First Penguin"?'

There were traces of a smile on Miss Parchment's lips as she replied with perfect calm: 'Well, really, Doctor, your tone of voice!'

'Miss Parchment!' This time his tone was sharp and menacing, and Miss Parchment seemed to realize it.

'I—I came to see a friend.'

'Which friend?'

'A Miss Trent. A Miss Steve Trent. Now don't tell me you've never heard of her?' she added, the faint smile coming back again.

Diana Thornley now spoke for the first time. 'How did you know Steve Trent was here?' she asked deliberately.

'How did I know. . .? A bird told me, Miss Thornley.' Diana Thornley looked at her sharply, not so much because of the queer humour with which Miss Parchment addressed them, but because she knew her name. It was, as far as Diana Thornley knew, the first time they had met.

'Not a little bird,' Miss Parchment was saying. 'Shall we say a pigeon?'

An idea suddenly struck Diana Thornley. 'Doc!' she exclaimed. 'She's only stalling for time. There's something in the wind. There's . . .'

As she spoke, the door suddenly opened. Her premonition was justified. It was Paul Temple.

'Drop that gun, Milton!' he ordered in a voice that brooked no denial.

'Temple!' Meekly the doctor put the revolver on the table, but his face blazed with anger.

'How the devil did you get here?' asked Diana Thornley.

'I came with Miss Parchment,' answered Temple. 'I regret not having joined you earlier, but I had a little difficulty in locating Miss Trent.'

Dr. Milton looked round, and became aware that his late prisoner had come quietly into the room behind Paul Temple.

Steve looked as fresh as ever. But, nevertheless, she clearly showed what she had been through. Her dress was torn, and her wrists showed the marks of the rope that had bound her. On her forehead was a deep cut on which the blood had now dried. Yet in spite of it all, Steve managed to look her crisp, attractive self. There was no hint even of the relief she must have been feeling, nor of the triumph that was justifiably hers.

'Steve!' continued Paul Temple briskly, never for a moment relaxing his watch, ready for any sudden move either of them might make. 'Take his gun!'

'All right, Paul!' She walked to the table and picked up the gun.

'Would you mind sitting over there, Miss Thornley?'

As he spoke, Paul Temple indicated a chair with his free hand. Diana had no alternative but to comply.

'Thank you!' he continued. 'Hold this gun, Miss Parchment,' he added, handing his heavy automatic to her. 'If either of them move while Miss Trent and I are making them comfortable, well, you know what to do!'

'Oh, er, rather, Mr. Temple!' she replied with a smile.

Steve Trent had carried a coil of stout cord into the room when she entered. She now picked it up from the chair and handed it to Temple.

'Thanks,' he answered. 'Now for a dose of your own medicine, my friends!'

First he started with Diana Thornley. Deftly he twined the string round her hands, binding them securely to the chair, then round her neck, followed by her ankles. Steve Trent kept her revolver trained on her while Miss Parchment kept Dr. Milton covered.

225

In a few moments Paul Temple had completed his task and had turned to the doctor. With the same quiet efficiency, he repeated the procedure. Then he went over all the knots he had made, testing their strength and making sure that escape was out of the question.

'What's all this jewellery on the table?' asked Miss Parchment when it was all over, and she was able to lay the gun on the table.

'It's from the Malvern job, unless I'm very much mistaken!' Paul Temple explained, examining the gleaming heap.

'Yes,' said Steve Trent. 'Horace Daley and two other men arrived with it. I could hear them talking.. . . Suddenly they seemed to disappear . . . I could hear some sort of a trapdoor being opened . . . and then what sounded to me like a splash of some sort . . . I had a feeling that—'

Steve Trent was still pale from the ordeal through which she had passed. The excitement of the last few minutes had brought some colour back into her face, but now the lines of anxiety showed themselves again as she recalled what she had heard. There was no doubt what had happened.

'Oh!' remarked Paul Temple. 'Oh, that's interesting. So you've been getting rid of the small fry, eh, Doc?'

'I'll get you for this, Temple!' was the venomous answer. 'I'll get you if it takes twenty years!'

But Paul Temple ignored the threat which Dr. Milton spat out at him. He was walking round the room on a tour of inspection. He stopped when he came to the curtains, and drew them back.

'Yes,' he said. 'Here's the trapdoor all right.' With Steve's help, he pushed the trapdoor back and listened to the sound of the water below. 'By Timothy, Steve!' he exclaimed.

They slowly released the trapdoor and stood up again. Paul Temple's lips were pressed firmly together.

'Steve,' he started, 'how many people arrived here tonight?'

'Three. Horace Daley; the man who admitted us to Ashdown House that time; and the other man we heard in Room 7. I think his name was Dixie. The doctor was the first to arrive; he came alone.'

'I see.'

'Just before the doctor came, I heard the telephone. It was Max Lorraine. I could only just hear what Diana Thornley was saying, but—'

'She's lying!' Diana suddenly shrieked out. 'She's lying! She's lying, I tell you!' she repeated desperately.

Steve Trent disregarded her. 'They were obviously planning a get-away. I heard the girl mention Salzburg. When the doctor arrived, she said the Knave would ring later.'

'Later!' repeated Paul Temple. 'By Timothy, if he rings again, we might trace the call!'

'I tell you, she's lying!' shrieked Diana Thornley, all her normal composure now fallen from her. 'I tell you she's lying!'

'You blasted fool, Temple!' Dr. Milton ejaculated. 'You don't really think that—'

At that moment, the telephone bell pealed out and drowned what he was saying. A hush came over them, against which the steady repeated ringing of the bell sounded with almost terrifying vigour.

'That's . . . that's him!' said Steve at last.

'Yes,' said Paul Temple quietly. 'I'll answer it.' He went to the telephone and took off the receiver. 'Hello! Hello!'

Then he turned away from the instrument, 'What's happened?' asked Steve.

'He's rung off!'

'Did he speak – did you recognize the voice?'

'No. But we'll trace the call!' he said with determination.

He pressed the receiver hook up and down to call the exchange.

'Hello! Is that the Exchange? . . . This is Paul Temple speaking.' He spoke with great authority in his voice. 'I'm speaking for Sir Graham Forbes, the Commissioner for the Metropolitan Police. I've just received a telephone call and I want you to trace it for me . . . Yes . . . Yes, just this minute . . . It's very urgent . . . This number is, er, Evesham 9986 . . . Yes, all right.'

He replaced the receiver and turned away.

'Is—is she tracing it?' asked Steve.

'Yes.'

Nobody spoke. All seemed to feel something strange hanging over them. Paul Temple walked up and down the room. At last the bell rang and he picked up the receiver again.

'Hello! Yes, yes, speaking . . . What! What!! . . . I see . . . Thank you.'

The little group in the room had been watching him with curiosity. But he rejoined them in silence.

'Well, Mr. Temple?' Miss Parchment was the first to put the question.

'Where did the call come from?' asked Steve Trent anxiously.

Temple looked down at them. 'It came from Bramley Lodge,' he said quietly.

CHAPTER XXIV

Recovery and Escape

Steve Trent looked at Dr. Milton with a feeling of horror. There was something devilish, almost inhuman, about the way he smiled. In some queer way he seemed to be triumphing over them, even now while he was still in their power. Suddenly he became serious again. A frown came over his face and he sat still, gazing down at the floor before him. Diana Thornley remained completely unconcerned, as if their respective positions were reversed.

Paul Temple had remained at the telephone with Steve by his side. Suddenly she laid a hand on his arm.

'Hadn't you better—'

'I'll get on to Pryce and see who's at the house!' he said quietly, lifting the receiver. After giving his number he replaced it, and walked across to the window.

'Paul—' Steve Trent looked anxious.

'Yes?'

'Oh, I know this sounds silly, but . . . How long has Pryce been working for you?'

Temple laughed. 'You don't have to worry about Pryce,

Steve. He isn't the Knave of Diamonds, I assure you. He looks far too guilty after snaffling one of my cigars – or perhaps it's the cigars!'

As he spoke, the telephone bell began to peal forth again. It was the call for which he had been waiting, and Temple lifted the receiver.

'Hello! Yes . . . What? . . . Oh, but there must be . . . Out of order? Oh . . . Oh, I see. Thank you.'

'What's the matter?' asked Steve.

The novelist slowly replaced the receiver, and half turned. 'There's no reply!' he explained. 'Or rather they can't get the number . . . . There's something funny, Steve!' His face had turned extremely serious. 'Look here, we must get back to Bramley Lodge as quickly as we can . . . I must find out who's been there!'

Steve Trent's eyes were shining with excitement. 'Paul!' she burst out, 'the Knave must be someone you know – otherwise Pryce wouldn't have admitted him!'

Paul Temple padded softly backwards and forwards through the room like a jaguar bent on its prey. He felt he was nearing a final solution of the whole mystery, yet still the prime mover behind the gang eluded him. He glanced at the two chairs in which were the tightly bound forms of Dr. Milton and Diana Thornley. Of the two, only the latter appeared unruffled. From time to time she glanced at the 'doc' as if to encourage him in his fortitude. Partly through this, and partly, it seemed, through sheer fear of her, Doctor Milton kept silent. Now and again, he seemed to be on the point of speaking, on the very point of revealing the secret the three watchers would have given so much to know. But each time he began to speak, a warning glance from Diana Thornley silenced him.

Miss Parchment was thoroughly enjoying herself. She was now sitting down facing them, with Paul Temple's automatic resting on her lap, her right hand gripping it in readiness. A slight smile flickered over her face as she watched them. It was as though she were beginning to taste the sweetness of a well-deserved triumph. Suddenly Paul Temple stopped near her chair.

'Miss Parchment,' he started, 'will you stay here with Milton and the girl? . . . It's imperative that I get back to Bramley Lodge. If the Knave has been there, and he obviously has, then this is the chance we've been waiting for.'

He spoke thoughtfully, but behind his quiet tones lay determination and the knowledge that events were moving towards a rapid climax.

'Yes,' answered Miss Parchment slowly, after considering his scheme; 'yes, all right, Mr. Temple!'

Diana Thornley's eyes flashed as she listened to the proposal. 'You can't leave us here – tied up like this!' she burst out angrily.

Dr. Milton rushed in to support her. 'Listen, Temple,' he started, 'if you think—'

But their protests did not interest the novelist, and Diana, realizing the utter futility of talking to him, relapsed into silence. Only two bright spots of colour in her cheeks revealed the bafflement and anger she felt.

Paul Temple put a hand on Miss Parchment's shoulder. He stood over her encouragingly. 'Miss Parchment,' he said, 'I'll get Sir Graham to send someone here immediately I get back to the house.'

As he spoke, Diana glanced at him. A tiny cynical smile appeared on her lips for an instant, then it disappeared again, and her features again were sullen and expressionless.

'That's all right, Mr. Temple,' answered Miss Parchment. 'I shall be quite comfortable.'

'Good.' Temple glanced round the room and suddenly noticed the diamonds lying on the table. So busy had he been with other thoughts that he had almost overlooked them. 'By Timothy,' he exclaimed, 'we'd better take these! Have you a handbag, Steve?'

Steve obediently passed her handbag across. The novelist looked at it with scorn and handed it back to her. Normally he was the first to laugh at the vagaries of feminine fashions, and the monstrous size of so many ladies' handbags was an unfailing topic for his satirical pen. But on this occasion even Steve Trent's handbag could not cope with the glittering heap on the table.

Fortunately, the attaché case in which Horace Daley had originally brought the gems was still on the floor, and Temple picked it up. Then, with a parting word to Miss Parchment, he took Steve Trent by the arm and they left the room.

Outside was the car in which he had arrived earlier in the evening.

'How long should it take us?' asked Steve, as she struggled over the gravel in her light shoes.

'About twenty minutes,' he answered. 'With a bit of luck, we—' Temple suddenly stood still, his eyes fixed straight ahead of him.

Steve looked at him, puzzled. 'Paul!' she exclaimed. 'What is it?'

'I say!' he replied quietly. 'Did you see that pigeon?'

'Why, yes!' she said promptly. 'There's a courtyard at the back full of them.'

'How do you know?' There was a strange urgency in his voice as he asked the question.

'Because I could see them from the room I was in.'

'By Timothy!' whistled Temple.

His seriousness made her smile. 'Paul,' she asked earnestly, 'what's the matter?'

'The constable commented on the pigeons at "The Little General"!' he said.

'Well?' The faint smile still played over Steve Trent's face.

'Steve!' he exclaimed. 'Wait here . . . I shan't be a second. . . . Start the car!'

Steve turned with surprise to watch Temple disappear round the corner. Then she gave up the problem and walked over to the car. Very obediently, she pressed the starter button and, after a couple of turns, the engine was ticking over quietly. Steve moved over to the passenger's seat, leaving the engine to warm up gradually so that they could start away immediately Temple returned from his mysterious errand. She sat there for what seemed an interminable period. Then at last she turned round and pushed open the door as she heard his footsteps over the path.

'What's all the mystery about?' Steve demanded, as he clambered into his seat.

'Sorry to dash off like that!' he said a little breathlessly. 'But there was something I rather wanted to check up on.'

'And did you?'

'Yes. I checked up on it—'

Steve began to gurgle with laughter. 'Of all the tantalizing . . .' She stopped. Her face had suddenly become very serious as an idea occurred to her, the idea that had already occurred to Paul Temple. 'Paul!' she exclaimed. 'I've just thought – They're—they're carrier pigeons!'

'Yes, by Timothy!' was the reply. 'They're carrier pigeons all right!' Temple paused. 'And now for Bramley Lodge,' he said softly, 'and the Knave of Diamonds!'

Inside 'The First Penguin', three people listened to the roar of the engine as it sped away. They heard it with strangely mixed feelings.

CHAPTER XXV

Amelia Victoria Bellman

'Miss Parchment, listen, if you don't . . .'

Dr. Milton had grown purple with rage. Every now and then, he struggled furiously with the bonds that still bound him securely to the chair, and his failure to escape from them only served to increase his anger. Even Diana Thornley smiled at his vain efforts, while Miss Parchment kept an air of good-natured calm. She interrupted him in the sweetest of tones.

'My dear Dr. Milton!' she protested. 'If I've told you once I've told you a hundred times. There is absolutely nothing to be gained by these, er, primitive outbursts. You're staying in that chair until Mr. Temple returns, and if there's any, er, funny business, I shall press this trigger, Dr. Milton. I shall press this trigger!' she repeated a little more emphatically, waving her automatic at him.

'My God!' he shouted with a voice that filled the room. 'When I get out of this, I'll—'

'Shut up, Doc!' exclaimed Diana. Her eyes, her looks, her tone, all indicated the utter scorn she felt for his raving. She herself had accepted her capture philosophically, and even now, while she was bound to the chair, she maintained a perfect equilibrium. 'There's nothing to be gained by kicking up a hell of a row!' she continued more quietly, now that Dr. Milton was reduced to silence. 'We're in a jam and we've got to make the best of it.'

'Ah,' breathed Miss Parchment, turning to her with a happy smile, 'you have a philosophical side to your character, Miss Thornley – I congratulate you!'

Silence fell on the room. Dr. Milton was clearly trying to master his feelings. In any case, a look from Miss Parchment was enough to make him desist. She appeared quite capable of making instant use of the automatic, which was all the while firmly clasped in her hand.

Diana was sitting perfectly still with her eyes closed. She might have been asleep, but for an occasional movement. Suddenly she opened her eyes and spoke.

'Miss Parchment,' she began, 'I've come up against a great many people in my time, and a great many – shall we say – awkward situations. But, well, you're sort of different.' She paused. It was clear that Diana, too, was puzzled by the secret of Miss Parchment's work and identity. 'How do you fit into all this?' she asked at length.

'So you're puzzled, Miss Thornley?'

'Yes . . . I'm puzzled,' Diana replied. 'And so are a great many other people, for that matter. Even Max can't figure you out,' she went on more thoughtfully, 'and the Knave isn't often puzzled by people or situations.'

'That, I can well believe, Miss Thornley!'

But since Diana had now started an attempt to solve the problem provided by Miss Parchment, she was not going to stop because of an evasive answer or two. 'First of all, you turned up at "The Little General",' she continued. 'By some means or other you discovered that it was called "The Green Finger" and that it was the headquarters of our organization. How did you discover that?'

'I made it my purpose to find out, Miss Thornley,' was the reply. 'I became interested in old English inns.'

'Yes, but . . . why . . .?'

'Because,' explained Miss Parchment after a moment's pause, 'I was pretty certain that the Knave would direct his activities in much the same way as he did in Cape Town – from a group of inns all situated in the same area.'

Both Diana and Dr. Milton looked at her in amazement.

'How did you know that?' she asked quickly. 'How did you know the Knave was ever in Cape Town?'

But Miss Parchment ignored her question. '"The Little General" was an obvious choice,' she explained. 'It had been for sale quite a little while. And then there was the passage from Ashdown House . . . I heard about that quite by accident, while trying to gather information about this place.'

'Miss Parchment!' Diana Thornley spoke with eagerness, but with the same note of alarm in her voice. 'You haven't answered my question. How did you know the Knave was ever in Cape Town?'

Miss Parchment hesitated. 'Do you remember a man on the Cape Town Constabulary named Bellman, Sydney Bellman . . .?' she said.

'Why . . . why, yes . . .' Diana Thornley's amazement was so intense that she seemed unable to speak.

'The Knave,' interrupted Miss Parchment quietly, '. . . murdered . . . him—'

Miss Parchment's face, never very bright in colour, had turned a deathly white. It was as if all life had ebbed out of it.

'Why . . . why are you looking like that?' asked Diana suddenly.

The doctor had been sitting in silence, listening to Miss Parchment with amazement. He now noticed that she was trembling violently, and he was watching with no small alarm the automatic in her hand. Suddenly, he could contain himself no longer.

'Good God!' he exclaimed. 'She's shaking! Put that gun down or it'll go off! Put that gun down, or—'

'Sydney Bellman,' said Miss Parchment slowly and deliberately, completely ignoring Dr. Milton, 'was—my brother.'

'Your . . . brother . . .!' It was Diana Thornley who spoke.

Miss Parchment paused. 'And now, my dear Miss Thornley, my dear Dr. Milton,' she said slowly, 'I am going to give you exactly thirty seconds to tell me – Who is the Knave?'

She had recovered her former calm. Her little smile had returned to her face. She once again seemed to be mocking them as she spoke. But both Milton and Diana recognized her determination.

Again it was Diana Thornley who remained calm. Dr. Milton was watching the automatic and the menacing finger on its trigger.

For some second he stared at it with a fixed expression. Then he could stand the strain no longer.

'All right! All right!' he ejaculated, in a voice of abject terror. 'Put that gun down . . . my God, it'll go off! Put—'

It was Diana Thornley who cut short his confession.

'Keep your mouth shut, you swine!' she suddenly exclaimed. 'If you so much as breathe a—'

Suddenly, from the wall behind them, came a strange rustling noise.

'What's that?' demanded Miss Parchment suddenly.

Dr. Milton had turned to Diana with a look of surprise. 'It's Horace!' he exclaimed.

The little innkeeper had been lying in the cupboard where he had been dragged by the doctor and Diana Thornley. It was clear that he was now recovering consciousness and sudden hope came to both Diana and the doctor.

'If we can get him to untie—' started Diana, expressing the feelings they both shared. She came to a sudden stop. The cupboard door was slowly opening, and, as it opened, Miss Parchment levelled her automatic towards it. 'Look out, Horace!' Diana shrieked. 'Look out!'

Simultaneously, Miss Parchment fired. The crack echoed and re-echoed through the room. The acrid smoke made the doctor cough.

They saw Horace Daley crawl through into the room and pick himself up. Miss Parchment had missed. The two watched each other closely. Miss Parchment was clearly a little nervous and uncertain what to do. On the other hand, although Horace Daley had recovered consciousness, he was still dazed and striving to understand the cause of the strange scene before him.

They were standing a yard or two apart, both motionless. Horace brought his hand to his forehead and rubbed it, as if in an effort to clear the daze in which he found himself. For some seconds the two stared at each other without speaking.

Then, quite suddenly, and without warning, Horace fell sideways on to Miss Parchment. At exactly the same moment, she fired. But she fired at the spot where the innkeeper had been an instant before.

Miss Parchment's struggles were useless. In a moment or two Horace was in command of the situation. He pushed Miss Parchment away from him, and with a broad grin on his face, looked from one to the other.

Then turning round to Miss Parchment again, his face became grim and determined.

'I don't know what the 'ell you're doing 'ere!' he started. 'But get in that cupboard! Get in that cupboard!'

Miss Parchment stood still.

'Mr. Daley,' she said, 'I must ask you to—'

But the innkeeper did not intend discussing the situation.

'Get in that cupboard or—'

He stopped. Miss Parchment was paying not the slightest attention to him. He put the automatic down on the table and walked over to her. Then, gripping her arms from behind, he forced her across the room into the cupboard. She was powerless to resist. Once inside the cupboard, he turned the key so that escape was impossible. Then he walked back to the table, picked up the automatic again, and faced Diana and the doctor.

'Get this untied, Horace!' exclaimed Milton suddenly. 'Quickly!'

But Horace Daley was still too dazed to listen to his plea. ''Strewth! My head!' he groaned, as he sank down into the chair Miss Parchment had recently occupied. 'It's like a blasted furnace!'

Neither Diana Thornley nor Dr. Milton were greatly anxious that Horace should fully recover his wits before their joint purpose was carried out.

'Horace!' It was Diana who now appealed to him in a tone that was part command, part wistful anxiety. 'Untie this – quickly—'

The innkeeper laughed. Although confused, Horace nevertheless retained an unpleasantly clear memory of recent events. He had been glancing around the room, and it had not taken him very long to realize that the diamonds were no longer on the table.

''Ello!' he exclaimed. 'Where's the stuff?'

But Dr. Milton was far more anxious that he should be speedily released than that Horace should be given a full account of what had happened. 'Horace!' he exclaimed. 'For heaven's sake don't stand there! Get this rope untied. We must get out of here—'

'Quickly, Horace!' added Diana, with the same suave kindliness that she had used to persuade him to drink his glass of whisky.

'Listen, you two!' he burst out, 'where's the stuff?'

Dr. Milton made yet another appeal. 'Cut the rope free, Horace, and then—'

'I'm asking – who's got the stuff!' shouted Horace in a blind fury. 'Who's got the diamonds?'

'Horace!' exclaimed the doctor in a voice of despair. 'We've got to get out of here . . . We've got to . . . No, don't!'

The innkeeper's patience had been exhausted. With a grip of iron, he had seized Milton's wrist and was twisting his arm round, through the ropes which still bound him.

'Horace, for God's sake!' he yelled.

'Now listen, Doc!' said Horace Daley, relaxing his hold for a moment. 'If you don't tell me where the stuff is, I'll break every bone in your blasted body!' And, by way of emphasizing his words, he once again twisted the doctor's arm.

'No! No!' Then, suddenly realizing that Horace very definitely meant business, the doctor nodded. 'All right,' he gasped. He paused. 'Temple's got it. He left about ten minutes ago with the girl—'

In an instant the innkeeper had put the automatic in his pocket and was making for the door.

'Where are you going?' called out Diana in alarm.

'To get the stuff back!'

'You've got to untie us first!' begged Dr. Milton.

'That's your guess, Doc!'

'Horace, listen!' began Diana in despair, 'Temple's after the Knave – he traced a telephone call – you've got to set us free! You've got to—'

'To hell with the Knave!' interrupted Horace briefly.

Diana Thornley had grown more and more alarmed. She was now pleading with him, begging him to release them. 'You've got to get us out of here. . . . You've got to—'

'For heaven's sake, Horace,' added Dr. Milton, 'listen . . . we must . . .'

'Temple's got the diamonds!' said Horace with satisfaction. 'Right! That's all I want to know!'

Ignoring their predicament, even rejoicing in it, Horace bowed sarcastically to Dr. Milton, kissed his hand equally sarcastically to Diana Thornley, and was gone. A few seconds later they heard his car accelerate.

'The dirty, double-crossing little swine!' began Dr. Milton furiously as he listened to the car driving off. 'When I get out of here, I'll—'

Another noise interrupted him. A hand banging on the door of the cupboard. Miss Parchment was struggling to be released.

'Let me out of here!' she shrieked. 'Let me out of here! Let me out of here, I say!'

But Miss Parchment was perhaps a little too optimistic.

CHAPTER XXVI

Horace and the Bridge

'Steve . . . You haven't told me what happened?'

They were now halfway on their journey to Bramley Lodge. Temple had kept the speedometer needle hovering between the fifty and sixty mark, which was as high a speed as most optimists would have claimed fit for the road. He was far too intent on his driving to devote much attention to conversation, but nevertheless this was the first time they had been able to compare experiences since Steve Trent had been captured.

'Well, there's nothing much to tell, really,' Steve replied. 'Early this morning, I received a telephone call which was supposed to be from the paper. It sounded quite genuine – but when I got outside the flat, I noticed a saloon car. It was drawn up close to the kerb. A girl got out of the car and came across to me. I forgot now what she said . . . but before I could do anything, a man came up from behind . . . took me by the arm . . . and well, the next thing I knew was that I was sitting in the back of the car. . . .'

'Well,' replied Paul Temple, 'thank heaven Miss Parchment knew about "The First Penguin".'

'Paul!' exclaimed Steve suddenly. 'Who is Miss Parchment?'

'Her name is Bellman,' he replied. 'Amelia Bellman. She's the sister to the man who helped your brother over the Cape Town–Simonstown robberies.'

A look of bewilderment spread over Steve's face.

'Sydney Bellman!' she cried. 'But—he was murdered – by—Max Lorraine!'

'Yes,' replied Paul Temple quietly, 'and from the very moment he was murdered, Miss Parchment made up her mind to track down the Knave. She knew quite a lot about the way Lorraine worked. In fact, if the Knave had known who Miss Parchment was, then, believe me, he wouldn't have wasted his time on kidnapping Louise Harvey.'

'Does Miss Parchment know who the Knave really is?' inquired Steve, shutting her eyes as a car seemed to rush out of a side road at them, and opening them only a moment or two later after she felt their own car swerve to safety.

'No. No, she doesn't. But I think she's got a pretty shrewd idea. We raided "The Little General" tonight, but the place was deserted.' He smiled. 'Except for Miss Parchment!'

Steve showed her surprise. 'What was she doing there?'

'Apparently she'd read somewhere or other that there was a passage between Ashdown House and "The Little General".' Temple chuckled. 'And she chose tonight, of all nights, to investigate the fact!'

'It's perhaps a good job she did,' Steve replied seriously. 'Or I might still have been at "The First Penguin" – waiting for . . . Max Lorraine. . . .'

Paul Temple turned his head for a moment and looked at her, almost as if to reassure himself of her presence beside him. Then his eyes were back on the road again. They were travelling far too fast to take such chances.

'Steve,' he said earnestly, 'you don't know how glad I felt when I broke into that room and saw you there. All the way down to the inn I was . . .'

Steve interrupted him with a smile, the same quick, flashing smile that had won so many hearts. 'Well, believe me, Paul, the relief wasn't one-sided!'

For a few moments neither of them said anything. A winding stretch of road took up all Paul Temple's attention, and Steve was giving herself up to a luxurious sense of ease and relief.

'It's rather funny about Miss Parchment,' began Temple, as he straightened the wheel. 'I guessed her identity after we'd visited Ashdown House. You remember I asked you the name of the man who assisted your brother in Cape Town. . . . At first, I had a feeling that Miss Parchment might have been his wife.'

'Does Sir Graham know about Miss Parchment?' Steve inquired.

'No, I don't think so.' Temple began to laugh. 'I'm afraid there are one or two surprises on hand for Sir Graham. And you'll be one of them, Steve, unless I'm very much mistaken!'

'Why do you say that?'

'Well, when I left "The Little General", I told him I was taking Miss Parchment back to Bramley Lodge. He'll get rather a shock to learn we've visited an outlandish inn known as "The First Penguin", captured the doctor and Diana Thornley, recovered the proceeds of the Malvern robbery, and rescued you into the bargain!'

Steve smiled. 'Yes, I suppose he will,' she said. She grew serious again. 'Why didn't you tell Sir Graham you were going with Miss Parchment to "The First Penguin"?'

'I don't think that would have been too wise, Steve,' he replied, after a moment's hesitation.

Francis Durbridge

Steve directed a puzzled glance at him. 'Why do you say that?' she asked, laying a tiny hand on his arm.

'When Skid Tyler was murdered,' he explained, 'it was in Sir Graham's office at Scotland Yard. When Sir Graham and I devised a little plan about an imaginary "Trenchman" diamond, the Knave got to know about it. When we decided to raid "The Little General" tonight, the inn was deserted.'

'Paul!' exclaimed Steve suddenly. 'You don't think Sir Graham is . . . the Knave?'

'I don't know who the Knave is, Steve, but I know that he has been to Bramley Lodge tonight, and when—' Temple broke off. 'I say, that car's coming up rather quick, isn't it?' he asked abruptly, glancing into the driving mirror.

A car, which a few minutes ago had been a mere speck in the distance, was now rapidly overtaking them. Steve turned. The car was obviously being driven all out. From time to time, it seemed to slither wildly across the road. Suddenly Steve recognized it.

'Paul!' she exclaimed in alarm. 'It's one of the cars from the inn!'

'But . . . it can't be—' There was amazement in Paul Temple's voice.

'It is!' she exclaimed. 'It's the red one that—' She broke off. Nearer and nearer it came. Steve stared hard at the driver, suspecting who it must be, yet still unable to believe her senses. She leaned hard over the seat, in an effort to see the car more clearly. Suddenly she jumped back and turned to Paul Temple.

'Paul!' she shouted over the noise of the two cars. 'It's . . . Horace Daley!'

'Daley!' repeated Temple.

'He's recognized us!' Steve was still watching him closely. Suddenly she saw him take his right hand off the steering

246

wheel and move sideways to feel in his pocket. A second or two later she saw the reason.

'Paul! He's got a gun!' shrieked Steve. 'He's—Look out, Paul! Look out!'

There was a crack, and a tiny hole appeared in the windscreen between them. The bullet had entered the back window and passed straight through the car. Horace Daley's car was still some twenty yards behind them, and it was not easy for him to aim straight. Nevertheless, Steve again saw his hand reach out of the window. Before she had time to do anything, Horace had fired again. This time the bullet hit the back of the car.

Then he pulled back his arm and set out to overtake them. In a few seconds, only five or six yards separated them, and the red saloon had swung out in an attempt to pass.

But their own car had still ample power in reserve. Temple pressed his foot down hard on the accelerator, and with tremendous acceleration the car leapt forward. Soon they were a safe distance away.

'Steve, listen,' he said suddenly. 'There's a bridge round the next bend. As soon as we reach it, I'll slow down and let him overtake us. Then we'll force him over the top. It's our only chance!'

'Yes!' answered Steve eagerly. 'Yes, all right!'

'Wrap the rug round your head and keep down!'

Steve obeyed, but she still managed to peer over the top of the seat, to see what the innkeeper was doing.

'Look out!' she shouted suddenly.

Paul Temple ducked. The front seat was high-backed and not divided into two separate seats. They were both well protected. As he bent down, another shot rang out.

'It's only the windscreen!' he shouted above the din made by the cars. 'Keep down!' he added imperatively.

'Paul!' ejaculated Steve in alarm. She had seen the stripe of blood on his face. 'You're hurt!'

'No . . . no, I'm all right!'

They were just reaching the bend. The needle of the speedometer fell as Temple released the accelerator, then crept up again as they shot round the corner, followed by Horace Daley.

Two hundred yards ahead was the bridge. Temple began to slow down and the big red car caught up with them. A second later, they were abreast. Steve could see the grim expression on Horace's face. The automatic was still in his hand, but they were both travelling too fast for the revolver to be of any use.

Paul Temple kept a lead of a yard or two. Then gradually, on the bridge itself, he turned his wheel slightly to the right. The innkeeper turned too. An instant later it looked as if he would forge ahead.

It was exactly what Paul Temple wanted. He gave him another yard, then turned his car straight into the red saloon.

'Hold on, Steve!' he shouted. An instant later there was a rending crash as the two cars met. Horace turned his wheel to escape, but it was too late. The impetus from Paul Temple's had succeeded. Over towards the parapet the two cars slithered, locked together.

Suddenly there was a second crash. The red car had hit the parapet. The stonework crumbled to pieces as the car ploughed through it. The red car tore itself free from the bumper and the off front mudguard of Paul Temple's car, and plunged into the river below.

As it fell, they saw Horace Daley pitched through the open sunshine roof.

Paul Temple had been braking hard. Nevertheless, his car followed Daley's through the parapet, and came to rest with the front wheels hanging over the river. The sudden jolt threw them both out of their seats.

'Steve!' Temple was the first to speak. 'Are you all right?'

'Yes!' she replied breathlessly. 'Yes . . . Yes . . . I'm all right!' Then she grew alarmed again. 'Paul! You're hurt!'

'No! No!' he repeated. 'It's nothing.' He drew his hand over his face and looked at the blood on it. 'It's only a scratch. I say,' he added suddenly, 'we'd better get out of here. The car's half over the bridge!'

On his side it was not possible to open the door. But Steve managed to raise the handle and push the door outwards. Then she clambered out, helped by Paul Temple, who had slid along the seat behind her.

Temple took her by the arm and together they walked round the car to the parapet, and peered over to the river below. They could see the roof of the car just above the surface of the water. It had fallen towards the side. Near the water's edge, lying on the ground, they caught sight of the prostrate form of Horace Daley.

They hurried across the bridge and began to clamber down the steep bushy slope to the level of the river. It was not easy going. The ground was wet, and thick bracken impeded their progress. Steve, especially, found it difficult. At last, Paul Temple turned to her, and without a word, picked her up in his arms and proceeded to carry her down. She succeeded in extracting a handkerchief from Temple's breast pocket and wiped the blood that had gathered on his face.

At last they got down to the river's edge. A small path ran alongside the water, and on this Temple set down his precious burden. Telling Steve to wait a few moments, he hurried off towards the spot where Horace Daley was lying. He knelt down beside the groaning body. Suddenly Horace opened his eyes and recognized the face of the man bending over him.

The innkeeper could do no more than groan a few words that were almost unintelligible. Paul Temple struggled to hear what he was saying, at the same time loosening his collar and tie.

'Horace, listen,' said Paul Temple gently. 'Who is the Knave?' He spoke slowly, deliberately. 'Horace,' he added, a little more urgently, as he saw him close his eyes. 'Horace!'

Just then Steve Trent came up. 'How—is he?'

'He's dead,' said Temple softly. For a few moments he knelt before Horace in silence. Then he stood up. It was time to be practical.

'We'll have to walk into the village, Steve,' he said. 'It's about half a mile, I think.'

He indicated some steps up to the bridge which they had not noticed before. When they reached the top the road was deserted. Together they set out towards the village.

CHAPTER XXVII

Conspiracy

It was a very startled Pryce who beheld his master standing outside the servants' entrance to Bramley Lodge, an hour or two later. As the door opened, Paul Temple put his finger to his lips in an urgent gesture of silence. Once inside the kitchen, a whispered consultation took place between the two.

Even the most disinterested spectator would have been amused by the spectacle of Pryce tiptoeing upstairs in front of the novelist, turning round every few yards or so to beckon him on. At last they reached the library on the first floor. Paul Temple closed the door as softly as he could, then walked silently over to a chair. Not till then did they speak.

'Well, this *is* a surprise, sir,' exclaimed Pryce, unable to restrain himself any longer, especially now that the elaborate need for caution seemed to have ceased.

'Pryce, listen!' Paul Temple spoke quietly, but urgently. He had no time to lose. 'Has anyone been here tonight, since I left with Sir Graham for "The Little General"?'

'Why, yes, sir.' Pryce was accustomed to queer moods as well as queer deeds from his master, but even he could not conceal the surprise he now felt. 'Inspector Merritt and—'

'Inspector Merritt?' put in Paul Temple quickly.

'Yes, sir. He's downstairs with Inspector Dale and Sir Graham. They're waiting for you in the drawing-room. Shall I tell them that you've arrived?'

Temple looked at him sharply. 'No,' he said. 'I don't want them to know I'm here; that's why I came in through the back entrance.'

'I—I see, sir.'

'Pryce!' The novelist's tones were still urgent. 'How long has Sir Graham been here?'

'About, er, two hours, sir. He rather expected to find you here, sir, when he arrived.'

'What did he say?'

'He asked me if I'd seen you – or a Miss Parchment. I told him that you had not been here since, er, yourself and Sir Graham left for "The Little General".'

Paul Temple nodded. 'Was he alone?' he asked.

'No, sir. Inspector Merritt was with him.'

'Inspector Merritt. . . . Oh, I see. Well, when did Dale arrive?'

'Much later than the others, sir. He came from Ashdown House, I believe.'

'Then what happened, Pryce?'

'I believe Inspector Dale and Sir Graham went back to the inn, sir.'

'Leaving Inspector Merritt here?'

'Yes, sir.'

'In the drawing-room, I presume?'

'Yes, sir. In the drawing-room.'

'Did Inspector Merritt use the telephone, do you know, Pryce?'

'Yes, I believe he did, now you come to mention it. I was passing through the kitchen and I heard the bell. . . . You know how it tinkles, sir.'

'Then I expect Sir Graham and Dale returned from the inn?'

'Yes, sir, and almost immediately two of them departed for Ashdown House again.'

'Which two?' asked Paul Temple anxiously. 'Merritt and Dale, or—'

'That I couldn't say, sir,' replied Pryce. 'I was in the kitchen getting Mrs. Neddy a cup of tea. I heard voices in the hall, and then the front door slammed.'

'What time would that be – about 10.30?'

'Yes. A little later, if anything, sir.'

Paul Temple nodded.

'After a short while they returned from Ashdown House, sir, and all three of them – Sir Graham Forbes, Inspector Dale, and Inspector Merritt – have been in the drawing-room ever since.'

Temple got up and started walking up and down the room. Suddenly he paused in front of the desk.

'Now, Pryce, listen,' he said. 'I'm going to write a short note. While I'm writing it, you slip round to the garage, get the small car out, and take it to the end of the drive. Miss Trent is there waiting. She'll take over. Is that clear?'

'Yes, sir.'

'And, this is important!' He spoke emphatically. 'Under no circumstances must Sir Graham, Inspector Dale, or Inspector Merritt know that I've been here. Is that understood?'

'Yes, sir.'

'Good! Now, where's the writing paper?' He rummaged about on his desk. 'Oh, here we are!' he exclaimed as he found the pad. 'Do you know, Pryce,' he said suddenly, and

253

there was almost a jovial note in his voice, 'I think this is going to be my greatest contribution to popular fiction! Yes, by Timothy, I'm sure it is.'

The faithful Pryce looked at him, wondering whether he was expected to laugh or remain serious. Then he gave up the problem, turned and closed the door noiselessly behind him. Quickly he walked downstairs. Even more quickly he walked through the hall, fervently praying that the drawing-room door would not open and somebody issue from it to ask him a series of awkward questions.

In a few seconds he had gained the safety of the kitchen. A little later, he was outside the house, armed with his duplicate key to the garage. The garage could also be reached from inside the house by means of a door in the hall, but under the circumstances Pryce was not anxious to disturb the gathering in the drawing-room.

It did not take him long to get to the garage, and he very quickly opened the doors and entered the little eight horse-power car Paul Temple kept in reserve. In a few seconds he was driving the car out of the garage, and down the drive. He stopped at the gate which closed the drive from the main road, but which had been left open all day owing to the frequent use that had been made of the drive.

Leaving the engine quietly ticking over, he got out of the car and stared into the darkness around him. There was no sign of Steve Trent.

'Miss Trent,' he called in a hoarse whisper. 'Miss Trent.'

Suddenly he heard a light footstep and a girlish figure appeared beside him.

'Oh, here you are, Pryce,' she said softly.

'Mr. Temple said you would take over from here, Miss Trent, and then—'

'Yes, that's all right, Pryce.'

Suddenly footsteps sounded behind them in the gravel, and they both turned. It was Pryce who recognized the newcomer.

'Here is Mr. Temple!' he exclaimed.

A moment or two later the novelist arrived. Temple had been hurrying and was obviously out of breath.

'Ah, you've got the car,' he began. 'Good! Now get back to the house, Pryce,' he ordered. 'And remember what I told you.'

'Yes, sir.' Pryce turned away from the car. 'Good night, madam. Good night, sir.'

They saw him vanish into the darkness, and listened to his footsteps receding as he neared the house. Paul Temple took Steve by the arm.

'Merritt, Dale, and Sir Graham are at the house,' he said softly. 'They've been waiting for me.'

'Did you see them?' she asked.

'No,' he replied. He paused. 'Now listen, Steve,' he said urgently. 'I'm going across the tennis court to the front of the drawing-room. They won't be able to see me from there. I shall be gone about two minutes.'

Again Steve was puzzled. 'But – what are you going to do?' she asked. Steve Trent had all the average reporter's curiosity, and Temple's habit of concealing his purpose inevitably increased her anxiety to know his intentions.

'I can't explain now, Steve,' he answered. 'But as soon as I get back to the car, let it rip!'

Steve nodded. Action, at any rate, she could appreciate, even if she did not understand its purpose. 'Yes, all right,' she said excitedly.

As she spoke, Paul Temple vanished. She listened to his footsteps disappearing. Then she got into the car and sat in the driver's seat in readiness.

CHAPTER XXVIII

The Message

'Well, I'm damned if I can understand it. We must have been here nearly two hours.'

The Commissioner was clearly not in the best of tempers. He was still in the drawing-room at Bramley Lodge, waiting for the arrival of Paul Temple. Indeed, Sir Graham was finding it difficult to contain himself.

'Did Temple say he was coming back here, sir?' asked Chief Inspector Dale.

'Yes, of course he did!' Sir Graham snapped. 'After the raid on the inn, he departed with Miss Parchment and said he'd meet us here, didn't he, Merritt?'

'That's right, sir,' Merritt agreed.

'Well, he wasn't at Ashdown House when I left,' said Dale thoughtfully.

'Of course he wasn't,' added the Commissioner abruptly. 'What the devil would he be doing at Ashdown House?'

'Well, wherever he is,' put in Inspector Merritt, 'I think he might have telephoned, instead of keeping us in the dark like this.'

'Yes, I agree with you,' said the Commissioner.

For a few moments, there was silence. Dale walked over to the telephone as if he were going to put a call through, then stood motionless before the receiver.

'Sir Graham,' he said suddenly. 'Perhaps this explains why we haven't received a telephone message from Temple.'

The Commissioner got up and joined Dale in the hall.

'Good lord!' he exclaimed with astonishment, as he looked at the spot Dale indicated.

The telephone cable had been cut. It appeared at first glance to have been hacked through with a penknife or a small pair of scissors. Merritt came over to them and picked up the ends. He was looking very surprised.

'It can't have been unless—' He paused.

'Unless what, Merritt?'

'I was going to say, unless it's been done quite recently,' he said.

'I say, Sir Graham,' said Dale suddenly, 'do you know anything about this butler fellow—er—Pryce?'

'No,' the Commissioner replied thoughtfully. 'No, I don't, Dale. And then there's the Irish woman. The woman who says she's Steve Trent's landlady . . . She's still in the house, remember.'

'Yes, you're right, Sir Graham,' Dale replied. 'And she delivered the gramophone record that time when Temple and Miss Trent had such—'

'Good heavens!' exclaimed Inspector Merritt. 'Why, Mrs. Neddy is out—' He did not complete the sentence.

There was a sudden crack in the room, followed almost immediately by the sound of glass splintering. On the carpet in front of them a small white object appeared.

'Good God!' exclaimed the Commissioner with a start. 'What's that?'

The three men looked at each other with curious expressions on their faces. Then Dale bent down to pick up the object that had been hurled through the French windows. It was a stone with a small piece of paper wrapped round it.

'Listen!' said Sir Graham suddenly.

From outside came the sound of a car starting, and then two brief pauses as the gears were changed.

'Well, that's certainly a quick getaway,' remarked Merritt. 'I say,' he went on, 'what does it say on the note?'

'Yes,' echoed Dale, 'what is it, Sir Graham?'

The latter had passed the note over to the Commissioner and put the stone in his pocket. Sir Graham unfolded the small piece of paper. A puzzled frown came over his face while the other two watched him closely.

'Well?' asked Dale at last.

The Commissioner said nothing. He was engrossed in the mysterious slip of paper.

'What is it?' It was Inspector Merritt's turn to show his curiosity.

The Commissioner slowly raised his head. His voice was shaking slightly when he replied. 'It says:

*'Temple caught .... First Penguin awaiting instructions.
... Malvern Pigeons despatched. ... Ludmilla.'*

CHAPTER XXIX

The Meeting is Adjourned

The Commissioner passed the strange missive across to Inspector Dale. Merritt, however, was the first to break the silence that had fallen on the room.

'Temple caught!' he murmured. Slowly, unconsciously, he began to rub his hands together. Then he walked over to the French windows and inspected the jagged hole the stone had made. For a few seconds he stood looking into the garden. Then, unable to see anything, he returned to the table.

'Ludmilla', said Chief Inspector Dale suddenly, looking more bewildered than ever. 'Who the dickens is Ludmilla?'

The Commissioner looked strangely at him. 'She's a friend of this man Max Lorraine, alias the Knave of Diamonds,' he explained. 'She's the girl who lived at Ashdown House with this so-called Doctor Milton.'

'Oh, yes,' came Dale's rather puzzled answer. He hesitated a while. 'But I say,' he continued, 'who's the "First Penguin"?' A queer smile spread over his face as he spoke the words.

'Heaven only knows,' answered the Commissioner abruptly. 'This business seems to get more complicated week after week.' He scratched his head and lit another cigarette. He had been smoking unceasingly ever since he had set foot in the drawing-room, and having exhausted his own supply, was now helping himself to a box of Virginia cigarettes that Pryce had thoughtfully set down on the table.

'What do they mean by "Malvern Pigeons despatched"?' inquired Merritt with a frown.

A strange light came into the Commissioner's eyes. 'There's some pigeons at "The Little General",' he remarked thoughtfully. 'I wonder—'

'Good lord, yes!' exclaimed Dale.

'Yes, of course,' put in Merritt quickly. 'Of course there are.' He jumped out of his chair and faced the other two. They were again sitting in the comfortable armchairs in front of the big coal fire. The weather had grown warmer during the last few days, but the evenings were still cold, and the crackle of the flames helped to make the room very inviting.

'Malvern—' said Dale thoughtfully, as if talking to himself: 'Malvern pigeons despatched . . . Why!' he exclaimed suddenly. 'It must have some connection with the robbery at Malvern. . . . Surely, that's why—'

An oath broke from Inspector Merritt. The Commissioner looked up at him sharply. 'What is it?' he asked.

'We are fools if you like,' answered Merritt. A strange light had spread over his face. 'That's how they've been getting the diamonds out of the country—'

Dale whistled. 'You mean . . . by pigeons . . . carrier pigeons . . .?'

'Yes,' said Merritt quietly.

The Commissioner clapped his hands together. 'Well, I'm damned!' he exclaimed.

Silence fell on them as they considered this new idea. It explained why they had never yet succeeded in discovering how the stolen jewels were smuggled out of the country. Never once had the police been able to lay hands on any of the property that had been stolen. Carrier pigeons!

'But, Sir Graham,' observed Inspector Merritt quietly, the obvious thought striking him, 'why should they give the game away, in a note like this. . . . "Malvern pigeons despatched." . . . They must have known we'd guess.'

'They're not worried about our guessing their little secrets now, Merritt,' the Commissioner replied. 'All they're concerned about is getting the whole matter straightened out, and then vanishing. And, by God, it looks as if they're doing it. . . . They've got Temple . . . and they've got the girl.' His voice had risen to a crescendo as he spoke and his expression showed the anxiety he felt.

'Yes,' put in Dale, 'but that still doesn't explain why this note should be thrown through the window, Sir Graham. The note was obviously intended for the Knave of Diamonds—'

Merritt hastened to his support. 'Yes, that's right,' he exclaimed.

'Then this girl—er—'

'Ludmilla,' supplied Sir Graham Forbes.

'. . . Ludmilla, must believe that the Knave is here. Here!' he repeated emphatically. 'In this house.'

'But there isn't anyone here,' said the Commissioner, almost helplessly, 'except for us and—'

'And Pryce,' added Dale, as the Commissioner hesitated.

'Yes,' agreed the latter, 'and Pryce.'

'Oh!' exclaimed Merritt. 'But Pryce is out of the question, why—' He broke off. 'Just a minute! Don't forget that old woman's still here, Mrs. Neddy.'

'Steve Trent's landlady—' The Commissioner cleared his throat. 'I keep forgetting her,' he added.

'The thing that really beats me is this "First Penguin" reference,' said Dale. 'What the devil, or who the devil, is the "First Penguin"?'

Merritt nodded. 'That's what I'd like to know.'

Sir Graham Forbes took his wallet out of his pocket where he had put the note for safety, and again inspected the message, hoping, perhaps, to find a solution to their problem. Dale looked over his shoulder as he read it.

'Can you think what it all means, sir?' he asked the Commissioner.

'I'm damned if I can!' was the abrupt answer. Sir Graham carefully folded up the slip of paper again and returned it to its compartment in his wallet. 'I say,' he went on, 'I hope Steve Trent and Temple are all right: if anything happens to them, then—' He paused, as if searching for words to express his full intentions.

'Yes,' replied Merritt, 'yes, I hope so too.'

Once again there was silence. Each man was busy with his own thoughts, speculating what was happening, wondering at the outcome of everything. It had become oppressive in the drawing-room. There was even suspicion and mistrust in the air.

At last, the Commissioner got up. 'Well, look here,' he started, 'it's no good staying here all night. I'm getting back to the Yard with the note. I'd like Henderson to have a look at it. He can make sense out of any dash thing.'

'I'll pick Turner up at "The Little General",' said Inspector Dale, getting up in turn. 'Then Mowbray and company at Ashdown House. Is that all right, Sir Graham?'

'Yes. I should bring Turner back here and let him keep guard on the house. He might keep an eye on this fellow—er—Pryce.'

'Yes.'

'Well,' said Merritt. 'I'm off back to Malvern.'

As he spoke, the door opened and Pryce made his appearance. He found three curious glances directed towards him. Behind him followed a surprisingly meek Mrs. Neddy.

'Yes, Pryce,' said the Commissioner, 'what is it?'

'I beg your pardon, sir,' Pryce began. 'But—er—Mrs. Neddy would rather like to speak to you.' And he stepped on one side to make room for Steve Trent's motherly old housekeeper.

'Yes, of course,' Sir Graham replied. 'What is it, Mrs. Neddy?'

'Sorry to be botherin' you now, sir,' the old lady started. 'But I'm that worried, I am, about Miss Trent an' I was wonderin' if—'

Sir Graham Forbes directed a severe and at the same time curious glance at her before he spoke. 'I'm sorry, Mrs. Neddy,' he said, 'but—er—well, so far we haven't any news.'

'Oh, dear,' she sighed. 'Oh, dear.' If possible, Steve Trent's benevolent Irish 'daily help' looked even more woebegone. She looked as if she might burst into floods of tears at any moment and the Commissioner, with trouble already on his hands, began to feel more than a little anxious.

'I'll see that a car is sent for you, Mrs. Neddy,' he said, 'so that you can get back to town. As soon as we have any news, we'll let you know.'

'Thank ye, sir,' she smiled gratefully at him, then looked sharply at Dale and Merritt, as if feeling that from them, at any rate, she was not receiving such kindness. 'You're very kind,' she added, with a very full-blooded attempt at an old-fashioned curtsey.

There was a discreet cough from near the door and Pryce made himself known. 'Sorry to have troubled you, sir,' he said apologetically.

Sir Graham Forbes seemed to become aware of Pryce's existence for the first time. He had always taken Paul Temple's manservant very much for granted, and even on the occasion of this present visit had not given him more than a passing glance. He now began to study Pryce more carefully. The idea that this man might after all be the mysterious Knave of Diamonds was a consideration to bear in mind, and Sir Graham looked hard into his eyes, hoping, perhaps, to see what lay behind them.

'That's all right, Pryce,' he said. 'As a matter of fact,' he informed him, 'we're leaving. If by any chance you should hear from Mr. Temple, ask him to get in touch with Scotland Yard. Whitehall 1212.'

Pryce bowed to him. 'Whitehall 1212,' he repeated. There was something rather mysterious in the way he spoke. It was, or so it seemed to Sir Graham, almost as if he were uttering a threat. 'Very good, sir,' he added.

Silently Pryce withdrew from the room. The door closed.

CHAPTER XXX

Even if it's the Commissioner!

It was a pleasant little Police Station outside which Steve Trent brought the small car to a standstill. Like many police stations in that part of the world, it was built of large grey stones and it had once, quite obviously, been a private house of no very great pretensions. Outside, a blue lamp warned the stranger that here was an outpost of the Warwickshire County Constabulary, while a noticeboard informed the farmers and other inhabitants of the district that the county constable's duties were not necessarily limited to the detection and prevention of crime.

Remarking that he would only be inside for a moment or two, Paul Temple jumped out of the car and disappeared inside the door. Steve switched off the headlamps, lit a cigarette, and lazily stretched out her graceful limbs. But she was far too excited to relax. The exciting events of the day, and the events that were still to follow, kept her very much on the alert. She thought too, with no small sense of satisfaction, of the marvellous 'story' she would be able to telephone to the office next morning. Completely exclusive too, she reflected, unless the local news-hawks got wind of it. And they could not in any case find out more than enough to whet the appetite of a sensation-loving public for her own complete account.

At the door of what was once probably a dining-room and was now pleasantly labelled 'Charge Room', Paul Temple paused. From the other side he could hear the voice of Sergeant Morrison raised in righteous anger. It was clear that the conduct of his subordinate officer, Police Constable Miller, was not all that he expected.

'The trouble with you, Miller,' Temple heard, 'is that you don't treat this place as a police station. You act as if you were in a . . . a farm house!' The worthy sergeant was even stuttering in his wrath.

'I'm very sorry, Sergeant,' P.C. Miller replied.

'Damn it, man, what's the use of being—'

But dearly as Paul Temple would have loved to have gone on listening, he was not too anxious to eavesdrop. In the middle of the sergeant's tirade, therefore, he pushed the door open and walked in. The sergeant paused in the middle of the sentence and turned round angrily to see who was now so preposterously disturbing his homily.

'Ah, good evening, Mr. Temple,' he beamed, becoming at once pleasant and affable, as he recognized his visitor.

'Good evening, Sergeant. Evening, Miller,' added Paul Temple, turning to the luckless subordinate.

'Good evening, sir,' replied the constable, gratified at being noticed.

'Well, what can we do for you, Mr. Temple?' the Sergeant inquired.

'I should like to have a word with you, Sergeant, if—er—'

'Yes,' answered Sergeant Morrison. 'Yes, of course. Right, Miller, you can go,' he added, dismissing P.C. Miller. 'Report to me again later, with Constable Hodge.'

'Yes, sir.'

'Sergeant, tell me,' began Paul Temple, as the constable left the room and closed the door, 'have you heard of a small inn known as "The First Penguin"?'

'No, sir.' The sergeant hesitated. 'I'm afraid I haven't. "The First Penguin",' he repeated thoughtfully, 'that's a new one on me!'

'It's about four miles from Harvington, tucked away down one of the side roads that lead to the river. There's an A. A. box on the corner, and a milestone with a name on it that looks to me very much like Bidford.'

Sergeant Morrison frowned. 'Yes,' he said at last, 'I think I know the spot you mean, now I come to think of it.' He paused. 'I say,' he went on suddenly, 'this "First Penguin"; isn't it that ramshackle-looking place with a grey roof and part of—'

'Yes,' put in Paul Temple quickly. 'Yes, that's right, Sergeant.'

Sergeant Morrison grunted and scratched his head.

'Now listen,' Temple went on, briskly, 'I want you to get as many men as possible and have them stationed at the corner near the milestone. If anyone leaves "The First Penguin" and comes towards the main road, arrest them. No matter who, or what, they are! Arrest them!' he repeated with emphasis. 'Is that clear, Sergeant?'

'No matter . . . who . . . or what . . . they are?' The sergeant repeated the words slowly and thoughtfully.

'Yes,' said Temple decisively. 'Even if it's the Commissioner himself!'

Sergeant Morrison began to laugh. 'Well, I hardly expect that we shall find Sir Graham Forbes,' he replied.

'You never know,' was the quiet answer. 'You never know, Sergeant.'

Sergeant Morrison looked up sharply, wondering exactly what to make of this remark. Then he suddenly appeared to reach a decision and to place supreme confidence in the novelist.

'When would you like the men stationed?' he asked.

'Well, the sooner the better.'

'Very well, Mr. Temple,' he replied. 'I'll do my best.'

'Keep the men well out of sight,' Temple ordered, 'and don't, under any circumstances, interfere with anyone who looks like making their way towards "The First Penguin". When you see a light in one of the windows – enter the inn.'

'Very good, sir,' he answered. He paused. 'Mr. Temple,' he asked at last, with a puzzled expression, 'if it isn't a personal question, who do you think will visit the inn tonight?'

Paul Temple smiled.

'The Knave of Diamonds, Sergeant! The Knave of Diamonds!'

CHAPTER XXXI

Enter the Knave!

Diana Thornley and Dr. Milton were not in the best of tempers. Horace had left them tightly bound in the uncomfortable hard chairs of 'The First Penguin' and all their efforts to escape had proved useless. From time to time, a distant car had raised false hopes. Dr. Milton had at length fallen asleep through sheer exasperation and exhaustion. A dog barking had suddenly awakened him and he had again started unburdening himself of his feelings.

'Can't you do anything except sit there and grumble?' protested Diana. 'We must have been tied up here for hours, and all you've damned well done is—'

'For heaven's sake, woman!' exclaimed Dr. Milton harshly. 'Shut up!'

Again there was silence. After ten minutes perhaps, Diana suddenly attempted to stretch her lithe body. She began to struggle with her bonds, summoning together every ounce of strength. 'Something's got to be done one way or the other,' she panted, pulling and twisting in yet another attempt to free herself. 'We can't just . . . sit . . . Oh! – this is tight!'

The words came out in jerks as if it were costing her more effort to speak than to fight against her bonds.

Dr. Milton looked at her contemptuously. 'It's no earthly use struggling.'

She went on writhing in a last desperate effort to free herself. She had kicked her legs outwards against the ropes until her feet felt lifeless. Now she fancied the rope must be loosened sufficiently for her to pull her arms through.

'It's no use, Diana,' exclaimed Milton. He had long since given up trying to escape.

'I hope Horace caught Temple before he got to Bramley Lodge,' said Diana anxiously.

'I wonder what on earth made the Chief ring up from Temple's place!' ejaculated Milton. It was somebody new to blame, and anything was better than blaming himself for his present predicament. 'That was a damn' fool thing to do, if you like!'

'Why was it?' demanded Diana. 'How was he to know that Temple was here, and would trace the call?'

'I say,' said Dr. Milton suddenly. 'What's that?'

'What?'

'I thought I heard something.'

Both strained to catch the noise. It was the horn of a car that Dr. Milton had heard. They heard it again, closer at hand. At last they could hear the engine of the car, then the tyres over the gravel outside. Finally it came to a stop. Doors were opened and closed.

'I hope to God it's the Chief,' breathed Diana.

Suddenly the door was flung open. With a look of horror, Dr. Milton recognized Paul Temple. His name escaped Dr. Milton's tongue as involuntarily as it did venomously.

'Yes, my dear Milton,' said Temple smoothly. 'You must forgive me for once again interrupting, but—'

Suddenly he felt Steve pulling at his sleeve. 'Paul!' she burst out. 'Where's Miss Parchment?'

'She left about an hour ago,' said Diana quickly.

'Why?' asked Temple. 'Why did she leave?'

There was a pause. Paul Temple looked from one to the other. Dr. Milton averted his eyes but Diana caught and held his squarely.

'Well, perhaps it's a good job you don't feel like talking,' Temple said at last. There was something in his voice, not threatening, but perfectly calm and composed, that alarmed the doctor.

'What are you going to do?' he asked sharply.

'Just gag you, my friend,' was the answer. 'We don't want you to be unnecessarily noisy when our distinguished guest arrives. You attend to the girl, Steve,' he said, pulling a large silk handkerchief out of his pocket, and handing it to her.

'Who's . . . who's coming here?' asked Diana sharply.

'A friend of yours, Miss Thornley,' Temple answered smoothly, at the same time forcing another handkerchief deep into Dr. Milton's mouth. 'A very close friend, if I'm not mistaken!'

'Not . . . not. . . Max!' she shouted. 'No! No!' She was still protesting when Steve rammed the handkerchief into her mouth so that only muffled protests could issue forth. Then Temple walked quickly over to the light switch and plunged the room into darkness.

'And now we wait!' he said slowly, softly, ominously.

'Paul.' Steve Trent was excited, but she kept her voice lowered. 'Is he really coming here?'

'Yes, I think so, Steve.'

'You're not certain?'

'One can never be too certain of people, least of all, people like Max Lorraine.'

'But, Paul, why should he come here?'

'Because I've laid a trap, Steve.' Paul Temple spoke quietly, but already there was a note of triumph in his voice. 'A rather neat little trap, with—' He hesitated.

'What is it?' Steve asked.

'Listen!' said Temple suddenly.

Both strained their ears, as Dr. Milton and Diana had done a little while before. It was a car. A few seconds later, they heard it stop outside the inn.

'Paul!' whispered Steve with obvious excitement. 'He's here!'

She moved up close to him and put her arm through his. As she did so she felt the cold steel of an automatic held ready for action.

'By Timothy, yes,' he replied. 'Now Steve,' he said, gently disengaging her arm, 'stand by the light. When I give the signal, switch it on.'

'Yes . . . yes, all right.'

She walked over to the switch while Temple took up his position immediately facing the door.

The footsteps outside came nearer, then entered the inn. At last, the door slowly opened.

'Ludmilla!' they heard a voice say softly. 'Ludmilla!'

'Lights, Steve!' exclaimed Paul Temple sharply. 'Drop that gun!' he ordered immediately afterwards.

At the same moment the lights went on and Steve Trent gasped. She was facing Chief Inspector Dale.

'Oh, Paul!' she exclaimed with amazement. 'It's Inspector Dale.'

'Yes, Chief Inspector Dale,' said Paul Temple quietly.

'Alias Max Lorraine, alias – The Knave of Diamonds!'

'Temple, are you mad?' asked the inspector sharply. 'What the devil does this mean?'

'Briefly, my dear Lorraine,' he replied, 'it means, exit the Knave! Steve,' he added briskly, 'ungag the girl.'

'Ludmilla!' exclaimed Dale, turning towards Diana. 'Why did you send that note?'

'Note?' echoed Diana, when Steve had removed the handkerchief. 'Which note?'

'Good God!' he exclaimed, the truth dawning on him. 'You don't mean . . . Temple!' he suddenly burst out.

'Yes, I sent the note . . . my method of delivering it was a little unconventional, I admit. But it seems to have answered its purpose,' added Temple grimly.

'You damned fool, Max!' Milton shouted with fury. 'You've played straight into his hands. Why—'

The door opened again, and he broke off. This time the visitors must have been even less welcome to the doctor. Sergeant Morrison led the way into the room, followed closely by Inspector Merritt. Behind them came Sir Graham Forbes and Police Constable Miller.

In the eyes of Inspector Merritt and Sergeant Morrison, there shone a light of triumph. Nevertheless, their expressions were as grave as the Commissioner's. Sir Graham Forbes seemed to be labouring under a heavy shock.

As Merritt explained later, they had been lying by the roadside, screened by some dense bushes, watching the inn, their surprise at the suddenness of events only exceeded by their amazement as Chief Inspector Dale arrived.

'So you've got Milton and—' Sir Graham found it difficult even to utter the name of his Chief Inspector. '. . . and Dale,' he said at last.

275

'Yes,' replied Temple gravely. Only too well did he realize the seriousness of the issue, of the evidence he had collected, together with the final proof of the identity of Chief Inspector Dale with the nebulous figure of Max Lorraine.

'I don't mind telling you, Temple,' went on the Commissioner in the same serious tones, 'that Merritt and I were staggered when the sergeant gave us your note, why—'

'Yes, I expect you were, Sir Graham,' Paul Temple replied.

The men turned round to survey the bound forms of Diana and Dr. Milton. Fear, even terror, could be seen deep in the doctor's eyes, but Diana looked calmer. She might have been some distinguished actress taking part in a play. Even her dress and stockings were comparatively unruffled.

'Have you searched him?' asked Inspector Merritt, turning to Temple.

'Not yet, Charles.'

'Then we'll wait till we get him back to the station.'

'Take Milton and the girl to the car, Sergeant,' the Commissioner ordered.

'Yes, sir,' Sergeant Morrison replied. 'Come along, Miller, give me a hand. . . . You untie the girl.'

He had gone over to Dr. Milton's chair and was examining the knots. Then he took out a huge jack-knife from his pocket and opened it. He proceeded to cut through the cords until at last Milton was able to stretch his arms and legs. While he was doing this, Miller was busy releasing the girl. Her wrists showed deep purple marks where the string had cut into them. But she made a little gesture of satisfaction when she stretched out her legs to examine her stockings and noticed that the silk had stood up to the very severe test and remained unladdered.

276

Both the doctor and Diana wearily stretched their cramped limbs. After a little pause Milton turned to Inspector Dale.

'Well,' he said, as he uttered a deep sigh of resignation, 'they say, give a man plenty of rope and he'll hang himself. And you've certainly made a good job of it, Max!'

Dale ignored him. As completely as he ignored everyone else in the room. In his downfall a strange dignity had come to him.

'Come along, you!' said Sergeant Morrison abruptly, taking the doctor by the arm. He led the way to the door.

Suddenly Milton halted. 'Goodbye, Mr. Temple,' he said. 'This time, I'm afraid, we shan't meet again!'

He smiled, then turned round again and allowed himself to be led out to the waiting car.

'Bring the girl, Miller,' added the sergeant over his shoulder as he was leaving the room.

The constable walked across the room and took Diana by the arm. For the first time she was face to face with Max Lorraine. She trembled slightly as she looked at him, but her features were still calm.

'So . . . it's goodbye, Max,' she said, in what was little more than a whisper.

'Yes,' he answered softly. 'Yes, it's goodbye. But—' He paused. 'Remember what I always said, Ludmilla. They won't take me!'

'Come along, miss,' said Police Constable Miller, with a self-conscious glance towards the Commissioner.

Diana drew back for an instant, desperately anxious not to be separated from the man at whom she was now gazing with the most intense devotion. Then she allowed herself to be piloted towards the door and out of the room to the waiting car. As she left, a little of Dale's moral resistance appeared to evaporate.

It was Inspector Merritt who broke the silence into which they had fallen.

'Well, you've certainly given us enough to think about, Dale,' he remarked.

'Yes,' said Sir Graham, 'but thank heaven we had the common sense to follow Miss Trent's advice and "Send for Paul Temple"!'

Inspector Merritt had been feeling in his pocket. 'I think we'll have the bracelets on, sir,' he said determinedly. 'Just to be on the safe side.'

As he spoke he pulled the handcuffs from a capacious pocket and slipped them over the wrists Dale held out to him.

'Well,' said Dale quietly, 'I've had a good run for my money. And I'm not grumbling. It's a pity you caught me on a cheap trick, Temple, but—I guess that's how things turn out sometimes.'

'Dale,' said the Commissioner, 'what happened that time when Skid Tyler was poisoned?'

A smile came to Dale's face. 'The poison wasn't meant for Tyler. I can assure you of that, Sir Graham.'

'Then it must have been meant for me!' replied the Commissioner, looking very grave.

Dale commenced to laugh. It was a long, slow, mirthless laugh, that made Steve shudder.

'I'll take him to the car, sir,' said Merritt slowly.

The Commissioner showed his relief at the suggestion, and Inspector Merritt put a hand through Dale's arm and quietly and very firmly led him out of the room.

'You look a little surprised, Miss Trent,' commented Sir Graham, as soon as they had departed.

'Well, I am rather,' she answered, in a bewildered voice. 'I can't quite see what's happened.'

'Then I should "Send for Paul Temple"!' he smiled, obviously amused at his own jest. A different atmosphere had come to the room now that Dale had departed.

The Commissioner looked a little anxiously at his watch. 'You have your car here, Temple?' he asked.

'Yes, thank you, Sir Graham.'

The Commissioner muttered a string of apologies, buttoned up his heavy overcoat, took his hat and gloves from the chair on which he had flung them down a little earlier, and left. Paul Temple and Steve Trent were alone together.

CHAPTER XXXII

And Exit the Knave!

'Paul,' Steve Trent turned a puzzled little face up at the novelist, 'why did the Knave come here? Did you know it was Dale? And why . . .?'

'One question at a time, Steve!' said Temple severely, but with his eyes nevertheless twinkling with humour. They were no longer in the room which had seen the inglorious end to the career of the Knave of Diamonds, and his fellow conspirators. Steve wanted to escape from it, and together they had set out on a little tour of exploration. They had come to a room which had once been some sort of lounge, and which appeared far more inviting to them both.

Neither of them felt tired, although it was now well past midnight. Both felt disinclined to leave 'The First Penguin' even in spite of the greater hospitality offered by Bramley Lodge. They sat down on a large and moderately comfortable settee that the room boasted. Temple produced a hip flask which, with remarkable foresight, he had filled with some of his famed cherry brandy.

It made them both feel considerably better after the wearying events of the evening.

'I'd had my suspicions about Dale for quite a little while,' he said at length, 'and when I got back to Bramley Lodge and found that he'd been there all night and had had ample opportunity of using the telephone, I was almost certain.'

'But he wasn't the only person at Bramley Lodge.'

'No. There was Sir Graham and Merritt. Sir Graham, of course, was really quite out of the question, although even with Sir Graham I found myself occasionally, well, wondering. I think it was those Russian cigarettes he smoked.'

'But there was Merritt!' said Steve, almost sharply.

'Yes,' he answered thoughtfully, 'and, quite frankly, he rather worried me. You see, Merritt was in Sir Graham's office the day Skid Tyler was murdered. Merritt knew that you were Louise Harvey . . . and he turned up tonight at "The Little General" when the inn was raided.'

Steve Trent nodded assent. She really was damnably attractive, reflected Temple, as he looked at her appraisingly. And she had stuck all these appalling adventures with singular grit.

'And there was one other point, too,' he went on. 'Merritt, apparently, according to Pryce, had used the telephone when Dale and Sir Graham had returned to "The Little General". This seemed to fit perfectly, but still, somehow or other, I didn't think Merritt was our man.'

'But,' asked Steve, with a little hesitation, 'when did Dale phone?'

'After Sir Graham and Merritt returned to Bramley Lodge from the inn, two of them went down to Ashdown House. Unfortunately, Pryce wasn't sure which two. We know now, of course, that it must have been Merritt and Sir Graham. It was then that Dale took the opportunity of ringing through here . . . to see if Milton and the gang had got clear with the Malvern diamonds.'

'Yes,' said Steve Trent, with even more than typical journalistic curiosity and perseverance, 'but I still don't see how you managed to trick Dale into—'

'I'm coming to that, Steve,' he answered. 'When I got back to the house and discovered that Sir Graham, Merritt, and Dale were in the drawing-room, I decided to find out, once and for all, who was the Knave. I scribbled a short note which said, *Temple caught. First Penguin awaiting instructions. Malvern pigeons despatched. Ludmilla.* This I pitched through the drawing-room window. Now the note would, I felt sure, read like utter nonsense to everyone in that room, except, of course, Max Lorraine. And Lorraine would, I felt confident, immediately assume that I had been caught and that Milton and Ludmilla, alias Diana Thornley, were waiting for him at "The First Penguin".'

He paused.

'I see,' said Steve, rather excitedly.

'The phrase, "First Penguin awaiting instructions" would, of course, sound like the most utter balderdash to Sir Graham and Merritt, who wouldn't even know what "The First Penguin" stood for. Dale knew perfectly well what the note meant, however, and he acted accordingly.'

'But,' pursued a puzzled Steve, 'what did you mean by "Malvern pigeons despatched"?'

'You remember I went round to the courtyard just before we were due to leave for Bramley Lodge?' Temple asked her in return.

'Yes – that was after you noticed the pigeon.'

'That's right. Well, in the courtyard was a basket of pigeons obviously all ready to carry the Malvern diamonds. That's how they've been getting the stuff out of the country, Steve, by carrier pigeon.'

'That's ingenious, if you like!' she exclaimed.

'Yes. And a reference to it in the note, which was, of course, supposed to come from Diana Thornley, alias Ludmilla, would, I thought, give the note an authentic touch.' Paul Temple paused and looked at his companion. She had taken a tiny notebook out of her handbag, and was scribbling in it, very industriously, very seriously, mocking Paul Temple's own seriousness, more seriously even than any of the beautiful reporters of fiction and their never-failing notebooks.

'When I got down to the station, Sergeant Morrison informed me that earlier in the evening Merritt had been through on the phone from Bramley Lodge to see if Morrison had seen or heard anything about Miss Parchment and myself. This, of course, accounted for the telephone call that Merritt had made, and to a very large extent cleared him of suspicion. While I was at the station, I wrote another note, which I addressed to Sir Graham and left with the Sergeant, on the strict understanding that he would deliver it to Sir Graham *only* if the Commissioner arrived at the police station accompanied by Merritt. The note, of course, expressed my opinion about Dale being Max Lorraine. The Knave would, I felt positive, get to "The First Penguin" as quickly as possible in accordance with the instructions in my first note.'

'Well,' said Steve at last, after listening to Paul Temple with wonderment, 'you certainly seem to have been exploiting your literary . . .'

Suddenly the door opened. They were sitting facing it, and recognized Inspector Merritt as soon as he came into the room.

'Hello, Charles,' exclaimed Temple, as he rose from the settee to meet him. 'What is it?'

Merritt's gravity of expression, as well as the urgency of his visit, showed that his errand must be serious. He looked from the novelist to Steve before he spoke.

'He's dead, Paul,' he said at last.

Paul Temple looked sharply at him.

'You mean . . . Dale?' he asked.

'Yes.'

Steve had risen from the couch behind Temple, and moved softly towards them. Her face showed the utter astonishment she felt.

'Dead!' she echoed.

'Just before we got him to the car,' Inspector Merritt began to explain, 'he asked for a cigarette. The Sergeant gave him one, and then Dale took a lighter from his pocket. Before we could do anything he had it to his mouth. I don't know what was in the lighter. But . . . oh, my God!' he suddenly groaned. 'He looked awful! I thought perhaps you'd like to know, Paul,' he added quietly.

'Yes,' Temple replied, after a moment's silence. 'Yes, thank you, Charles.'

They shook hands. Merritt indicated that he still had an unfortunately large number of matters connected with the case to attend to before he could award himself the much needed luxury of a bed. He left the room and made for his car.

Temple took Steve's arm, and they strolled together to the window to watch the inspector's departure. They heard the engine begin to purr as he pressed the starter, and presently watched the lights swing round and then light up the main road.

Paul Temple reflected with satisfaction that, at least as far as he was concerned, all was over. His evening's work had been completed. Nevertheless, he felt a little sorry for Steve. She had just reminded him that her life was given up to her newspaper, and that the story they would print on Monday would be one of the most sensational *The Evening Post* had ever had. Before she could go to bed the story would have to be partly completed, and ready on the news desk in her office.

They discussed the main outlines of the story, and decided to complete it a little later at Bramley Lodge. There they could type it out and phone it to the office for a telephonist to take down. Early next morning, however, as Steve explained, she would have to leave for town. The details she would telephone that evening would be sufficient for the early editions of the paper, in which they could not afford to reveal too many secrets to their rivals. Then for the Monday evening editions she could write out a fuller version at the office.

They drew back from the window and decided it was time to make for their car and return to Bramley Lodge. Before they left Temple picked up the telephone to ring Pryce and give him instructions. Then he suddenly remembered that the line had been cut. It would mean waiting a little for the late supper he hoped Pryce would cook for them.

'Steve,' said Temple suddenly, the thought of food in the immediate future possibly giving him the idea.

'Yes?' she said, with a curious smile.

'I was wondering if, er, you . . .' He broke off. For perhaps the first time Paul Temple knew what it meant when he used the word 'bashful' in one of his novels.

'Well?' prompted Steve.

'If you'd—er—care to have dinner with me on . . . on Thursday?' he said.

'Thursday? Yes, of course,' she said happily. 'I'd love to.'

'Good. I shall be in town, so perhaps we can . . . er . . . lunch together, too?'

'Yes,' she smiled. 'Why not?'

'We might even manage to have tea together, as a sort of, er—

'I'd love to,' she replied softly.

'Oh, er, splendid,' he said. 'Well, that's about all. Of course, there is breakfast, but—'

'I always have breakfast in bed.'

'In bed?'

'Yes, in bed.'

'Well, that's a bit awkward!'

'Of course,' put in Steve a trifle glibly, 'we could get married.'

'Yes, I suppose we—' Temple suddenly gasped. 'I say . . . are you proposing?'

'What do you think, Mr. Temple?' she asked brightly, in a voice that was a perfect imitation of his. 'What do you think?'

He burst out laughing. 'Well, of all the unconventional little devils, you simply—'

They had left the room in which they had been sitting, and were now in the passage on the way to the car and Bramley Lodge. As they neared the door of the little parlour in which Temple had brought about the capture of the Knave of Diamonds, they heard a loud banging noise.

'What's that?' asked Steve abruptly, seizing his arm.

Paul Temple flung open the door, switched on the light, and inspected the room. 'It's from the cupboard,' he announced.

'Yes,' she replied. 'Yes, what is it?'

'We'll soon find out!' he proclaimed, taking his automatic out of his pocket again. 'Stand on one side, Steve,' he ordered, as he turned the key of the cupboard. 'Stand on one side!'

Francis Durbridge

As Temple suddenly opened the door of the cupboard, a gasp of amazement escaped from him.

'Why, it's Miss Parchment!'

'Miss Parchment!' repeated Steve, with astonishment.

Quickly Temple placed his gun on the small table, and put an arm round Miss Parchment's waist to support her. She was deathly pale from her confinement in the cupboard, and looked on the point of collapse.

'Oh, dear! Oh, dear!' she moaned, as Paul Temple piloted her very carefully to a chair. Suddenly she glanced round the deserted room. 'Where's Milton and the girl?' she asked quickly.

'They've gone, Miss Parchment,' Temple told her. 'They've been arrested. And the Knave's gone, too,' he added, after a slight pause. 'He's dead. It was Dale – Inspector Dale, of Scotland Yard.'

Miss Parchment looked at Temple with complete bewilderment; after a second or two she turned her gaze to Steve.

'You mean to say that all this has been going on while I've been in that—blasted cupboard!' she ejaculated.

Paul Temple nodded.

'*By Timothy*!' said Miss Amelia Victoria Parchment.

288